on the
kalalau trail

Book 2 of the Trailblazer series

Robin Reardon

IAM Books
www.robinreardon.com

ON THE KALALAU TRAIL
Book 2 of the TRAILBLAZER series

Copyright © 2019 by Robin Reardon

Cover and formatting by Sweet 'N Spicy Designs

Cover photograph by Alex Calder

The events and characters of this book are entirely fictional. Any similarity to events or people, living or dead, is entirely coincidental.

ISBN: 978-0-9988414-9-6

To Laura Richards, General Manager of the Hanalei Colony Resort

After more than fifty inches of rain fell on the island of Kaua'i in the spring of 2018, Richards devoted the Hanalei Colony Resort in Ha'ena to housing and feeding locals whose homes were destroyed or unlivable.

Richards also provided classroom space for forty-eight local students.

God hides the fires of hell within paradise.

— Paulo Coelho, Brazilian novelist

Wherever you find the greatest good, you will find the greatest evil, because evil loves paradise as much as good.

— Wallace Stegner, American novelist

PREFACE

I was on the island of Kaua'i in the summer of 2001. Like Nathan Bartlett, I traveled the east and north coasts of the island along the Kuhio Highway. Once I left Princeville and headed west along the northern shore, the road became progressively less like a highway and more like a country road—picturesque, and often too narrow for two vehicles to pass without accommodating each other carefully.

I stayed in the Hanalei Colony Resort in Ha'ena for a week, and I hiked the Kalalau Trail south to Hanakapi'ai Beach and followed the stream in to the Hanakapi'ai waterfall.

Much has changed on the island since I was there. In the spring of 2018, fifty inches of rain fell in a mere twenty-four hours, washing out much of the northern section of the highway, destroying homes, and ultimately causing nearly $20 million in damages.

Because a stretch of more than four miles of the northwestern section of the highway was closed, there was no access to the famed Na Pali Coast and, of particular interest, the Kalalau Trail, for many months. When the story in this book takes place, the trail had recently been opened again with caveats for hikers, and road repairs were ongoing.

The Hanalei Colony Resort, the closest facility of its kind to the Kalalau Trail, was damaged by the flood but not destroyed; in fact, General Manager Laura Richards devoted the resort to housing and feeding locals whose homes were destroyed or rendered unlivable. She also provided classroom space for forty-eight local students.

Then in July of 2018, the property suffered $3 million in damage from a fire. Although I have Nathan staying at the resort for this story, it had not yet finished repairs and was not open to the public at the time when Nathan would have been there. I very much hope the property can recover fully and once again provide reasonably-priced guest rooms on Kaua'i's magnificent north shore.

Note that while reading all three of the Trailblazer books in order will take you on Nathan's journey with him—his first love, his successes and failures, and the maturity he gains along the way—each book can be read and enjoyed individually.

— *Robin Reardon*

CHAPTER ONE

"You're crazy. He's nothing like Daniel." I shook my head for emphasis.

On one level, Nina was wrong to say the two men were similar. Conroy's charm was studied, whereas Daniel's had been genuine, even a little vulnerable.

But she was focused on a different level. "He's another loser, Nathan."

There's nobody like a big sister to tell you what she thinks, whether you want to hear it or not.

Nina was only one year older than I was, but—I hated that this was true—she had proven herself to be considerably more mature.

Of course, she'd inherited her position as the oldest sibling in the family when our older brother Neil had died. That didn't necessarily mean that I followed her advice.

Neil. Our big brother.

Neil had been born five years before me. He and his best friend, Jeremy Ford, started claiming mountain peaks together when they were in their mid-teens. I lost track of how many mountains they climbed together. And when I was eighteen, just over two years ago, they had died. They'd been hiking in the Priest Wilderness in Virginia, an extremely remote area.

I'd never heard of a fire tornado before, but that summer I learned it was a thing. Neil and Jeremy were unable to get out of the path of one of these hell-spawned monsters. Neil called me from the satellite phone he'd brought for the trip, as he and Jeremy huddled inside the portable fire shelter that might have saved their lives if the fire had been smaller, or less ferocious. Neil had told me the same thing I think anyone would say when facing certain death: Tell everyone I love them.

I heard my brother die. I can still hear the screams.

I met Conroy, the man Nina and I were arguing about, the summer before my senior year at UNH. It was on Cannon Mountain: four thousand one hundred feet above sea level, a qualifier for the Four Thousand Foot Club. Before he'd died, Neil had been aiming for the honor of membership in this club, whose members have climbed all of New Hampshire's forty-eight peaks with summits four thousand feet or higher, at least once each. His goal, cruelly interrupted, was now mine.

I parked my grandmother's Subaru along the side of the highway; even though I'd left the house in Concord where I lived with Gram at O-dawn-thirty, there were enough people already at the Lafayette Place campground that there was no more parking available there. I assured myself that most of the people from these cars were here to ride the aerial tram up the mountain. I didn't expect to see a lot of hikers on the tough trails I planned for the day. I liked rugged trails. The more rugged the better. The fewer other hikers the better.

Toward the beginning of the trail, about half a mile from the Lonesome Lake trailhead, I turned onto the Hi-Cannon Trail, and by that time there was no one else in sight. It was a gorgeous day in late August, with the warmth of summer in the process of giving way to fall.

About a mile up the trail, when it had grown steep, I came to something that a lot of people who consider climbing this mountain will hike a different trail to avoid. It's a ladder, or a couple of them: wooden slats nailed to paired two-by-fours climbing at a moderately steep angle for about twenty feet. Mind you, I wouldn't want to fall off the thing; for the ascent, the right side is attached rather precariously to a vertical granite face, and the left is open to a steep fall into the forest below. It's a true ladder; there are no handrails. I'm pleased to say I had no problem on it.

Past the ladder, the Hi-Cannon climbs up a lot, and down a bit, and up a lot more, around huge boulders and over granite faces that forced me to use hands as well as feet. It's not technical rock climbing by any means, but it's not an easy trail.

At one point I came out onto a massive granite ledge, the lower Cannon outlook. Facing east, I could see for miles as my eyes followed the massive ridge connecting Mount Liberty in the south to Mount Lafayette, pretty much due east of where I stood. The sky was so bright and clear I could almost pick out Gram's car, parked way down along Route 93. There's nothing like this kind of view to validate the work it takes to climb this high.

The freckled granite of the ledge, heated by the sun, was almost too hot to sit on. The backs of my legs below my hiking shorts settled onto the gritty surface, and gradually my skin grew accustomed to the temperature. I filled my lungs with mountain air that was scented with pine and with that earthy decay from fallen leaves. Legs dangling over the sloping ledge, I pulled out a hunk of cheese, tore a handful of bread from my large sandwich roll, and settled in for a snack, relishing the solitude.

I'd barely swallowed a couple of mouthfuls when I heard the scuff of someone's boots on the granite behind me to my left.

Shit.

I decided to pretend there was no one there. At least it sounded like just one person, not a group of people who would completely spoil the spot for me.

"What a sight."

It was a man. A man whose voice started somewhere near his feet, gaining resonance and dimension as it rose through his body.

5

Former intentions aside, I turned enough to see a pair of brown hiking boots with dark red laces, the legs above the green tweed hiking socks decorated with light brown hairs catching sunlight. My eyes moved up the tanned skin on his calves, over his knees to the hem of dark olive shorts. From the edge of my vision I could tell he was gazing into the distance, so I allowed my gaze to linger on his crotch, even though the thick material and heavy zipper prevented me from getting much of a sense of what lay beneath.

A motion of his head warned me to move my eyes up, past the sleekly muscled arms, over the broad shoulders to the face. Sunglasses hid his eyes, but there was no hiding the jawline that made me think of the granite ledges I'd crawled over on my way up the trail. Fashionably tousled light brown hair polished off the look, with a few longish curls teasing his forehead.

In so many ways, he was the opposite of me. This guy was practically Aryan, while anyone looking at me would almost certainly guess at my somewhat-diluted Chinese heritage. If my slight build wasn't a clue, my board-straight, nearly-black hair would give it away.

His face toward me, he asked, "Mind if I join you?"

He waited until I extended my left arm toward the granite beside me before dropping his pack between us and settling onto the warm rock. I guessed his age at mid-twenties. Once he was sitting, I could tell he wasn't especially tall—just a little taller than me, probably. He positioned himself so he could extend his right hand in my direction.

"Conroy Finnegan."

"Nathan Bartlett," I responded. His grip was firm, the handshake just one downward plunge and a definite release.

He busied himself pulling out a water bottle and a small ziplock bag that held gorp.

"You hiked Cannon before, Nathan?"

"Not Cannon, no. First time on this one. I'm working my way through." I waited to see if he'd know what that meant.

He did. "Notched my boots for Owl's Head a couple of weeks ago. You got that one yet?"

Owl's Head was one of the peaks I would have to climb to join the four-thousand-foot club. He hadn't actually notched his boots, of course; that was just an expression some hikers use.

"Not yet," I admitted. "Good climb?"

He chuckled. "It's one of those peaks you do just because you have to. I decided to get it out of the way."

"Tell me more."

"Summit's not above tree line, for one thing, so that's not much fun. The lower part of the trail is kind of flat, and some folks bike it. Mountain bikes, of course. But then they have to lock their bikes someplace, because once you hit the rock slide part of the trail, it's painfully slow going. Dangerous, actually. Not a fun climb, unless you like that kind of thing. I don't mind the danger, but I don't like a slow pace."

"But—biking? That doesn't count."

He finished a swig of water and shook his head. "Not toward the patch, no."

I knew he meant the patch awarded hikers who've proven their qualification for the club. Biking any part of a trail, or traveling it by any means other than on foot, would not qualify you for claiming that peak.

"How many peaks do you have so far?" I had to know.

"This today is number nineteen. And, of course, twenty and twenty-one, because I'll do the ridge loop over the Kinsmans."

I nodded, trying to look knowing. On the drive up, I'd decided to see what Cannon was like before setting my sights on North and South Kinsman, just south of Cannon, each of which is over four thousand feet. It's one of those perfect loops that gets you more than one qualifying peak in a day's climb, if you're up to it; I just hadn't been sure how tough

Cannon would be.

Cannon was only number eight for me. I was hoping he wouldn't ask what my total was. Neil had started claiming peaks in his mid-teens and had been well on his way before he'd died. I reminded myself I had gotten a late start.

So instead of volunteering my score, I took a side trail in the conversation.

"Had a crazy experience last fall. Climbed Lafayette twice. By accident."

I took a swig from my own water bottle, going for a dramatic pause.

"Thereon on hangs a tale," Conroy said, his voice implying that he wanted to hear it.

"My college roommate and I decided to do an overnight. We parked near the head for Falling Waters Trail—"

"Love that trail. You went up and over Little Haystack and on to Lincoln, then."

Was he showing off? This was *my* story.

"Anyway," I continued, "yes, so I claimed Lincoln for the club, too. El Speed isn't going for the patch, but—"

"El Speed?"

Okay, so that interruption might reasonably be warranted. "Yeah. Larry Speed. Taking the initial 'L'—"

He laughed, and his laugh had the same character as his voice: deep, resonant, compelling. "I get it! Fun."

I sighed inwardly. Was he going to let me finish? I gazed east toward the mountain in question. "After the Lafayette summit, we headed a little way down the Greenleaf Trail to make camp. In the morning, when he went to put on his frame pack, one of the straps broke."

"Man!"

"We tried a few ways to fix it, but nothing worked. So we put as much as we could into my pack, hid his, and finished the loop down, taking turns wearing the pack. At the car, we emptied my pack and hiked with it back up to get what we'd left hidden. We were so far back up the mountain we said, fuck it, let's just do the summits again."

Conroy laughed again, and again the richness of it pulled at me. "That's not how you're supposed to do a loop!" He pushed the bridge of his sunglasses down his nose a little, revealing clear blue eyes and very long lashes, and gave me a teasing glare from under his eyebrows. "You do realize that doesn't mean you can claim four peaks."

"Yeah. Tempting, though."

We had finished our snacks, but neither of us made a move to leave. I lifted my legs, one at a time, off the pocked surface of the granite, feeling with my fingers where the skin was temporarily dented. I could reasonably have gotten up, wished Conroy a great hike, and headed off. I'm not sure why I didn't. Sure, the guy was attractive and friendly, but he didn't know I was gay, and it was unlikely he was. It was also unlikely I'd ever see him again. Still, neither of us made a move to leave.

After about a minute of silence, in which we both gazed into the gorgeous distance, he said, "Did you see anyone on the ladder?"

"You're the first person I've seen since I left the lower part of the Lonesome Lake Trail."

He paused, no doubt for effect. "I had to wait for this couple who were part-way up the ladder when I got there. Man and a woman. They had a mixed-breed dog with them, maybe the size of a pit bull. The woman was about five feet up from the bottom, following close behind the guy and—well, the dog."

"The dog. On the ladder."

"Not exactly. So, the guy is going up the ladder backward, one arm around the dog, which is kind of hanging onto whatever portion of lap the guy can keep available. The guy hitches himself up slat by slat, very slowly, very carefully, while the woman stays a couple of slats below him on the ladder so she can break the fall of the dog if the guy can't hang onto it."

He lifted his pack, set it to his left so it was no longer between us, and pulled a phone out of one of the pockets. He shifted himself close to me as he swiped through his photos.

"You gotta see this."

He'd shot a short video of the trio. Their progress was slow and looked painful.

Conroy leaned closer. "Watch the expression on the dog's face."

I could smell Conroy's sun-warmed skin. It was hard to concentrate on the phone. But as I watched, the guy lost his grip on the ladder for a second and nearly dropped the dog, and the dog's eyes—already unnaturally wide open and glaringly white against the dog's dark grey coat—grew even bigger. Conroy and I both laughed, and he settled back onto his own spot on the rock.

"I take it they all survived?"

"They did. Though it was a bit of a pain waiting for them to get all the way up. I passed them on the trail as soon as I was up the ladder."

"Wonder how they'll make it down again."

"That will be a challenge. Don't think I want to watch."

As if on cue, a man's voice behind us called, "Here, boy!" I heard something crashing through the trees behind us, and then panting noises grew louder.

"Uh oh. Well, that's it for me." Conroy closed his pack and started to stand up.

"Wait!" I was almost too late, but Conroy sat down again just as the dog skidded out onto the rock and plowed into him. If he'd been partially standing, or all the way up, the dog might have sent him careening over the ledge.

A woman's voice called, "Sorry!"

I grabbed the dog's collar and held on as Conroy rolled away from the edge of the granite ledge and got to his feet. Pack gripped in one hand, he turned toward the two people approaching us.

I couldn't see Conroy's face, but I knew he was not happy. The dog's people were grinning, their apparent good humor obviously covering up nervousness. Conroy said nothing to them, just pulled out his phone again.

"Nathan, is there a tag on the collar?"

I twisted the collar to see. "Yeah."

"Would you hold it still?" And Conroy took a close shot of the tag. He turned to the couple. "I've already got photos of the two of you." He let that hang in the air, possibly so the people would wonder what that was going to mean for them.

Conroy hefted his pack and shrugged into it. "Do you have a leash for the dog?"

The man said, "Um, well, yeah, but—"

"Put it on him." The man started to protest. Conroy moved over to him, stopping mere inches from his face. "Put. It. On. Him." His voice was not loud, but it was heavy with threat. "Now."

"Teddy," the woman said, obviously frightened, "go ahead. It's probably better, anyway."

Teddy said nothing, didn't move a muscle. So the woman dug into a pocket in his pack and came up with a leash. She held it out to Teddy, but he didn't take it.

Conroy did. He tossed it to me and told Teddy, "I was in the process of getting up when your dog crashed into me. If my friend hadn't warned me to sit down, both your dog and I would have gone over the edge. Do you know what's down there? Do you think either of us would have survived?"

Teddy shrugged and backed a few inches away from Conroy. I fastened the leash to the dog's collar, but I was close enough to the edge that I didn't want to try and stand up while controlling the dog, who was not exactly settled. I held the other end of the leash out to the woman behind me, who came and took it.

As I got to my feet I heard Conroy tell Teddy, "If I see you on this trail, or any other trail, and you have an off-leash dog, I will report you."

He moved away, back toward the trail, and I followed, shrugging into my pack. I was barely past Teddy when I heard him grumble, "Asshole."

I froze, turned toward him, and glared. The woman said, "Never mind, Teddy. Let's have a water break." She coaxed him toward the ledge where Conroy and I had been sitting, and I turned back toward the trail.

Conroy was waiting for me. "Sorry if that seemed harsh. And, by the way, thanks for saving my ass."

"No problem."

"I hate dogs.

"Really? How come?"

"Don't know, actually. Just always have. You, uh, you wanna join up for a bit here?"

I did, even though I wasn't altogether sure what to make of Conroy; I mean, how could anyone hate dogs and not know why? Was it like "I was mauled by my neighbor's dog when I was a kid," or something like that? Plus, he'd been a little—harsh was his word, and I guess it fit. But he was still intriguing, and I could pump him for information about trails I'd need to consider if I was ever going to earn that patch.

As we hiked we talked trails, in New Hampshire and elsewhere, and I got the impression that either he was showing me how well he could maintain breath control by talking non-stop while climbing up steep sections, or he was testing me, or both. It didn't matter; we were well matched in terms of ability and physical conditioning.

He'd hiked in the Rockies. He'd hiked in Austria. He'd hiked in Alaska, and Canada, and Norway.

At one point I asked, "What, not in New Zealand?"

He grinned at me. "Maybe that'll be next. I've been working my way in that direction. Ever hiked the Kalalau Trail?"

"Never heard of it." There was no point in being coy, in trying to seem more experienced than I was. I knew that whatever I'd done, Conroy had done so much more. "Kaua'i. Absolute paradise. And in some ways, absolute hell. That island is the whole ball of wax."

As we continued toward the summit, my favorite bits were when the trail was too narrow to walk side by side. Either I was in front, and I wondered if he was watching my ass, or he was in front, and I was definitely watching his.

By the time we were approaching the observation tower at the summit, it was obvious we would not be there alone. Far from it, in fact. There was an easier trail to the summit than the one Conroy and I had taken—one without a ladder—and there was that aerial tramway that brought people up from the base as well.

Conroy had set us a very fast pace, and it wasn't quite noon yet. As we stood near the base of the tower, he didn't say much to me. He avoided the tower and just did his best to position himself so that he could see as much of the distant mountains as possible while maximizing the distance between himself and other people. It wasn't clear to me whether he was also maximizing the distance between the two of us. Was this his opportunity to be off on his own again? Should I take a hint and go back to my own plan of a solitary hike?

The answer became moot when I realized that Conroy was nowhere in sight.

To hell with Conroy, I decided. I wanted to get a view from as great a height as I could. I climbed the steps up the observation tower to the viewing platform.

On one hand, it was worth every step of the climb up the tower. On another—maybe it shouldn't have surprised me to see so many people up here, but I wasn't quite prepared for the masses of them. There was an older couple with a small, fluffy dog in a carryall. There was a young couple so androgynous-looking in their black leather clothing and boots, and silver piercings, and colorfully-dyed hair, that I couldn't tell whether either of them was male, female, or neither. A short, plump woman wearing an orange sari nearly bumped into me as she stared at the screen on her phone, experiencing the vista on that tiny window so she could watch it again, hours later, on that same tiny screen. There were also people whose hiking gear identified them as having arrived at the summit, like me, under their own steam.

I managed to find an opening on the platform that afforded me a great view to the south. I leaned my arms on the railing and let my gaze blur into the distance, past Lake Winnipesaukee toward Concord, where Gram was either working in the small vegetable garden behind our house, or taking a nap, or putting a dinner together for the two of us. Nina was in New York City, making friends with her two new roommates, about to start an internship at a fashion magazine.

Every time I left for a hike, usually in Gram's car, leaving Gram at home alone, I felt a wrench. She'd been our mother and father and everything else a good parent can be ever since my folks and Gram's husband had died in a traffic accident, when I was all of one year old. If Neil had been alive, he'd already be married to Cotton, the girl he'd met at grad school, and he'd be living someplace other than Concord. Nina had finished her undergrad years and might be headed for more school in New York. I was the only one left, and I know Gram felt lonely, even when I was home with her.

I stared into the hazy distance and wondered whether every youngest child with only one parent felt like this. Did I owe Gram anything? I owed her everything. And yet it was her job to prepare me to leave her behind, and she'd done it well.

That didn't mean it wasn't supposed to hurt.

Almost unconsciously I became aware that someone had taken a position close beside me. Conroy was back.

"Penny for your thoughts."

I wasn't sure how that made me feel. The closest I could come was slightly annoyed; he disappears without a word, and he just pops in again as though he hadn't left? Who does that?

Without looking at him I said, "They're worth more than that."

He laughed. "I like that. Think I'll save it for when I might need it."

"You may quote me."

He leaned on the railing beside me, both of us staring into the same distance but thinking our own thoughts, until Conroy said, "Let's blow this scene, eh? You up for the Kinsmans?"

He pointed toward the two closest summits to the south. They looked green and welcoming. Plus, I knew that the hardest part of the hike was behind me; although we'd need to go back down the Hi-Cannon for a little way, claiming the two Kinsman peaks would be a relatively small matter of some ups and downs as we walked the ridge. We wouldn't need to start at the highway.

I turned my wrist so I could see the face of the Garmin Forerunner hiker's watch that Gram had given me for my birthday last year. It was just past noon. Before I could reply, Conroy whistled.

"Nice watch. Does it have GPS?"

"It has about everything. Um, sure. Let's do the loop."

As we descended the tower stairs, he said, "I figure we can put some distance behind us, find a spot on North Kinsman for a lunch break."

"Sounds good."

Back on the trail again, he asked where I lived, I told him, and I mentioned I was about to start my senior year at college. I asked where he lived and learned he was house-sitting in

Wolfboro, on Lake Winnipesaukee, for the summer. Before I could ask why the owners wouldn't want to be in their own lake house for the summer, he went on to say that he had another house-sitting job lined up for the winter. I didn't ask about his work or question his apparent peripatetic lifestyle; each to his own, I figured.

We didn't talk much after leaving Cannon, but that was fine by me. And anyway, having a hiking companion who didn't chatter meant I could pay attention to the trees, to the feel of the occasional breeze on my face and arms, to the solid feel of my boots on the granite. The quiet also gave me the space to relish the slight burn in my thigh muscles as the trail climbed, and when the trail descended I could take pride in the work I'd done to condition the muscles above my knees and alongside my shin bones. If those muscles aren't in good shape, the work of constantly lowering your entire weight onto surfaces below you will wreck them to a point where walking downhill the next day will be a real struggle.

There was one distant view that appeared suddenly between the trees on the way to North Kinsman that made me freeze in my tracks. We were going along at a good pace, and I was in front at the moment (for once). Vistas were appearing between the trees or above open ledges, too many of them to count, and certainly too many to stop for each one, or we'd never get where we were going. But this one spot....

It felt as though someone had put it there just for me, someone who knew I would be right where I was on a day like today. There was some color on distant hills, slopes that rolled downward one behind the other, all pointing more or less toward the pristine, level plane of a pure blue lake.

Where had I seen this before? Why did it have such a powerful effect on me? Why did it feel so painfully bittersweet?

Conroy nearly bumped into me from behind. He stopped short and moved to stand beside me, and we both stared into the distance. I couldn't speak.

ON THE KALALAUA TRAIL

He could. "Another gorgeous vista." He heaved a sigh, part leftover exertion and part appreciation, and then he headed off along the trail, leaving me standing there. My heart felt swollen. Tears welled up in my eyes. I heard myself whisper, "What *is* it?" I'd never been on this trail before, and yet that scene felt so familiar, so agonizingly familiar. Finally I had to move on, but the image—and the mystery—stayed in my head.

The rest of the hike to North Kinsman was rugged, and when we reached the summit I feared that it wasn't going to be lunch-with-a-view; there was a lot of open granite, but the trees grew up along the sides of the trail, blocking a good bit of the vista. However, after Conroy planted his boot on the summit marker, he headed away from the trail as though he knew right where he wanted to be. I followed. He stopped on an open granite expanse from which the view was fairly open. We sat on the warm, prickly granite and gazed silently for a minute or two. I looked for my vista, the one that had moved me so much, but it was gone. At least, I couldn't see it from here.

I'd packed my usual hiking lunch: peanut butter on whole wheat with honey; an apple; a chocolate bar; and lots of water.

Conroy had cheese and bread, an orange, and more gorp. He watched with amusement as I had to lick my fingers where honey dripped out of the sandwich.

"You're enjoying that, aren't you?"

"I love honey."

He tilted his head in a way that might be teasing, or it might be insinuating, or it might be both. "I was referring to the licking."

Something about his voice made me look harder at his face. Did that tone carry some meaning? His eyes on mine, he used his teeth to tear a hunk of bread off the large piece in his hand, exaggerating the action as though making a point. But what point?

Before I could figure anything out he turned his head to gaze into the distance, at the limited view that was open to us from this spot.

CHAPTER TWO

On the trail to South Kinsman, which was as rugged and rocky as any trail I've been on, I might as well have been hiking alone. Conroy took the lead immediately and didn't relinquish it for the entire short distance to our third and final peak for the day. I had no trouble keeping up with him, though it did seem as though he was trying to see if he could leave me behind, or at least gain some space. Again, I felt a slight irritation; was he testing me? Was this his way of demonstrating how much more experienced a hiker he was?

The wind had picked up. It wasn't enough to make me strain against it, but it lifted Conroy's hair and ruffled it, and the loose ends of our pack straps whipped around, slapping against the nylon of the packs.

I reached the large cairn at the South Kinsman summit within seconds of Conroy and shrugged out of my pack, setting it on the ground beside where he'd put his. He stood on one side of that pile of stones and I stood on the other, each of us admiring the impressive view silently. There was no one else in sight. After a few minutes I took out my phone, stepped a little away from the cairn, and took a shot of it, carefully avoiding including Conroy on the shot. I slid the phone back into its pouch on my pack just as a group of three people, two women and a man, approached the summit, chatting and laughing. They greeted us with the standard, "Hi!" and we responded in kind. One of the women approached Conroy and asked him something about trails. I couldn't quite hear what they were saying.

Each of the other two people added a stone to the cairn, and the woman who'd spoken to Conroy asked him to take a shot of all three of them around the pile. Then they headed back to the trail they had come from and disappeared.

Conroy wandered a short distance away, found a stone slightly larger than his hand, and brought it back to set onto the cairn. I'd been thinking of doing that, but I decided against imitating his action; I hadn't enjoyed always being the follower on the last part of the trail, and I didn't mind giving up the privilege of adding to the cairn if it meant asserting myself even this little bit.

He looked at me. "You should take another shot."

"Why?"

"It's got my stone on it now."

I gave a short laugh as if that was slightly amusing and left my phone packed away. The way he'd looked at me after the comment about licking honey, and even the comment itself, had left me feeling off-balance. If he wanted to let me know something, he should do it. Or was he waiting for me to give him more of an opening? Maybe that was the off-balance feeling; I didn't know what to do.

I wasn't especially shy about letting a complete stranger know, in a setting where no one else would hear or care, that I was gay. It wasn't any of Conroy's business, though, unless he was gay and was trying to establish a connection. But what kind of a connection?

I'd had a few months of something approaching bliss with a man named Alden Armstrong my freshman year at UNH, and since then I'd had some number of very casual, very brief encounters with guys I met on campus, guys I mostly didn't see again, guys I didn't especially want to see again. I'd gotten pretty burned when Alden had disappeared from campus—and from my life— without a word. It hadn't helped that I'd fallen for another guy after that, a guy who'd proved to be nothing like what I'd thought he was. So I was leery of letting anyone past some kind of outer perimeter. But surely I knew the danger signs well enough by now to avoid making that mistake again. Right?

Watching Conroy's face for a reaction to my refusal to preserve an image of "his" rock on the cairn, I had to admit there was something about him that pulled at me more than any of those causal-encounter guys. Should I be concerned that he might be another mistake?

Fuck. I had no idea.

All I cared about right now, this moment, on this mountaintop, was whether he had come on to me, how I could figure that out, and what I might like to do about it if he had. And all I knew was that I wasn't going out on a limb to find out.

So I tried a test of my own. "Think it's time I headed back. You staying for a bit?"

I couldn't read his face. He was silent for several seconds, and then he walked closer to me, slowly enough that it was evident he wasn't headed for the return trail. He didn't stop until his body was mere inches from mine. I didn't back away.

Did I want this? And what was it? My brain felt disconnected from the rest of me. As for the rest of me, the chill of the wind was a fascinating counterpoint to the warmth that had started somewhere in my belly and was making me wonder if the glow was visible. Was this the casual sex, the one-off-with-a-near-stranger that had been my diet since my sophomore year?

Sure. Why not?

Conroy tilted his head, one side of his mouth lifted in a slight smile, and he answered my question about whether he was leaving or staying. "Depends."

We were so close that I had no more doubts about his intentions. I lifted my chin a tiny bit. "On?"

"Are you enjoying my company as much as I'm enjoying yours?"

I dropped my eyes to his mouth and opened mine just a smidge. My message: *I'm here. The next move is yours.*

He moved. It was quick, and it was slow. Suddenly, and yet over the course of what seemed like minutes, he leaned toward me and oh, so gently placed his lips on mine and then pulled away. I heard myself gasp despite the sound of the wind whipping around us. In his eyes I saw lust, desire, and something that wasn't exactly courage, just something that didn't care that other people could appear any second.

His hands grasped both sides of my jaw, essentially claiming control of my head. I'm not sure what my hands did, but they hung onto some part of his body, kneading hard through the dark red synthetic clothing he wore. As his tongue thrust into my mouth, I lowered my hands to his ass and pressed him against me. It felt instinctive, perfect, natural. It was all of those things.

Oh, God! Why did Conroy feel different from anyone I'd been with, ever? For reasons I didn't understand, my mind came up with an image of Alden's tall, slender frame. Conroy was muscular, solid, overtly masculine without being bulky. I loved it. I wanted it. Badly.

I had a moment of hesitation in which my brain said, *Really? You're going to fuck a complete stranger, outdoors, on a mountaintop? The guys you've been with at school were not complete strangers. You know nothing about Conroy, and if that's not enough you're in full view of anyone who rounds the bend of that trail and heads toward the cairn on the summit!*

Then: *Why not? And: Is there a better place for this than a mountaintop?*

Conroy pulled his head back, eyes half shut, breath coming in short pants. He took my hand and half-led, half-pulled me toward our packs. Without pausing, we grabbed our own packs with our free hands, and I let Conroy lead the way to a group of scrub pines a little distance from the cairn. In the dubious shelter of the spot, we nearly ripped open our packs and pulled out any extra clothing we'd brought.

Rain ponchos strewn with polar fleece vests protecting us from the ground, we lowered our shorts and then our bodies onto the pile. His body was as I would have expected: firm, compact, with subtle but definite muscle definition, and very little body hair above his waist—essentially, in my opinion, perfection. After a rather abbreviated (by my usual standards, anyway) period of kissing and stroking and squeezing, Conroy positioned himself so that he could take my dick into his mouth.

Wow, I thought; *he's not wasting time.*

His hard dick was now practically in my face. As I got ready to wrap my lips around it, I noticed it had a particularly distinct curl to the right which I found charming; it was as though there was one thing about this man's physique that wasn't absolutely perfect, and only someone who saw him naked and hard would know about it. It gave me the odd feeling of having been let in on a secret.

In standard sixty-nine position we licked and sucked and kneaded and squeezed. This wasn't the first time I'd had sex outdoors, so I was ready for the amazing sensation of cool, fresh air flowing across intimate areas that had just been warmed by a man's moist mouth. I did my best to make sure this was part of Conroy's experience as well, moving from his belly to his balls and on to the end of his dick, leaving a trail of warm moisture as I went.

Sex with Conroy, once he took me fully into his mouth, was hard, insistent, and immediate. Finesse had nothing to do with it, affection had nothing to do with it, and there was no time—or any inclination—to think.

When he lifted his head away from me, one hand massaging my balls and the other pulling on the end of my dick, I followed his example. We came within seconds of each other.

With the salty, musty taste of Conroy teasing the sides of my mouth and the warmth of his cum oozing onto my chest, I lay back onto our impromptu mountain bed and panted. There was a slight odor of mushrooms; was that Conroy, or had we made our bed on top of some phallic fungi?

As my breathing calmed, my eyes gradually focused

enough to see dark evergreen needles on stiff branches overhead, framing a section of bright blue sky with whiffs of white cloud skittering across.

Conroy was ready to get up before I was. He wiped himself off with a paper towel from his pack, no doubt originally intended as a lunchtime napkin. Then he repacked the bits of clothing that were his, stood, and shrugged into the pack.

"Hope we meet again, Nathan Bartlett. I like hiking with you. Among other things." He grinned, turned, and was off. He disappeared quickly, and the sounds of his boots snapping twigs and shuffling through everything else underfoot faded into the distance.

I pulled myself together and sat up, elbows on knees. My mind wandered as I stared through the brittle pine branches at partially visible ledges of granite and at the sections of sky that weren't obscured by trees.

Here's where my wandering mind went. Nina is fond of musicals. A few years ago, I sat with her and watched a recording of Steven Sondheim's *Into the Woods*. There's a scene toward the end where a character known only as The Baker's Wife is walking through the woods, and she comes upon Prince Charming, whose wife (somewhere far away) is Cinderella. He's not a terrible fellow, just a terrible husband, and he seduces Baker's Wife. Mind you, she doesn't exactly resist, though she has moments of hesitation. When it's over, he says, "I shall not forget you," and he disappears. She looks around at nothing, stunned, and says, "*What* was that?"

As I heard her words in my head, I nodded. Aloud, I said, "Exactly." And then I sighed, took a long swig of water, dressed, repacked my gear, and went to find the trail so I could retrace my steps, reconnect with the Hi-Cannon Trail, and make my way back to Gram's car before it got dark.

I didn't expect to see Conroy again. Certainly I had no way of contacting him; as far as I know, there is no listing for where house-sitters are at any point in time. Plus it wouldn't be long before I had to return to campus for my final year at UNH, and although I was pretty sure El Speed and I would do some fall hiking, that "some" would not be a lot. And there were a lot of mountains. It was unlikely Conroy and I would find ourselves on the same one again.

Alone for the descent, I had a kind of conversation going on in my head, starting with a voice that thought what Conroy and I had done had been great.

Voice one: "That was a really wild thing to do."

Voice two: "That was kind of a *dangerous* thing to do, and not because of the mountain. When have you ever fucked a guy you didn't know at all? Your encounters have been with college students. You knew where they lived. Or you knew their friends, or what their majors were, or friggin' *something* about them!"

One: "Yeah, but—why not let it happen?"

Two: "Okay, but is that who you are? Really? Be honest."

[Silence for several seconds.]

One: [reluctantly] "No."

Two: "And what about the way he made you feel? Was that really as casual as you're pretending?"

One: "Well...."

Two: "So...."

One: "Look, it's not gonna happen again, all right?" [No response.] "*All right?*"

It went on like that for a while, with one version of me heady and excited about the encounter, and another version knowing something outside of me had taken over and allowed that to happen. I did my best to put it behind me by assuring myself it had been merely a romp in the woods à la Stephen Sondheim.

And I decided not to tell anyone, not even my best friend. As comfortable as El Speed was with my being gay, and far from prudish though he was, I wasn't sure what he'd make of how I'd celebrated claiming three peaks in one day.

In the trees. Fucking Conroy.

El Speed didn't know much about my sexual encounters. For one thing, I didn't consider them worth talking about. And for another, I'd never known him to be with anyone other than his girlfriend Ellie, at least not as long as I'd known him. If my encounters with any of the guys I'd fucked had been—or had turned into—something with some staying power, he would have wanted to know, and I would have told him. But I wasn't sure what he thought of my casual approach to sex, or what he thought of me for indulging in it.

Yeah, best not to test El Speed with Conroy.

INTERLUDE I: POOR JUDGEMENT

When Neil had died, I'd just finished my freshman year at the University of New Hampshire, UNH, the alma mater for all three of us kids. Our family didn't have a lot of money, and the state school was the best financial choice for us, a benefit we could take advantage of because we lived in Concord. It had served Neil especially well, because of the environmental program. He was a mountain man, through and through, and wildlife management was where he was headed.

The summer after he died, I stepped into his hiking boots, in a manner of speaking.

I'd never hiked with Neil, though he'd invited me a few times. My first climb—still not with Neil—had been a profoundly ill-advised hike up Mount Chocorua in March of my freshman year. In a snowstorm. Without proper equipment, and with absolutely no common sense. And it isn't even in the four-thousand-foot group. It was a misadventure that never would have happened if I'd been hiking with Neil.

This is where Daniel comes into the story—the "Daniel" Nina had said was a loser. Daniel Cooke was a couple of years older than me, he was my supervisor at my job in a campus dishroom, and he was hot. I had wet dreams about him. His chops in terms of mountaineering rivaled Neil's. Unfortunately for me, or so it seemed at first, he was more interested in Nina than in me. I could tell, as soon as he met Nina, that he was attracted to her somewhat exotic appearance, attributable at least in part to our Chinese maternal great-grandmother. Plus, you know, Nina is very pretty.

Another problem was that I gave him too much credit for being like Neil. Where Neil was organized and careful, Daniel was spontaneous and impulsive. He had been so impulsive that he'd done only a cursory job of reviewing my hiking equipment, which had left me woefully unprepared for a long climb in winter conditions. He hadn't researched the trail system on the mountain and didn't even know there were multiple trails. He hadn't known that the trail we took would not lead to the cabin where he'd planned for us to spend the night, so we spent the night in the snow. And in the morning he'd nearly led us down a trail that would have left us nowhere near the car, stranded in the dark, in no condition by then to survive another night in winter wilderness.

So I was mistaken on two counts. Yeah, he was hot, and he gave me a lot of attention, but even though he'd told me he was straight, I'd been blinded by lust. And despite being "a mountain man," he was nothing like Neil. Together these mistakes had nearly cost me my life and had left me with frostbitten feet.

The residual effects of the frostbite, as my podiatrist explained to me, were that my feet lost the ability to regulate their own temperature, so that in hot weather they got hot and needed help cooling down. In cold weather (which, in New Hampshire and by the standards of my injured feet, was between sometime in September and sometime in May), they got cold very easily, very quickly, and couldn't warm themselves up. Warmth usually had to come externally in the form of a warm-water bath or some other heat applied directly. The alternative was aerobic activity, so I could still do the kind of skiing I loved—Nordic—as long as I kept moving, but there would be no more winter hiking for me. Anytime I was inactive for more than a few minutes, the cold would set in, the feet would react by sweating (which only made things worse, because evaporation cooled them further), and then they would become painful. Really painful. The kind of pain that stops short of agony but that pretty much keeps me from focusing on anything else.

The frostbite that had damaged my feet would be a life-long reminder of poor judgement.

As I headed into my senior year at UNH, I was determined not to repeat my youthful mistakes. In support of my intentions, I would complete my undergraduate degree in a subject I was sure would guide me: psychology. It was a choice born of my need to help myself learn how to navigate life as a gay man, to help me reject the shame I felt society tried to make me carry, and to help me trust that I had as good a chance as anyone else of finding love. At least, that was my first reason. Before the end of my freshman year, I had two other reasons to feel drawn to a career in psychology.

Reason number two was that Neil's death left a gap much bigger than the loss of a brother, tragic though that would be for anyone. Neil had stepped as well as he could into the shoes my father would have worn if he and my mother hadn't died when I was barely a year old. "As well as he could" is a bit of an understatement. Neil was not perfect, but in my eyes he was as close to it as a real human being could get.

Neil had been the first person I'd come out to. I remember being scared shitless, even though it shouldn't have surprised me that he'd been as accepting as he was.

"I want to know about *you*," he'd said. "You need to be who you are," he'd said. "My best friend is gay," he'd said.

Every time I remember that scene, how loved he'd made me feel, how hopeful, my eyes start to water.

Reason number three has to do with addiction.

Addiction can come in a number of forms. It's not out of the question to say that in a certain way, I'd been addicted to Neil, or at least to Neil's love, to his support. I can tell you that his sudden death—and the manner of it—sure made me feel like I was going through detox of some kind. But I don't mean to make light of substance abuse, or of the struggle to live with the constant pull it has on people in recovery. It took one of my friends away from college in his freshman year, and it destroyed my first romantic relationship.

I was determined to understand, as well as I could, the need, the compulsion, the pull that addiction has. And I wanted to help people who suffered from it.

CHAPTER THREE

El Speed and I were in our room after dinner one evening, in late September, sort of doing classwork, sort of not. I'd been thinking of a specific climb—Mount Madison, five thousand, three hundred and sixty-seven feet above sea level. Definitely a four-thousand-foot qualifier.

I told my roommate, "I think it's time for a hike. Maybe Columbus Day weekend? Give you an extra day to recover."

He looked sideways at me. "You wanna drag me up another massive mountain?" His tone told me that, as I expected, he was feigning reluctance. With most of our hikes, the dynamic was that I'd suggest, he'd teasingly resist, I'd cajole, and he'd pretend to capitulate—pretend, because he actually liked hiking together.

"Madison is a great climb. Remote, so not a lot of other hikers. No ski slopes, so you won't bump into people in tank tops and flip-flops who rode a ski lift to the summit. I think it'll make a great overnight climb."

"Yeah. Just like Lafayette. I haven't forgotten that fiasco."

"That was a blast! How many times have you dined out on that story? And anyway, you got a new frame pack out of it."

He glared at me from the corners of his eyes. "Well… but I can't go that weekend. Promised Ellie I'd go home to Maine then. Spend that weekend with her."

I didn't mean for there to be an edge to the look I gave him, but I'm sure he saw it. But it had always seemed to me that he spent an inordinate number of weekends at home in Lewiston, Maine, with Ellie. She was at school in Orono, and

I wondered if her roommate or friends there felt like I did sometimes, when she returned to Lewiston to be with "Larry." What I felt like was a little deserted.

El Speed went to his bureau and opened a top drawer. As he fished around inside it, he said, "Y'know, one of these days you're gonna meet someone special, and all of a sudden you won't have any time for me."

I was about to protest when I noticed that what he'd pulled out of the drawer was a little grey velvet box. My eyes followed it as he brought it closer to me and opened it. Inside, predictably, was a ring. An unusual ring. A single dark stone was surrounded by tiny diamonds, set into a silver-colored metal. I think my jaw dropped.

"The black diamond was in a ring my grandmother had. She gave it to me in her will. I had the white diamonds set around it. White gold." He gave me a minute to gawk before adding, "I don't suppose I have to tell you what I'm going to do with it."

I looked up at my best friend's face, and the softness, the vulnerability I saw there made me drop my eyes back to the ring. "It's incredibly beautiful." I swallowed. "Are you asking her that weekend?"

He snapped the case shut and replaced it in the drawer. "Our first date in high school was a long walk in the woods Columbus Day weekend. Senior year." He sat in his desk chair and swiveled it toward me, his elbows resting on his knees, hands gently clasped. El Speed is tall and long-limbed, and there was something elegant about his posture at that moment.

He chuckled. "It was kind of a test. I'd broken up with a girlfriend who always seemed to think I should be spending money on her. I didn't mind springing for movie tickets or the occasional hamburger, but every time we got together it seemed like she wanted to empty my wallet. So when I asked Ellie out the first time, what I said was, 'How would you feel about a walk through Riverlands?' That's on the Androscoggin. I know that won't mean much to you, but it's a long network of trails along the river, just north of Lewiston. It would be a date, but one where I wouldn't spend more money than gas for the car."

His eyes looked away from me just a little and he seemed to be seeing something from a memory. A good one. So I prompted, "I take it she agreed."

He grinned his lopsided grin. "We must have walked five miles that day. All through the woods, along the river. The leaves were amazing, every color in the world. And Ellie," he had to stop for a wide grin here, "Ellie had packed a picnic lunch. So we ate that and then wandered. And wandered. We talked and talked... I'd never felt like that with anyone before."

I grinned back. "Sounds like you need to be in Maine for Columbus Day weekend, all right. So what about Madison the weekend before? I can't go too late in the season because of my feet."

"Right. The frostbite. Okay, so we'll go the weekend before. But I ain't hikin' it twice!"

I almost wanted to thank El Speed for telling me about that first date with Ellie. It had felt like an intimate moment between us, and I cherished those. Our relationship had been as perfect as it could have been, right from the start of freshman year. I loved him like a brother. And I'd spent enough time with him and Ellie to believe that they were meant for each other in a way few couples are.

The first time I'd met her was just after the end of freshman year. El Speed had invited me to spend a few days in his family's cabin, on a remote lake in central Maine. Maybe I should have realized that Ellie would be there, too, but when I saw a tall, strawberry blond young woman with a Victoria's Secret body dressed like a lumberjack, it surprised me. Not in a good way.

She was every bit as comfortable in the wilds of Maine as El Speed. It didn't faze her that there was no indoor plumbing or electricity in the cabin. She and El Speed had spent enough time there that they had the food issues all figured out, the most annoying of which was that although we could cook with eggs and cheese, meat would have spoiled without refrigeration. She made fun of me when I complained about the mosquitoes that were sucking my blood all night long, and she committed a horrendous faux pas by trying to make me feel unreasonable because I'd wanted Neil to come home before going hiking in The Priest Wilderness. As it turned out, his change in plans—going to meet Cotton's parents in San Diego instead of coming home between the end of school and the start of that hike—meant I never saw him again.

To her credit, she and El Speed came to Neil's funeral, and she felt terrible about the way she'd spoken to me about Neil. So we made friends, and the better I knew her the more I knew she was the perfect mate for El Speed. I knew he'd been thinking of marriage since our freshman year, and I was a little surprised there'd been no development on that front up to this point. Guess that was about to change.

Madison was every bit the challenge Neil had once described to me. El Speed and I went up the same route Neil and Jeremy had climbed once, up the south side of the mountain and through the Great Gulf Wilderness. A good part of our trail was little more than a dried-up stream bed, paved irregularly with rocks and boulders of different shapes and sizes, some stable in their spots and some ready to wobble under our boots and send us tumbling head-first onto yet more rocks. It was a crisp, brilliant day, perfect for the exertion necessary for this climb. I relished every step. My roommate? Maybe not quite so much.

"Whose idea was this, anyway?" El Speed grumbled as he struggled to maintain his balance after yet another rock tried to topple him.

"Yours. I'm sure of it."

Five minutes later: "Are we there yet?"

"Sure. Which pile of rocks would you like to make camp on?"

It went on like that for a good part of the climb. There'd be long silences punctuated by a "Shit!" or a "Fuck!" from El Speed. Every once in a while we'd come upon a moderately easy incline through woods instead of over treacherous rocks, which would put him in a better mood and we'd chat about nothing in particular.

At the top of one particularly challenging rocky stretch, the trees to my left opened up enough that if I stood in just the right spot, I could see for miles to the west. I stood still, breathing deeply, and waited for my grumbling roommate to catch up with me.

"Man," he said, breathing hard from exertion, but unable not to admire the view, which he could see over my head. "I'm pretty sure we can see the Green Mountains in the distance, all the away into Vermont."

"I think you're right."

He took a few more deep breaths. "Will you tell me why it's easier for a little short person like you to climb these monsters than it is for me?"

I laughed. "My center of gravity is lower. Probably means I'm more stable."

"Yeah, but you're faster on *all* the trails."

I didn't respond; I knew he didn't expect me to. But the feeling his comments gave me felt like powerful validation of my decision to pick up where Neil had left off. And today, I was truly walking in his footsteps, and doing a very creditable job of it. I needed to think he'd be proud of me.

We weren't planning to hit the summit until the next day, but it wasn't quite late enough yet to begin scouting for a good campsite. After that last rocky bit, we followed the trail into a relatively flat section of woods where we lost the trail markers. All around us were young white pines, the lower parts of their dark brown trunks empty of branches because the sun didn't penetrate through the upper boughs.

El Speed wandered off slowly toward the left, with his head down to spot any rocks that might have a trail marker painted on them, and I wandered mostly straight ahead and a little to the right, also looking down, until I saw something as dark brown and as straight as the pine trunks, but much thinner. There was a black hoof on the bottom of it.

My head snapped up, and a sharp intake of air made my chest expand. I smelled my own fear: sharp, even acrid. Towering over me—or so it felt like, and probably close to true—was a moose. She was maybe ten feet ahead of me. She eyed me casually, her jaw moving slowly on whatever plant material dangled from her mouth.

I backed slowly away from her, and when I was far enough to feel as though I could take my eyes off of her, I looked for El Speed.

"Hey!" I called in a hoarse whisper.

El Speed stopped, looked at me, saw the moose, and gasped. "Fuck me dead!"

We both froze, and the moose kept her gaze on me.

"Don't look directly at her," El Speed whispered. "Back away slowly."

I could tell that behind me, he was moving away as well, and then I heard him start running, so I turned and did the same. We didn't run far, just far enough that we couldn't see the moose any longer.

Between panting breaths, El Speed told me, "It's rutting season. It isn't the females we need to worry about. But if she's here, a cantankerous 'he' might not be far away. And any of those creatures can kill you easily."

"Look," I pointed to a painted marker on a boulder.

"She did us a favor, looks like."

"Or maybe she just wanted to get rid of us so she and another moose could have some privacy."

36

"Oh, yeah," he said, his tone wrapped in pretend sarcasm. "I'm sure that was it."

We made camp below the tree line. With the tent set up and my camp stove ready to make dinner, we took a brief rest and sat on a log we'd rolled into a good spot near the front of the tent.

El Speed took a sip of water. "Guess I'll have another story to dine out on, thanks to your moose."

"My moose? Why is it my moose?"

"I been thinking. This wasn't my idea, no matter what you said."

I loved this banter. Much as I had adored my actual brother, there had always been something serious about him, probably because he saw his role in our family as a very weighty one. El Speed was a good-natured peer, teasing out of respect as much as fun and never from a place of superiority in any way.

We sat on the log to eat our reconstituted beef stroganoff and carrots, chocolate bars for dessert, and once we'd finished we sat there as what light was left of the day seemed to drift farther and farther away from us.

After a few minutes of silence, El Speed said, "You know why I like this?"

"Hiking?"

He gave a kind of snort. "Actually, I'm talkin' about hanging out in the woods, listening to the trees talk to each other, passing their communication from one of them to another and another in the wind."

I turned to look at him, or as much of him as I could see in the low light. "How many times have we hiked," I asked him, "and you've never said anything like that before?"

He shrugged, like it didn't really matter. But to me, it did. I just wasn't sure how to respond.

Then he said, "You've never told me what you get out

of this either, you know. I mean, beyond notching those boots of yours with four-thousand foot tallies."

I shifted my body to face him. "That's crap. You know I started hiking after Neil died."

"Cuz you never hiked with him. Yeah, I get that. But that can't be the only reason."

Was he right? I re-settled myself so that, like El Speed, I was gazing at the nearly black space between tree trunks on the gentle downward slope.

"So why do *you* like this?" His tone told me he really wanted to know. And the only place I knew to start was with Neil.

"You know, I asked Neil that question. He told me about how he felt small and massive at the same time. Small, because he could die on a mountain, and it wouldn't care. Massive, because at the summit, he'd get this feeling like he was part of everything there is."

El Speed took that in. "Okay, but I think my granddad got that feeling sailing. He'd take a small boat out onto the ocean. I'm thinkin' the ocean wouldn't care if you died out there, either."

"And d'you think he felt like he was part of everything out there?"

Another shrug. "Probably."

Maybe there were similarities. I wracked my brain to remember what else Neil had said, and my brain cooperated.

"So another thing I asked was why he liked hiking in the White Mountains in particular, where so many trails are much like the one we climbed today. He said, 'If you can hike in the Whites, you can hike anywhere.'"

"Meaning?"

"All the little things you have to pay attention to, like not shifting all your weight onto an unstable rock, or like finding the best place to cross a stream, are like everyday life. All those little details might seem unimportant, or like they don't have a lot of meaning in themselves. But Neil said they're the paving stones of life. And then, when you get to the summit and the whole world opens up to you, you're no longer focused on those particulars, those details. You might not even remember them. The feeling of being one with the majesty all around you is overwhelming. And the challenge is to remember that those fussy details of life are what got you here. They aren't unimportant. They're essential. They are the journey, and all together they make up the universe. They're part of the universe, just like us."

El Speed gave that some space and then said, "That's way too deep for me."

I chuckled. "I doubt that." And I did.

A bird call, nearby.

"Crow," said El Speed.

And then a different call. I asked, "Was that a hawk?"

El Speed shook his head. "Could be a sharp-shinned hawk, but I'd put more money on a falcon. It's higher, with a quicker repetition of the note."

We sat through a few minutes of silence punctuated by tiny rustlings in the fallen leaves around us. I focused on listening for those conversations the trees were sending to each other on the wind. Then I heard a few short hoots followed by a longer one. "Great horned."

"Nope. Barred owl. It's a similar pattern, but the great horned's call is richer and deeper."

More rustlings.

I asked, "D'you think Ellie's expecting your proposal next weekend?"

I'd been thinking about El Speed's plan a lot since he'd described it to me. For most of my life, marriage had been something not considered possible for gay people. Sure, I'd known Massachusetts and a few other states were making progress, but that would still have left me out of the picture if I'd moved to, like, Wisconsin. And then, just as I'd finished high school, came the Obergefell v. Hodges decision from the Supreme Court. That had surprised me, not just because all my life I'd bought into the idea that any partnership I formed wouldn't be recognized by law, or by most people, for that matter. It also surprised me how much it had meant to me to have it happen.

El Speed was very fond of a folk singer named David Wilcox. I couldn't say how many times I'd heard one song, "Hurricane," with this line in it: "You can get what's second best, but it's hard to get enough." That's how long-time gay relationships had always seemed to me, because of the little regard society sent our way. But now that I was out, now that I was ready to be who I am, I also knew what I wanted.

Someday, I wanted to be married.

I heard El Speed's low chuckle before he answered my question about Ellie. "I think if I didn't make my move soon, she'd make the arrangements and tell me where to be and when."

"But do you think she knows it'll be this weekend?" I poked his ribs with an elbow. "Does she know what a sentimentalist you are?"

He resettled himself on the log. "Nathan, women are a mystery. My mom has this book. It's called, *What Men Know About Women*. You open it up, and all the pages are blank." He picked up a stone and threw it into the darkness. "In a way, you're lucky. You're a guy, and you want a guy, and you know more or less what guys are like."

I snorted. "Hasn't helped me find anyone yet."

"But when you do, I expect it'll be easier for you to figure out what to do than if you were me."

I thought back to the only guy I could reasonably be said to have had a romantic relationship with. I'd fallen in love with Alden, or had at least been on the verge of it. But because of his history with—and return to—fentanyl, I would never know what I'd meant to him.

"I doubt it," I told him. And I meant it.

Almost immediately came a weird, braying kind of call from a tree very close to us. I looked at El Speed, not really able to make out his features in the dark. "Donkey bird?"

He laughed. "Eastern screech owl." He shifted his position again. "Time to turn in."

We crawled into the tent and into our respective sleeping bags, and I switched off the camp light. We bid each other good night, but before long I knew I had to pay attention to my feet. They were cold and starting to hurt. As quietly as possible, I sat up and pulled one sock-clad foot up toward my hands. I squeezed and released to encourage blood flow. I rubbed the ball of the foot rapidly. Finally I took the sock off and held as much of the foot as I could in my hands.

"I wish you didn't have to do that."

"Sorry," I said. "I won't be much longer."

"No. I mean I wish it hadn't happened to you."

In the morning, when I unzipped the tent door, everything outside was white. There was about half an inch of snow on the ground. It was exactly what Neil had told me had happened when he and Jeremy had claimed this peak.

It was a cold climb to the summit. We stood on either side of the obligatory cairn and gazed into the distance. It was a little cloudy, but the visibility was good. The wind, however, was biting right through my clothing layers.

"Man," El Speed said. "I'm beginning to understand why you do this."

"Finally!"

"Don't get excited. I'm not at all sure why *I* do this."

I could see his grin, and it made me feel a little warmer. "It's friggin' cold, though," I admitted. "Ready for our descent?"

"Thought you'd never ask."

"And that's what Ellie will say."

He laughed his loud, barking laugh, and the wind carried it away as we turned to head down.

When we got to the wooded section where we'd seen

the moose, we looked around carefully. El Speed stopped once, listening.

"Thought I heard a bull moose for a second."

"Deep? Thrumming?"

"Ha. You've never heard a moose call? They have this super high, ear-piercing kind of whistle that carries for miles. Kind of a metallic sound. Surprised the hell out of me the first time I heard it. But the ladies seem to find it irresistible."

"The straight ones."

He chuckled. "Right you are."

"You know," I started, and then wasn't sure I wanted to go on. My mind had traveled back several weeks to a certain mountain top where the call of the wild had ended in sex, if not procreation.

"Know what?"

Nothing for it; I hadn't thought I'd ever tell him, but— what the fuck. "I, uh…. Did I tell you the most interesting part of that climb I did last summer? Cannon, and the Kinsmans?"

"I doubt it. None of it sounded all that interesting, except the dog on the ladder."

"Yeah. Well, I mentioned meeting with that guy Conroy." Would he guess?

He did. And he froze in his tracks. "Nathan. Tell me you didn't."

I turned toward him and shrugged. "I could do that, but I'd be lying."

He rested one hand on his hip. "Fuckin' A."

"No, we didn't go that far."

He laughed so hard he had to sit on the ground. I don't know why that simple response touched me as much as it did, but I looked down at my roommate, my best friend, who was helpless with delighted laughter over a joke that related directly to an important difference between us, a difference that did nothing to diminish our friendship.

Rather than make El Speed feel self-conscious if he

caught me smiling at him, I looked up and gazed into the distance to the south. And I nearly gasped.

There it was. Or, almost. It was a scene very similar to the one that had affected me so powerfully during my hike with Conroy, the distant hills sloping down to blue water. Recognition hit me so suddenly I took a step back to keep my balance.

It reminded me of the tapestry that had been on the wall in Alden's living room, the one that later had helped me to know the best way to honor my brother.

INTERLUDE II: TAPESTRY OF LOVE

Alden Armstrong. Two years older than me, even though he
was a sophomore the same year I was a freshman. The reason
for the gap wasn't something he talked about. At least, not
right away.

Anyway, my first time, my first times, sexually, were
with Alden. He'd started things so casually, September of my
freshman year.

"I'm asking if you'd like to fuck," he'd said across a
café table from me. He wasn't looking for romance, he'd said,
just a fuck buddy.

The sex hadn't started right away; he hadn't realized I
was a virgin. But before too many more weeks had gone by,
I'd decided I was ready, and he was still interested.

I learned a lot from Alden. I learned what it felt like to
have a man, with a man's strength and a man's immediacy
and a man's insistence, hold me in a way that made my heart
and my dick throb in concert with each other. I learned and
loved the feel of having an end-of-day shaven face press and
rub against my own, and against my neck, against my belly
and my thighs. I learned the feel of the warm, wet inside of a
man's mouth, not just with my tongue but also with my dick.
And I learned the insane joy of holding another man's dick in
my hand, in my mouth, and—yes, eventually, in my ass. That
final ecstasy happened only once, our last time together as
things turned out. I never got to return the favor, as it were,
with Alden, though since then I've discovered that I like both
roles very much.

And, also because of Alden, I had learned the joy and
the pain of having a lover and then having him leave me
behind.

Alden's family had money. Lots of it. His mother had renovated the upstairs of a slightly rundown, colonial-style house outside of town for him to live in while he was at UNH. It held nice furniture and a few pieces of art. I particularly liked a figure about six inches high of dark green stone, carved to resemble a pile of rocks stacked in the shape of a rudimentary human form. Alden said it was an inukshuk, a small version of what Inuit people would use for trail markers.

My other favorite was a tapestry.

I'd noticed it on my very first visit. About two feet across and just over a foot high, it had hung on the wall between the two front windows in the living room. There were slightly abstract mountain shapes in lots of colors with the blue of a lake in the lower right.

"That's a Sarah Warren," Alden had told me. "Amazing weaver. Lives up in the northern part of the state."

Maybe Alden hadn't been looking for romance, but he'd found it. We both found it, I think. By December, I was in love with him. And I believed he felt the same. Maybe he did. But I'll never know for sure.

Alden disappeared after my first semester. Winter break. I went home to Concord, and Alden went home to St. Louis. When we parted just before the break, I knew I'd miss him like crazy, but I wasn't worried. I expected we'd communicate at least a little—the occasional text, maybe even a phone call or two. I wasn't looking for long, breathless conversations. I wasn't looking for phone sex. Maybe I'm the kind of person who trusts a little too soon or a little too much, but I'm not clingy, and neither was Alden. So a few connections would have been enough for me.

There was nothing. N-O-T-H-I-N-G. Or as good as. I texted him on Christmas Eve just to say I was thinking of him. All I got back was, *Same.* I felt dismissed. I didn't try again, and he didn't contact me. I hoped like hell I was being too sensitive, that he was just distracted with things at home. I wasn't worried that he'd met another guy, or that he'd rekindled some old flame—not because I thought it couldn't happen, but because that's not the way I think.

He was distracted, all right. And perhaps I might have considered the possibility of how that happened, because by then I knew some of his history. But for whatever reason, I never suspected.

Fentanyl is a wonderful thing, and it's a terrible thing. It's useful and good when used responsibly by medical specialists. But used in other ways, it's a killer. Alden didn't die, as far as I know. But he died to me. Or maybe I died to him first.

Once I asked him about the age gap between us, the apparently missing year, but all he said at the time was something cryptic like, "Have you ever seen the polar bear invasion in Churchill?" The truth, which he told me eventually, was that because of fentanyl he'd been in a rehab center in Canada—a very expensive one, thanks to his wealthy parents.

I'll never forget one of the things he said to me. He was describing substance abuse, and being addicted. He said: "When you're in it, what you're addicted to feels like your friend. It's a place where you can at least temporarily stop whatever emotional downward slide you're on. It seems better than suicide. It's a substitute for hope in a hopeless situation. So, giving it up.... Fuck. That feels like letting go of the only thing that's keeping you alive."

Over winter break, Alden went back into that place. Back into that darkness. Back to that "friend" that seemed better than suicide. I wish he *had* gone back an old boyfriend.

Christ. Just thinking about that hurts like hell.

Before Alden and I had started our relationship, I'd fallen in lust—never quite love—with Daniel Cooke. Daniel treated me like... well, somewhere between a little brother and someone he has a crush on, a crush he won't quite admit to having. He even had a nickname for me: Nota Bene. My initials are NB, he found out I loved to sing, and he twisted the typical meaning so that it stood for Beautiful Note. The way he said it, with a bit of an Italian-style lilt, made me feel safe, and like I belonged to someone, to something. At the time, Neil—who had always made me feel safe and like I belonged—was in Colorado at grad school. I must have missed him more than I admitted, because, looking back, I'm convinced that for me, Daniel was a Neil substitute. Methadone for my heroin addiction.

Once Alden and I started seeing each other, I stopped having wet dreams about Daniel. I'd never talked with Daniel about Alden. But during winter break, that period when Alden was so silent, Daniel came back into the picture. He invited me on a three-day Nordic skiing trip, and I went. I went, and I had a fabulous time. We stayed in a primitive cabin. We bushwhacked around the lower parts of Wildcat Mountain. In the evenings we took alternate swigs from a bottle of bourbon Daniel had brought. He asked me to sing for him, and I did. Mind you, I was still in love with Alden, and I truly wanted things to work themselves out with him when he got back to campus. But—damn, Daniel's attention felt good. It felt almost like Neil's.

After winter break, back on campus, I tried again to reach Alden, but calls and texts went unanswered. I left a few messages and then, one evening, I got pissed off, and I hitch-hiked out to his house. Parked out in front was a big, black car I'd never seen. There were lights in his windows. I rang the bell, got no answer, and rang it repeatedly until a woman opened the door. It was Alden's mother.

She asked who I was, and when I told her she said, "You'd better come in."

She struggled to maintain her composure as she explained that Alden was back in Canada, back in rehab, back trying to recover again from fentanyl. She explained, gently and with compassion, that I couldn't contact him. It was unlikely I would ever hear from him again.

I've heard people say, "I was so shocked!" I'd probably said it myself before that night. But unless someone has gone through something like what I went through that night, they have no idea what it means. I hated him. I loved him. Sitting in that beautiful living room surrounded by wealth and art and packing boxes, I was furious with him. And I pitied him. I pitied myself.

Alden had told me his parents accepted him, and his mother seemed to acknowledge that he and I had been in a relationship. But I didn't expect the offer she made.

After saying that Alden didn't want to keep anything from the apartment, she asked, "Is there anything you'd like to take?"

At first I couldn't think of anything other than the inukshuk, but I figured that was probably more costly than she had in mind, so I said nothing. But I stayed for a few hours to help her with packing, and a few pieces of memorabilia tempted me. She was glad to let me have them. And later, just as I was about to leave, something did occur to me.

"Mrs. Armstrong? Um, there is one other thing I'd like, if it's all right with you."

"Name it."

I pointed to the tapestry Alden had described as "A Sarah Warren," the mountain scene with slightly abstract slopes pointing down toward a lake. I said, "Alden really loved that tapestry. And I love it, too."

If she had given even the slightest indication that she

had any doubt, I was going to tell her to never mind. I had no idea of its financial value. But she smiled.

"It's yours."

I took it with me, and I stashed it under my dorm bed, unsure about the best thing to do with it, because every time I thought about it, I hurt. When I went home for the summer, it went under my bed there. And then I lost track of almost everything in my life when Neil died.

So it wasn't until some weeks after his funeral that I was in my room, and I dropped something that rolled under the bed. I went to retrieve that and found the tapestry, along with the other things Mrs. Armstrong had let me take.

It took my breath away for a second. I spread the tapestry out on the floor and stared at it. And stared at it. And stared, until I could imagine Neil climbing those mountains. And something he'd said the last time he'd been home came back to me, something he'd said during a conversation about why I hadn't ever hiked with him.

"I love the trails," he'd said. "The rocks, the streams, the meadows and woods. I love the struggle when it gets super steep, and the way I feel when there's an opening in the trees and I can see other mountains in the distance. But what I really love?"

He'd looked beyond me at nothing, and yet at everything, and then brought his eyes back to mine again.

"The best part, Nathan, the reason I climb, is the profound feeling of perspective it gives me when I get above tree line, when I can see forever, and when I realize how very small—how infinitesimally small I am. You know, I could fall, I could break a leg, I could *die* on a mountain. And the mountain wouldn't care."

I think I'd made some kind of scoffing sound at that point. "This is a good thing?"

"It's the only good thing. Because as small as I am at that precise moment when I realize it, I'm also massively huge. I'm also part of everything there is. It's like I'm one with the mountain, and the next mountain, and the next one and the next one on into infinity."

His voice had taken on a breathy quality that I knew he was not doing for effect. It was genuine, and there had been no doubt in my mind that he'd believed what he was saying with everything in him.

Staring at the tapestry, I felt something like a hint of that existential experience Neil had described. And suddenly, like a flash of light, like a lightning bolt inside my head, my path was clear.

I would pick up the baton Neil had been forced to drop and do what he had invited me to do many times, invitations I had declined. I would climb mountains.

That tapestry, as I discovered with a little bit of research, had probably cost Alden more than a thousand dollars. I can't help wondering if Mrs. Armstrong knew what she was letting me walk away with, or if she'd thought I knew what I was asking for. But its price tag did nothing to change the value it had for me. I could not value it any more if it had cost far more than that. It represents three things to me: Alden, Neil, and my personal quest.

CHAPTER FOUR

A week before Thanksgiving I got a call from Gram. I almost didn't answer, because I was hurrying to a class.

"Nathan, do you know someone named Conroy?"

I froze in place. "I—What did you say?"

"This person named Conroy Finnegan called and asked for you. He says he met you hiking."

"Um, yeah." *Conroy?* Conroy called my grandmother's house? "I, uh, we bumped into each other on Cannon last August. He called?" Had I given him my phone number? Well, no, because if I'd done that, it would have been my cell, not the land line at home.

"He asked if he could have your cell phone number, but I told him I'd have to ask you first."

"Yeah. Thanks, Gram, that's good. But, well, did he leave his number?"

"Yes."

"Can you text it to me, or something? I'm on my way to a class."

She sighed. "I'll have to find my own cell phone, but I should do that anyway. I'm sure it needs charging." Gram wasn't exactly a Luddite, but she preferred talking on her land line.

Conroy. What the hell…. Straining my memory back to that hike, I remembered I'd told him I was from Concord, and I'd given him my last name. That must have been how he got to Gram. But why was he calling?

By the time I got to my class, Gram had texted me Conroy's number. On one hand, I was dying to call him and find out what he wanted. On the other, I wasn't entirely sure I wanted to connect with him again. Sure, he was attractive, and sexy, and interesting. And older. And kind of a nomad, which had a certain intrigue for me, having lived in the same house all my life. But that encounter on the summit of South Kinsman.... I'd thought of that as a one-time thing.

He'd called my *grandmother*.

Calm down, Nathan. It wasn't like he'd known who would answer the phone. Shit, it could have been my father who answered, for all Conroy would know; I hadn't told him my folks were dead. So—was it better or worse that he wouldn't have known who'd answer?

I was going around in circles, and I forced myself to stop. I also decided to wait some amount of time—maybe even twenty-four hours—before calling.

I waited, like, two hours. He answered on the third ring.

"Nathan! Hey. Was that your mother I spoke to?"

"Grandmother. Good work finding my home number."

He chuckled. "No great mystery." Maybe not, but it meant he'd remembered everything I'd told him about me. "Listen, I don't remember whether I told you that my current house-sitting job is in Durham. You're at UNH, right?"

Shit! He's *here?* Had I mentioned UNH to him? So much for never seeing him again. It was a little surprising that I hadn't seen him before now. Durham is not a big town.

"Yup. And no, you didn't mention." And why hadn't he? The only thing I could think of was that he wasn't sure he wanted me to know until he'd decided what to do about it. He wanted the control.

He said, "Anyway, I thought it would be fun to get coffee or something sometime. You up for that?"

Think fast, Nathan. Let him know you're not expecting anything else. Maybe don't even want anything else. "Sure, that's fine. Just coffee, though."

He laughed his rich, deep laugh. "There's no way *that* will ever be as good again!" We both knew what that meant. "So, what about tomorrow?"

We agreed to meet at Breaking New Grounds, a coffee shop in town. I didn't suggest Zeke's. Not only was it on campus, which might not appeal to Conroy, but also it had been over a table at Zeke's that Alden had asked if I wanted to fuck.

I wasn't sure what to tell El Speed when we were both in the dorm later. He'd already told me all about his proposal to Ellie, which—along with the ring— had been received with predictable delight. Would he even want to know Conroy was here, and that I'd see him the next day? But if I didn't tell him, and then (for some reason I couldn't quite imagine at the moment) it turned out I saw Conroy again another time, that would be bad.

I worked it into our dinner conversation. We'd gone to the dining hall with another couple of guys from the dorm, and they'd both had evening classes, so they left earlier than we did.

"So I spoke to Conroy today. The guy from my Cannon hike? You remember?"

El Speed's hand, wrapped around a spoon loaded with chocolate soft-serve, froze half-way to his face. "Okay."

"He called. Seems he's in Durham. He'd told me he was house-sitting for the winter, but he hadn't said where. Turns out, it's here."

"Okay." The ice cream went into his mouth.

"I don't see this going anywhere, just so you know, but I'm having coffee with him tomorrow afternoon."

"Does *he* see this going anywhere, do you think?"

I laughed, trying not to sound as nervous as I felt. "Doubt it."

El Speed took another mouthful of ice cream and sat back in his chair. "What's your take on the guy? Do you, y'know, like him, or what?"

I shrugged, probably unconvincingly. "He's interesting."

He let his spoon drop into the bowl. "Well, that seals it, then. 'Interesting' will hook you quicker than almost anything else, in my experience."

"Let's not get ahead of ourselves. Besides, like I told him already, it will be coffee only."

"And he said—?"

"He said something along the same lines."

El Speed smiled and nodded. "Yeah. Interesting. Well, I guess we'll see."

Conroy was already at the café when I got there. I'd deliberately timed things so I'd be ten minutes late, hoping that would send a quiet message. I wasn't ready to admit to him— or even, really, to myself—that I'd wanted very much to see him again. After all, when he'd disappeared from the mountaintop, he'd been pretty clear that any future meeting would be by chance. And yet... and yet he had called me.

I had prepared an insincere apology for my planned tardiness. But when I stepped inside, there was Conroy, half-leaning over the order counter, a mischievous expression on his face as he flirted with the young female barista, who seemed to be enjoying the attention.

So he was bi? It wasn't necessarily the case, but somehow this made sense to me. I stepped up beside him, a couple of feet away, leaned on the counter, and smiled at the barista. She glanced at me, looking a little confused. She was very attractive: long, dark hair pulled back except for a few strategically-loose tendrils; dark, sparkling eyes; a small, pink mouth perfectly positioned in the heart-shaped face.

Conroy didn't shift his position as he turned his smile to me, which told me he didn't mind my seeing him flirt with a young woman. I felt a bubble of something like jealousy expand in the middle of my chest, and I didn't like it.

"Hey, Nathan. This is Janice. I haven't given her my

order yet. D'you know what you want?"

I glanced at the long list, and my eye fell on one in particular. "What's Ethiopian yirgacheffes like?"

Janice corrected my pronunciation and added, "It has a fairly light body. Slightly sweet flavor. One of our most popular beans."

Conroy and I both ordered that. Neither of us offered to pay for the other's coffee. We found a table and sat across from each other, Conroy taking the chair that faced the counter, maybe so he could see Janice. We'd barely settled when he opened the conversation.

"Claimed any good peaks lately?" He watched my face over the top of his cup.

"Of course." My tone was, how could you even ask? "Just did Madison, up through the Great Gulf. Nearly trampled by a moose. We camped below the summit and finished the climb the next day." Let him wonder who "we" might be.

"I love that peak. Though I haven't been through the gulf. What's that trail like?"

I described it to him in just enough detail to let him know it was very rugged without, I hoped, making it sound as though I'd had any trouble with it. I didn't return the inquiry; that is, I didn't ask where he'd hiked recently. What I wanted to know, but had to figure out without asking, was whether he had an agenda regarding me. But he volunteered about his exploits.

I'd nearly finished my coffee by the time he was done with his tales of adventures. He'd added four more four-thousand-foot peaks to his list. The last had been Mount Washington.

"I was looking at my list," he said, "and I realized I hadn't been up Washington yet. To tell the truth, I've always kind of avoided it." He drained his cup.

"Oh? Why is that?"

"I have this reluctance to work my way up a mountain

that other people drive up in cars."

I nodded; I'd heard Neil say something very like that once.

He wasn't done. "Just did it a month ago, actually. Got snowed on. Not surprising. Fucking cold up there!"

I nodded again. "It wasn't exactly warm on Madison. We got snowed on overnight, and that was in early October." There was just enough silence for me to consider whether I wanted to tell him more about myself, and then just enough more silence to make me do it without really making a decision.

"I couldn't hike any later in the season than I did. Not anymore." I drained my cup. Let's see what he says.

"Oh? You can't, or you don't want to?"

I sat back in my chair. "Frostbite. My feet can't tolerate cold. It's not a problem when I'm moving, but if I stop for any length of time...." I shrugged, as though it was what it was, and that's all it was.

"How did you do that?" His tone implied it had been my own fault. He wasn't entirely wrong.

So I gave him a thumbnail sketch of my first hike. I didn't name the mountain; let him think it was a qualifying peak. I didn't mention that I hadn't actually made it to the summit on that first climb. But I told him about the snowstorm, about the incredibly challenging work of trudging through snow that would sometimes come up to my ankles and sometimes to my hips, and about how often I'd had to take off my borrowed frame pack just so I could climb out of deep snow. I told him my watch had frozen. And I told him about having to spend the night in a make-shift shelter, in the woods. At the end of my tale, I told him it had been my first hike, that I'd been with an experienced mountaineer, that he had underestimated the climb, and that if I hadn't corrected our direction he would have led us down the mountain on a different trail from the one we'd come up, a trail that would have left us stranded.

"Shit. That would have been the end of both of you, it sounds like."

"We would have been nowhere near the car. In the dark. In the freezing cold. So, yeah, I guess that would have been possible."

"That was your first hike?"

"Yup. I went back that summer, alone. Overnight."

Thank you, Jeremy. Jeremy had told me to do that, in a conversation just before he and Neil had left for their fateful trip to Virginia. When I'd asked why he thought I should hike alone, he'd said, "You're the only one you need to prove something to." He'd been right; and yet, here I was feeling like I had to prove something to Conroy.

Conroy's turn to nod. "Impressive. And you've been hiking ever since. How long ago was that?"

"It was March of my freshman year." I let a beat go by. "D'you want another coffee?" I still hadn't learned whether he wanted something besides a comparison of hiking exploits.

By way of answer, he looked in Janice's direction. I couldn't see her, but it seemed she was watching him, because all he had to do was hold up two fingers and point down to the table.

"Let me get this one." And he stood.

Fine.

As Conroy set the cups down, I said, "Thanks. Janice was right; this is great coffee."

He chuckled. "I'll never be able to ask for it again. Can't pronounce it any better than you did."

"So where's this house you're sitting in?"

He took a sip. "Garden Lane. Little ranch house. The professor who owns it is on sabbatical."

Garden Lane. I'd been by that street only once, with Alden. We'd walked down to the swan pond. That was where he'd told me he couldn't stop thinking about me.

"Hope they don't have a dog."

He looked at me blankly for a second. "Oh, right. The

dog on Cannon. No, or I wouldn't have accepted the job."

I decided to ask again: "Why don't you like dogs, anyway?"

"They look at you like they expect you to save them from something. Like you're God." He took a sip of coffee and shook his head. "I don't want that responsibility. And I don't respect them for trying to lay it on me."

I decided to change the subject. "So house sitting is a job. Do they pay you?"

"Sure. Wouldn't do this otherwise."

"So, is that like, your real job?"

He laughed. "Hell, no. I didn't tell you?" I shook my head and didn't point out that, also, I hadn't asked before. "I lead hikes. Just got back from one, actually. The Ozarks. I have a website where people can read about the hikes and sign up."

I blinked, surprised only for a moment, and then nodded. "Of course you do."

He laughed again. "You know, on Cannon? I was pretty impressed that you kept up with me. When I'm leading a hike, I have to make sure I don't outstrip the slowest person in the group. But that day, I didn't hold back. And you were right there with me." He lifted his cup and held it toward me for a second. "To you, Nathan." And he took a mouthful.

It's hard for me to put words to how that made me feel. Like I've said, I never hiked with Neil. There were lots of reasons, but the main one had been that he'd given me so much of himself, and so many other things, that I'd decided to let him keep hiking for himself, he loved it so much. But after he died....

By the time Conroy and I parted company that afternoon, I'd invited him to Gram's for Thanksgiving dinner.

INTERLUDE III: GRAMS, BEING GAY, AND LOVE VS. FENTANYL

My first year in college, I told my grandmother I was gay.

I knew she still loved me. I knew I was as much a member of the family as ever. I know that's not the case for a lot of kids when they come out to their families. So I knew I was lucky. But it still hurt to know that if she could, she'd change something so basic to the foundation of who I am. Maybe it doesn't define me, but it sure as hell colors the way some people think about me. And so it sometimes colors the way I see myself.

Most people are straight. I get that. I also get that this means most straight people don't put a whole lot of thought into what it means to be straight. And as wonderful as Gram has always been to me, as wonderful as she continued to be even after I came out to her, there have been gaps.

I'd told my family over Thanksgiving dinner. Of course. It's traditional, right? Anyway, I'd already told Neil over a year before, and he'd been beyond supportive. I knew what I wanted from Gram, and I almost got it. At first she seemed kind of sad, worried that "some people would make life difficult." She said something about going through a phase, or a stage, something like that, which I immediately contradicted.

About this time Neil came to my rescue and voiced staunch support. After that, Gram stopped arguing and made it seem as though she accepted it, but I couldn't tell whether that was real. She said something about already having her grandkids (that would be the three of us, of course), and I gently disabused her of the notion that gay people don't have children.

It had been a short conversation that had felt about an

hour long to me. At the end of it, despite the feeling that I'd gotten only token acceptance, I was glad it was out of the way.

But Gram cornered me later. She called my announcement "a step." Not quite knowing what that meant, I replied that it was who I was, not a "step" at all. She started to say that being gay was not... was not.... She couldn't finish.

I finished for her. "Not normal? Not natural? Not moral?"

She just stared at me, looking worried, or confused, or both.

"Gram, you know, this isn't a choice. No one chooses their orientation. Hell, no one even chooses who they fall in love with, whether they're gay or straight."

She still just stared.

"How do you know you're not gay, Gram?"

"What?"

"Seriously. How do you know?"

That took her by surprise. I said nothing else until she did; whoever spoke first would lose.

"Well, I... I fell in love with your grandfather."

"But what if he'd been a woman? Would you still have fallen in love with him as a 'her?' Would you have felt romantic about 'her?' Would you have married 'her?'"

"Nathan, that's not the question."

"Of course it is!" I hadn't meant to raise my voice, but it felt like she was being obtuse. "Sorry. But, Gram, it *is* the question. Because if you couldn't love a woman like that, you're straight. *I* can't love a woman that way, either."

She looked both hurt and ashamed. "I just want you to be happy, Nathan. You know that. And I don't see how that's possible if this is true."

"Trust me. It's possible. This is the only way it is possible."

I guess she couldn't think of a reply to that, because she wrapped her arms around me for a quick, hard hug.

So that's how it had gone at the time. After that, every so often, she'd feign nonchalance (or so it seemed, and I'm convinced I was right) and ask, "Any romance on the horizon, Nathan?"

I know she was always relieved when I'd shake my head. "Not right now, Gram."

The truth was that there hadn't been any romance for me since Alden had ripped himself out of my life. Sex, yes; romance, no. I'd given a lot of thought, and shed tears, trying to understand why fentanyl meant more to him than anything else in his life. My research into substance abuse had helped me understand that when you take fentanyl recreationally for the first time, the high is so extreme that it leaves all other highs, whatever the source, in the dust. In fact, from what I've read, even fentanyl can't deliver the same high again. But once you've had it, you know it's there, and you keep trying to get it back.

When I started to fall in love with Alden, I was (and I still am) pretty sure the euphoria, the obsessive focus on the person, is the same *kind* of high you'd get from fentanyl. And yet—even though I'm certain Alden was falling in love with me, too—the intensity of that feeling for him evidently paled in comparison to the high he knew fentanyl could give him, the high it had given him once and that he craved again with a desperation that made him leave everything else in his life behind. Even me. Even love.

So what Alden felt for me was inadequate. *I* was inadequate. And even though I knew fentanyl was the cause, even though I knew it wasn't some inherent lack within me, the sting of knowing I could never have meant to him what he could have meant to me stayed with me. It hurt. A lot. It wasn't front-and-center most of the time—just when some guy expressed more than a passing sexual interest in me. Then it roared into life, and some instinctive self-preservation took over and pulled me back.

El Speed had noticed it. "I thought you liked Cody," he said to me once when I turned down a second get-together with a guy who lived in Hubbard Hall. "Hell, *I* liked Cody. I mean, you know...."

For this type of conversation, I had at my command a tone that was as dismissive as possible while staying in the realm of friendship. That is, I was dismissing relationships in general, not El Speed's opinion or his concern. "He's fine. Just not quite in the mood for getting something started." The tone carried a subtext: *Not your business, guy. Back off.*

He shrugged and left it alone. And it went like that any time El Speed brought the topic up, which he did less and less frequently over our years as roommates, finally giving up altogether.

El Speed's comments and questions came from a place of friendship, concern, and absolute acceptance. Gram's came from a place of concern, but it had a different character. Gram really, really, *really* didn't want me to say, "Glad you asked! Yeah, I met this really great guy. We've been seeing each other for about two months now...." No; she didn't want to hear that.

Bottom line was she gave me a lip-service level of acceptance, and I gave a lip-service belief in that acceptance. I can't be sure how much, or in what way, this gap in our relationship affected our love for each other. I just know it did.

CHAPTER FIVE

After I'd come out to Gram my freshman year, she'd made it clear that while she wouldn't hold being gay against me, while she still loved me and accepted me, she didn't understand it or entirely accept that part of me. I'd felt nervous about the idea of introducing her to Daniel for fear she'd jump to conclusions, but circumstances had prevented her from ever seeing him.

When I called to tell her I'd invited Conroy for Thanksgiving dinner, all she said was, "That'll be fine, Nathan. I'm happy to meet one of your friends, and there'll be plenty of food."

I let a beat or two go by to see if she wanted to know more, but the line was silent. So I said, "He'll give me a ride to Concord and leave after dinner. I'll stay through the weekend."

"Sounds good."

Her lack of curiosity left me a little nonplussed, and I suspected she was already wondering about the nature of my relationship with Conroy. Hell, *I* was wondering about the nature of my relationship with Conroy. So the idea of Gram's scrutiny made me uncomfortable enough that I had second thoughts about the invitation. Had I been overcome with good intentions, having concluded that Conroy would otherwise spend the holiday alone? I had no idea if he had family, or where they might be. Whatever. I had no good answer, so I did my best to put the question aside.

"Nina's coming, too," Gram told me. "She wasn't sure at first. One of her roommates will be here as well. Isabella. She's from Peru, so Nina might have stayed in the city with her. But I suggested they both come up."

"So Isabella and Nina will stay for a few days, then?"

"That's right. And—well, Isabella will be in Neil's room, Nathan. Just so you know."

Gram knew that having someone stay in Neil's room would be difficult for me, and probably for her and Nina as well. No one had slept in that room since Neil had died.

After that horrible forest fire, Gram, Nina, and I had spent long, tearful days going through Neil's things, deciding what to give away, what to keep, what to throw out. There was now a kind of unofficial memorial in the basement where we'd put the things we couldn't bear to part with. His old room was ready for a visitor; it was just that there hadn't been one yet.

I'd never met either of Nina's roommates. When she'd said she was moving to New York, I'd been thinking I might visit her. But with two female roommates, that seemed unlikely to happen.

Once upon a time it wouldn't have occurred to me to consider visiting Nina anywhere. We were never enemies, but we were never close, either. We're such different people. She's acerbic and sometimes sarcastic, and I'm—well, I hate to say that I'm an open book, but it's probably true. At least, that's a term Nina has used to describe me. And there's something about me that prevents me from being able to carry off sarcasm. But Nina and I developed a new respect for each other after Neil's death. I realized she had a loving and courageous heart and a sense of integrity she'd kept hidden from me until then. I think she's better at protecting herself than I am. I don't know whether that's a good thing or not.

After coffee with Conroy (sounds like a play, doesn't it?), I looked for his website. I hadn't asked him for the name of his business, but a quick search yielded "Finnegan's Walks," and there was his smiling face off to one side of an inviting photograph of a wooded hiking trail.

Clever name, I thought, and then wondered if it really

was. Probably a lot of people would make the connection with the novel *Finnegan's Wake*, but—like me—would have little idea what it was about, or why it was significant. But it didn't matter, really; "Finnegan's Walks" would be memorable for some and just catchy for anyone else.

The site advertised hikes and walks and even ski trips. Only a few of them had upcoming dates, so it seemed that he limited himself to only a few active trips in a given year. I didn't see anything truly wild and crazy; no hikes up Kilimanjaro or K2 or Denali. Most of the trips were fairly tame, which probably meant he'd have more takers.

El Speed drove home to Maine on Wednesday to be with his family and, of course, his fiancée. As he was getting ready to leave, I told him I'd invited Conroy home.

Duffle bag hanging by a strap from one shoulder, door halfway open as he was about to leave, he looked at me for a few seconds. Then, "Interesting." And he left.

Our first two years at UNH, El Speed and I had shared a room in Hunter Hall, the dorm where Neil had spent all four of his college years. I had requested it for my freshman year, both because it was familiar and because at the time, I had been terrified about this new phase of my life. But mostly I think it had been because Neil had been there. I hadn't known El Speed before that.

I could not have asked for a better roommate. From the start, his gentle acceptance of life in general had felt like a buffer between me and the rest of campus life. I think it was the first or second day when I saw him lift a pair of his used undershorts, sniff them, and decide they could get another wearing after all. He loved the nickname El Speed, which Nina had given him before he'd met her; he'd sent me a letter before the school year started—an actual letter, handwritten—in a blue envelope with a return address starting "L. Speed." Nina had taken it from there. He'd thought it was especially funny because, as he'd put it, "Not much about me that folks are likely to call speedy."

As for me being gay, the first time he'd mentioned his girlfriend, I'd told him I didn't have anyone special yet, but it wouldn't be a *girl*friend. He'd accepted that with a shrug, saying, "That's cool."

El Speed had taken me to the infirmary after my disastrous winter hike and had been incredibly helpful during my recovery from frostbite. He'd never questioned whether we'd room together a second year; it had been a given. As I've said, I loved him like a brother, and I'm pretty sure he felt the same.

About half-way through our sophomore year, one evening as each of us sat working on something at our respective desks, El Speed had said to me, "Y'know, homey as it is here and all, I think I want to live in one of the mini houses next year." He waited for me to look over at him.

Was he saying he wanted a different roommate? Or maybe a single room? I braced myself for rejection. "Yeah?"

He nodded and turned to his computer screen. "Yeah. Take a look."

I got up and stood behind him, leaning in slightly to see the screen better. One after the other, he displayed four different buildings that looked more like houses than dormitories: modern shapes, wooden clapboards painted grey or brown. I'd known the minis were there, on the far south end of campus, but I'd never been in them. El Speed browsed from Richardson to Marston to Eaton and finally, like a salesman who shows you the car or the house he knows you're going to want after he's shown you everything else, El Speed landed on Hall. As he browsed through, he talked about each of them.

"There's a bit of a risk, of course, cuz there's only about fifty residents. Less buffer, if there are some folks you don't like. Some rooms are single, some are double. And each house seems to have a kind of theme. Richardson is the smallest, so that's their appeal, along with a gender-inclusive bathroom. Marston goes for the eclectic and lets the residents kind of drive things in terms of how the place is run. Eaton seems to be all about the arts. And Hall," here he turned to look at me, "is for people who love being active outdoors. You know, like hiking."

A huge wave of relief washed over me as surely as if I'd been in a warm and gentle ocean. He wasn't trying to leave me behind! The magnitude of feeling took me by surprise. I mean, sure, it would have been very hard to hear that El Speed wanted a different roommate, or a single. But I felt near tears, and at first that seemed excessive. Then I realized where the feeling was coming from.

Neil had been my anchor, the one person in my life who'd made me feel like I belonged someplace. Maybe I should have felt like that about Gram as well, but my feelings about her—while full of gratitude for what she'd done—felt more like tenderness than solidity. I needed a solid place to be.

El Speed, whether he knew that or not, was my solid place.

I shook myself mentally and did my best to sound normal as I asked, "So have you been to look at these minis?"

He turned back to the screen. "I have." He looked back at me again, maybe a little sheepishly. "Hope you don't mind."

"Hey, you've done the footwork. How hard is it to get in?"

"Okay, well, see, I've already applied. For both of us. No commitment yet."

I laughed. Maybe I should have been a little pissed at his presumption—not that we'd room together, but that I'd be interested in the move. But I was too happy.

Tongue firmly in cheek, I said, "Have you, indeed.

Should I guess which one?"

He lifted one shoulder and dropped it. "Don't think you could miss."

We lucked out and got into Hall House starting our junior year, and we'd loved it enough to stay through the end of our final college year. So when Conroy came to pick me up at Thanksgiving, it wasn't in front of Hunter, where (in my mind) I could still see Alden's white BMW convertible waiting to take me star-gazing (he was quite the amateur astronomer) or back to his place for... well, you know.

Conroy texted me from the parking lot on Evergreen Drive, as I'd said to do. When I got there, I felt an all-too-familiar lurch in my chest. It was a lurch I knew indicated that I had strong feelings for this guy, and so far I'd seen no indication that he felt anything like that for me.

Duffle bag strap draped across my body, I trotted over to where Conroy leaned against the driver's side door of a cobalt blue Jeep Wrangler Sport. *Of course*, I told myself, *he has a four-wheel-drive.* He wore dark grey slacks and a soft blue crew-neck sweater over a white shirt: simple, understated, and not jeans. Silently I approved of his choice. And every part of me approved of how gorgeous he looked.

Memories of other guys who had waited for me by their vehicles flashed through my mind. Not only was there the wealthy Alden, who liked driving with the convertible top of his BMW folded down in chilly weather because it made him feel alive. There was also Daniel, who had little money of his own and had driven an old-model Jeep Wagoneer, the color of which he'd described as mung, a not-quite-dark brown. It would seem Conroy's finances lay somewhere between the two.

Conroy nodded in my direction when he saw me, and I made my way to the passenger side. As far as anyone watching could have told, we were just friends in a platonic, casual relationship. And, I told myself with very little conviction, that's all it was. I threw my bag into the back and hopped in.

"Do you know how to get to Concord?"

He tapped on a GPS screen. "Just give me the street address." I did, and we were off.

"Great car," I told him, knowing he'd expect a comment.

"I like it a lot. And it takes me where I need to go."

We headed out of town, neither of us saying anything until we joined up with Route 4.

"So tell me a little about your family. Who are these generous people who're allowing me to share their holiday feast with them?"

"I can't remember how much I've already told you, so I'll just start at the beginning." I told him about the accident that had taken my parents and Gram's husband. I told him about how Gram had raised us kids, and once or twice I mentioned Neil without any details. "Nina will be there, with one of her roommates. She's living in New York City doing some kind of internship at a fashion magazine."

"So she's older than you?"

"By one year, yeah. She'll go on with grad school at some point. She wants to be a fashion designer, or maybe a personal stylist, so she's getting some experience under her belt, as it were."

"And Neil?"

I heard my own sharp intake of breath. I swallowed once or twice. Conroy glanced toward me briefly, no doubt wondering why I was taking so long to answer.

"Neil died in a forest fire. Two and a half years ago. He was hiking with a friend in the Priest Wilderness in Virginia." I wanted to keep details to a minimum.

Road noise. That's all I heard for maybe ten seconds that felt longer.

"Shit." Conroy stared straight ahead as he drove. "I'm

sorry, man."

Another ten seconds.

"I've hiked through there," he said finally. "It's gorgeous country. So remote, though." He didn't add anything about how deadly it would be to get into trouble that far away from civilization, but he didn't need to.

About a mile later Conroy changed the subject. "So I didn't see which dorm you came from. You're in one of the mini houses? They all have, like, some kind of focus, right?"

Silently I wondered why he knew so much about campus dorms. Just how many men, and how many women, had he made friends with in Durham? How many of them were students? And how many of them had he fucked? It amused me rather than bothered me, I told myself, to wonder about his exploits.

Aloud I replied, "Hall House. Its focus is outdoor activities."

He barked a laugh. "Should have guessed. And how does it live up to this idea, other than housing people like you and your roommate?"

Wow. He really did remember everything I'd told him.

Mention of El Speed reminded me of something we'd both tried recently. "Okay, well, one thing is teaching each other things. Like, there's one guy who's a self-proclaimed expert on slack-lining. He teaches anyone in the house how to do it for free. So El Speed and I both tried it last spring. I think I might be decent with enough practice. But El Speed is so tall, it's harder for him. Maybe it's a center-of-gravity thing."

"Cool. I love slack-lining. I have a demonstration vid up on YouTube." *Of course you do.* "If that guy gets tired of working with you, let me know."

"Thanks." Tempting. I had enjoyed the little I'd done, but spending more time with Conroy was a question mark.

My turn to change the subject. "I went to your website. Looks like you've been all over."

ON THE KALALAUA TRAIL

"Well, I've been at this since college."

"Um... how old are you, if you don't mind my asking?"

"Twenty-nine."

Shit. I had figured, maybe, twenty-five. Did more years make a lot of difference? I shrugged internally; not to me, I decided.

"How many people do you usually have on one of your hikes?"

"Depends on the hike. The more technical the skill set has to be, the fewer people sign up. In fact, the fewer I *want* to sign up. Those trips are more dangerous. Ice climbing in Austria is not something I want more than four other people on. Even a day hike up Katahdin shouldn't be a group bigger than seven or so. But Acadia? That's a pretty easy set of hikes, as long as you stay away from The Precipice."

"What's that?"

He let out a slow breath. "It's amazing to me how many people climb that thing and don't die. It's not a technical climb, or anything. No pitons, no rappelling. There are ledges, some quite narrow, and nothing like a guardrail anywhere. In places you have to hang onto metal rods stuck into the rock, or climb up them. It's a pretty sheer drop, almost all the way up. People fall off it and die, every once in a while."

"Have you climbed it?"

He glanced briefly at me, and one side of his mouth rose a little. "What do you think?" When I didn't say anything, he added, "Twice. But I never took a group up it. Wouldn't do that."

That statement reminded me of something that had occurred to me after our coffee chat. "So, you said you don't like that dogs make you feel like they think you're God, and that you don't want that kind of responsibility. But aren't you taking on responsibility for people when you lead hikes? Especially if it's a dangerous hike?"

He was shaking his head before I finished my question. "A hike lasts for a finite amount of time. Four days. Seven days. That's it. And I always screen people for their skill level. They have responsibility for that. I do the administrative stuff, I have expertise, I know the territory, and—sure, I'm responsible. But only for certain things, and only for a few days. I'm not 'God' to anyone."

We were quiet for a few minutes, and then I turned the tables. "You're about to meet my family. What about you? Family? Siblings?"

"I grew up in western Montana. It's where I learned to love the mountains. No siblings, so I got used to hiking alone. Mom died when I was fifteen. Dad and I never got along."

Grim. I didn't know what to say, so I went with, "Guess I'm not keeping you from any family gathering of your own, then."

"Nope."

Since Nina had been around sixteen, I'd seen her as very attractive in a slightly exotic way. Like me, she's fairly short and has nearly-black hair. Hers is cut in a short style that frames her face. Her skin is flawless, setting off the very dark eyes nicely. That impression of Nina didn't change when I saw Isabella Fernandez, but—wow.

Isabella was a knock-out. Her rich skin color, her long dark hair, the deep eyes with the long lashes, all that was compelling. But where Nina was slight, Isabella was... well... stacked. She had what I think is referred to as the perfect hourglass shape: round hips, a slender waist, and a lot of heft to fill out a bra. She wasn't much taller than Nina, but her neck could have graced a Latina swan. She wore navy slacks and a dark magenta sweater of some fuzzy yarn that clung to her figure without being tight. The sweater wasn't cut low, but it didn't need to be to do more than hint at what was under it.

The disdain in the expression on Nina's face as Conroy bent over Isabella's hand to kiss it was palpable.

Conroy, obviously smitten, smiled his charming smile and said, in what I would have said was an excellent Spanish accent, "Encantada de conocerte."

Once again I had cause to suspect that he was bi. I gave Nina a tongue-in-cheek glance as I excused myself to help Gram in the kitchen. Nina glared at me.

Our dining room wasn't large, but we could seat six comfortably (or eight in a pinch) around the table. Nina took the chair beside Isabella, rather purposefully, I thought. Conroy moved to take the chair across from Isabella, while I sat at one end, opposite Gram.

Conroy was obligingly appreciative of everything he was served, complimenting Gram's cooking enough to register without going overboard into obsequiousness. Like, "Great stuffing! I prefer this classic style to recipes that call for weird stuff." And, "Whole berry cranberry sauce! You made this yourself, didn't you?" And, "I'm glad you mashed the skins into the potatoes. So much better this way."

When he asked her about life in Concord, she told him some things I hadn't known, or things that maybe I'd heard but had gone in one proverbial ear and out the other.

"I'm so impressed," Conroy told Gram, "that you've raised your grandchildren all by yourself." I was terrified that he'd refer to Neil, but he avoided that landmine skillfully. "The results do you credit. Nina seems to be well on her way to a glamorous career, and Nathan is a responsible student and quite a mountaineer. Is this the house where you worked these miracles?"

Gram blushed and pushed at her pile of mashed potatoes with the tines of her fork. "My husband and I had turned this house over to my daughter and her husband. When they died," she set down her fork and took a deep breath, "I moved back in."

He smiled and glanced briefly around. "It's obvious that you love your home. It has a warm, loving feel, almost like an embrace."

"Thank you. I do love it."

"And are you still working outside the home?"

"Oh! My goodness. No, I never did that."

"Gram," Nina interrupted, "you're being too modest." I thought she might say more, but she clammed up quickly, almost as though she hadn't meant to say anything at all.

Conroy picked up on the comment, though. "That sounds interesting." His face, turned fully toward Gram, had an expectant, almost excited look.

"Oh, well, I suppose Nina's referring to my volunteer work." She stopped speaking, and one look at her told me that she didn't believe anyone would find that work interesting.

Conroy proved her wrong. "Such as?"

Gram waved a hand as though to dismiss the issue.

I wanted her to get some credit. "Gram, tell him about that project you ran for the middle school. The books, and supplies, and stuff."

She looked at me and shook her head. "I don't think Conroy wants to hear about all that."

Conroy did, though, because he prompted her. "Is this one of those situations where the teachers end up paying for supplies out of their own pockets because there isn't enough money in the school system?"

"Well, yes," Gram admitted almost grudgingly. "They—well, I was particularly interested in the arts, you know. So I ran a fund-raiser to purchase art supplies and music. Books too, of course."

"Music!" Conroy's eyes got big. "Like, band music?"

"Yes. And music for the chorus. Vocal music has always been a particular interest of mine." She glanced almost shyly at me, and I knew it was because of how much she had encouraged me to sing when I'd been in high school, and how much I had loved it. "But that's enough about that."

Maybe Conroy's studied charm was an artifact of how he needed to act with strangers when he was leading them through the wilderness. It was studied, yes, but it felt honest. He asked Gram a few more questions, and she warmed up to the attention. It seemed to make her feel good, and that alone made me glad I'd invited him. Then he turned to Nina and asked her about her work in the fashion industry. And he hit kind of a brick wall. Or maybe it was made of rubber, because things kept bouncing back at him.

"I'm guessing," he said admiringly to my prickly sister, "that you designed and made your outfit." She wore a short black skirt over dark green tights that picked up a green in the pattern of her silk blouse, which had a high, round neck and long, full sleeves with wide cuffs. In the silk, the green was not a prominent color, but when she'd walked into the room earlier, the color of the tights had pulled the whole outfit together. Black suede ankle boots completed the look. My favorite thing, though, was that the blouse was made from three different silk fabrics, with different geometric patterns, and somehow they worked together to great effect. I don't know how she did it. I'd seen this blouse before, and she had referred to it as her "Mondo" blouse. Evidently Mondo is a designer famous for successfully mixing patterns that most people would never think to combine.

When she didn't respond, he tried again. "Such a creative field. It amazes me how many different ways there are to design clothes to cover a form that's essentially the same from person to person."

She chewed a mouthful of turkey slowly, eyeing his clothing the whole time, any critique of them remaining unknowable. After she swallowed she took a sip of water. "Yes." And she put a forkful of peas with onions into her mouth.

He seemed unfazed by her brevity. "How do you come up with so many different ideas?"

Peas swallowed, she said, "It's a gift."

It went on like that for maybe four or five questions from Conroy and barely-veiled condescension from Nina until he evidently gave up making any points in that quarter. I already suspected that the attentions he'd paid to Gram and Nina were obligatory, and that he was winding up his pitching arm for Isabella. His attitude so far had been interested and polite but nothing more. Giving up on Nina, he turned to her friend.

And there it was. The smiles, the tilting of the head, the intensity of his glances, and after she responded to a few easy questions that revealed her charming Peruvian accent, he engaged her in earnest. But with her, unlike with Gram or Nina, almost every one of her answers led to a morsel of unsolicited contribution from Conroy.

First he told her that his business was leading people on various kinds of hikes. "You're from Peru, Isabella?" He pronounced her name convincingly, again as though he knew Spanish. "What an engaging country! I led a group of people up Machu Picchu two years ago." He raved about that destination for a few sentences.

And later, "You've lived in Manhattan for a year? I wonder if you've visited any of the sights I took a tour group to see. Usually I lead hikes in the mountains, or at least in natural settings, but it's possible to walk almost everywhere in New York City. We covered ground from Battery Park to the caves in Inwood. I really enjoyed the Cloisters and Fort Tryon Park."

To his credit, he encouraged her to talk about the sights she *had* seen, though unlike Conroy's sights, they seemed fairly predictable: the Statue of Liberty, the Empire State building, Rockefeller Center, St. Patrick's Cathedral, and the Central Park Carousel.

"Have you ever hired one of the hansom cabs that go through the park?" Conroy wanted to know.

Isabella's bronze complexion seemed to flush a little.

"Oh, I have not the money for that."

Conroy gave her a smile that was part understanding and part insinuating. "A lovely girl like you shouldn't have to pay for her own carriage."

I wish I could have taken a picture of Nina's face at that point, about as sour as Gram's cranberry sauce would have been if she'd forgotten to add the sugar.

Isabella asked a question of her own: "Have you ever travelled in Hawai'i, Conroy? It's a place I want to go."

For a few seconds he was speechless. I knew he had been there, and I was a little surprised at the momentary silence. He closed his eyes for maybe three seconds and then opened them full on Isabella's expectant face.

"If I were a god, I would live there." He let that startling assertion sink in around him before going on. "I've spent more time on Kaua'i than on any of the other islands. There's a primal feel to it I don't sense anywhere else in the world. The whole center of the island is a crater, the Waimea Canyon. The colors are deep reds and intense purples and rich browns. I was hiking the upper rim once, and I glanced down into the canyon. I watched the backs of raptors as they scoured the canyon floor for prey, I was that far above them."

He took a deep breath and let it out slowly. "The north shore is where they filmed parts of the film *South Pacific*, if you've ever seen that."

Nina interrupted him, using a belittling tone. "Wasn't that the island where they shot *Jurassic Park*?"

Conroy's glance darted to Nina. "Probably." And his eyes went back to Isabella. "Magnificent doesn't come close." Unperturbed by the distraction, he sat back, somehow holding everyone in thrall (with the probable exception of Nina).

He turned his gaze upward as though he could see the paradise he'd told me the place felt like to him. "It's like— okay, now," and he lowered his gaze to the table, "I know this will sound corny or hokey or whatever. But I'm going to tell you honestly."

Again he looked directly at Isabella. "When I stand on Ke'e Beach at the northwest corner of the island and gaze south down the western shore, with those steep, knife-edged points of land plunging into the pounding surf," and here he held up a hand, fingers separated and pointing down at a steep angle, "it feels as though I've found the nexus."

There was an intensity to Conroy's voice, and to his posture even, that seemed intimate. I felt myself leaning a little in Isabella's direction as though to capture some of that intensity for myself. I wanted him to talk to me like that. I wanted him to focus on me like that. But he didn't.

Nina must have decided it was time to remind us all we were still earth-bound. "Nexus." One word, no question mark at the end, inflected as only Nina could do, to carry an undeniable mixture of skepticism and condescension that would make most people stop talking except to mutter some babbled excuse for not explaining further.

Nina's attitudes had always had the effect of making me feel small, or stupid, or some combination. At that moment, I was torn between being embarrassed for Conroy and annoyed at Nina; Conroy's intensity had sucked me in, and I was waiting for more.

At any rate, Nina's tone didn't stop Conroy. He glanced at her, apparently either ignoring her tone's intent or immune to it, and his gaze was intense. "Nexus."

Back to Isabella. "You know what I mean? I see a bridge between the physical and the spiritual. It's everywhere, especially in nature. But there?" He sat back and shook his head slowly. "There's no bridge there. No need. Life and death, the sacred and the secular... they exist together. Nothing between them to bridge. In that place, it's all one."

He smiled at Isabella and then at Gram, both of whom seemed—like me—to be hanging on his every word, and then he looked at me. "I'm going to lead another trip down the Kalalau Trail. I'd been thinking about it, waiting for them to finish repairs after last spring's floods." He nodded. "Yup.

I've just decided."

Conroy left at around eight o'clock, expressing what I'm sure was sincere delight at the packet of Thanksgiving banquet remnants Gram put together for him. Nina and Isabella both donned aprons to help Gram and me with cleanup. I liked Isabella, and I chatted with her as we worked, following up on some things she'd told Conroy during dinner. I felt totally ignorant about Peru, but Conroy had made it sound appealing, and I liked Isabella's accent.

Nina said very little, but that wasn't necessarily a sign of anything so I shrugged it off. But when I went upstairs to my old room for the night, something stopped my door from closing. I turned and saw Nina's hand pressing the door open.

"Can we talk?"

I shrugged and walked into the room. She closed the door and took my desk chair as I sat on the side of the bed, and she wasted no time.

"What's the story with this Conroy character?"

I didn't want to let her get a rise out of me. "What story would you like to hear?"

She exhaled through her nose, a mildly exasperated gesture. "I seem to recall you were once head-over-heels in lust with a straight guy who nearly got you killed." So she didn't like Conroy; I got that. But the comparison was uncalled-for.

"You're crazy. He's nothing like Daniel."

"He's another loser, Nathan."

I scowled at her. "You don't know anything about him."

"I saw how he worked the room tonight, flirting with Isabella and Gram, trying to flatter me. They ate it up. He's done this before. It's how he makes his way in the world, isn't it?"

"What are you talking about?"

"Let me guess. He either has no family, or he's not in close contact with them. He moves around a lot. Part of that is his business, and part of it is his home life. He's, what, nearly thirty in years, but more like sixteen emotionally." She stopped and regarded me carefully, as if to see what parts of what she'd said had hit a mark.

I wasn't convinced she was right about his emotional level, but everything else was so spot-on it scared me. No one but me knew about his house-sitting approach to living quarters. I went for the one place I knew she was wrong, one way he was not like Daniel. Probably. "He's not straight."

"Neither was Daniel. Not really." She paused, and her expression changed from one of certainty to something like concern. "Wait. How do you know?"

I hoped to God I didn't blush. I'm sure I did, though. "We've had sex. His idea."

Now her expression was one of profound sadness. "Oh, Nathan."

"What? Are you the only one in the family allowed to have relationships?"

She actually blinked. Hard. "You think he's going to have a *relationship* with you? Did you see how he fawned over Isabella, right in front of you?" She gave a kind of snort. "Nathan, don't take this the wrong way. You're very attractive. But if he'd had sex with anyone here tonight, it would not have been you."

Now I was angry, despite her assessment of my looks. "There's no way you can know that! And anyway, I'm already fairly sure he's bi."

"*Fairly* sure?" Her arrogant tone was back. "That says worlds about how deep this 'relationship' isn't."

We glared at each other for several seconds.

"Look, Nathan, I just don't want you to get hurt again. The look on your face during some of his little speeches told me you're already in deeper than is probably good for you."

"I find him intriguing, okay?"

Everything about her softened. Her face, her posture, her voice. This was a Nina I'd seen only a few times during my lifetime. But it was one I knew to be true.

"Nathan, here's the thing. I'm a hard ass. You're a sweetheart. I keep people at bay so I won't get fooled, or hurt, or taken in. You want to like people. You want to trust them. You let them in. And this guy?" She shook her head gently once or twice. "He's going to hurt you."

I kept my voice low and soft. "Okay, Nina, I love you, too. Now just let me live my life."

We watched each other's eyes for several seconds. Then she nodded, stood, and shut the door quietly as she left the room. She left me alone to wonder why I kept finding myself attracted to bisexual men.

CHAPTER SIX

El Speed got back to campus after I did on Sunday night, full of news.

"We've set a date," he told me, an expression on his face somewhere between excited and terrified. Or maybe that was just my interpretation.

"For the wedding? That's great!"

"June twenty-second. Ellie's dad knows a guy who owns a function hall we can use for the reception. Otherwise—man, you wouldn't believe how booked up things are! We might have had to wait until next year. Or maybe set up a huge tent someplace."

"Will it be a big event?"

He nearly collapsed onto his desk chair. "We've both lived in Lewiston all our lives. We both have extended families. You do the math."

"Church?"

"Ellie's folks are Presbyterian. My family is more live-and-let-live. So it'll be Ellie's family's church. We've already got an appointment set up with the minister for over Christmas break."

This confused me. "An appointment for...?"

"I guess he wants to make sure we've discussed things like what we want out of life, whether we both want kids. Or a dog. Hell, I don't know." His tone told me he expected to be grilled, or at least interviewed.

"Wow. I thought it was only Catholics who required that sort of thing."

"Pre-Cana. Yeah, nothing that rigorous. But, you know, I guess it's a good idea. Ellie's dad says it helps make sure we've thought about things that will happen in the future. Like, stuff we might take for granted and assume the other person does too."

"Makes sense." It did, too. I wondered how many people there were like that minister who wanted to help prepare gay couples like this. I was willing to bet they'd be hard to find. But that wasn't El Speed's fault, or his problem.

"Honeymoon?"

"Ah. That, there's no question about. Ellie and I have both always wanted to go to Nova Scotia."

I nodded; wouldn't have been my first choice, but it wasn't my honeymoon.

"Anyway, Nathan, I, uh...."

"What?"

"Listen, I wanted to ask you to be best man. But there's this friend at home, someone I grew up with. We sorta promised each other that role years ago. I'd feel bad going back on that."

It honestly hadn't occurred to me. "I get it. No worries."

"Thanks. Well anyway, put the date on your calendar."

I grinned. "Wouldn't miss it for the world."

That night I had trouble getting to sleep; couldn't have said why, but these things don't always have obvious reasons. I got up and positioned my laptop screen so it wouldn't shine toward El Speed, plugged in my earbuds, and for some reason I couldn't have explained I googled Conroy's slack-line vid. No surprise, he was a natural in front of a camera. He was photogenic, he spoke clearly and with just enough enthusiasm, paused just long enough in all the right places, grinned when appropriate, and he explained everything he was doing and why. Made me want to go right out and try it again.

I went back to his website, Finnegan's Walks, and poked around. He had links there to videos of himself instructing viewers in all kinds of things: how to cross a fast-flowing river; what equipment you need for rock climbing, and how to use it; advice about sleeping mats and bags; a discussion of hiking watches and GPS devices; what packs to use for what kind of hiking, and what to put in them; reviews of tents, boots, and other equipment. Each vid included a short intro about how he does not accept payments for endorsements.

"I'm not an influencer," he said with intensity, a close-up of his handsome face looking right at you. "I'm a professional."

That week it snowed. Not a whole lot, not enough for me to take my Nordic skis over to College Woods. It had disappeared by Friday, melting into the earth that was still too warm for snow to stay in frozen form. Walking back to Hall House after my last class, my phone chimed: text message.

Conroy.

Hey, you up for a slack-line lesson? Got trees?

I stood still on the sidewalk staring at the little screen as people walked around me on either side, like I was a pebble tossed into a bubbling stream, stuck in place as life went on around me.

At first all I thought was that one of us was prescient; I'd just watched his video demonstration. But my thoughts moved on. Maybe what I decided to do about this invitation was influenced by knowing that El Speed really was getting married, and I was not. Maybe it was feeling tired of jackin' the beanstalk. Gland-handing. Freeing Willie. Maybe I wanted to see just how "bi" Conroy was, to see if we could lose the slack in slack-line. Hell, maybe I just wanted to join the bubbling life I felt was leaving me behind. Whatever.

I typed, *Interesting. The wood is hard, the line is slack. You think I need a lesson in that?* I added a winky-face.

Seconds after I hit send, I wanted to take it back. More people moved around and past me as I stayed rooted in place, eyes glued to my screen for what felt like an eternity. Had I gone too far? *Of course you've gone too far, you blithering idiot.*

I was just about to put the phone away and trudge onward, ready to hurl curses around the inside of my skull, when I got a reply.

You surprise me. In a good way. Tomorrow afternoon? Say, three-ish before it starts to get dark?

My phone went crazy trying to auto-correct, my fingers hit so many wrong letters just to get two words onto the screen, but finally I sent back, *Sounds good.* I was tempted to add more, but I forced myself to stop. I'd already said more than was wise. And I wasn't entirely sure what "surprise" meant to him.

When I got to the room, El Speed had left already for Lewiston. If I'd thought he disappeared a lot before, well... he was setting a new standard since getting engaged. I won't say I was pissed at him, but I will say it made me think maybe my message to Conroy hadn't been such a bad idea after all.

Defiant. I think that's the best word for how I felt.

Conroy showed up at three-fifteen. He didn't ask to see my room, and I didn't offer. I was already dressed for being outside, and that's where I met him. We nodded at each other.

He grinned. "Let's go find ourselves some wood."

That stupid text message. I might have blushed.

Scratch that. I blushed. But Conroy had already turned to walk around the building.

I showed him where the slack line had been set up last spring.

He looked sideways at me. "Let me guess. There were two lines. One to walk on, one to hold onto. Yeah?"

"Yeah. So?"

He laughed and added a joking tone to his voice. "That's not for the likes of us, Nathan." I shook my head, not understanding. "If you've got two lines, you could use trees farther apart. You and I, kid?" He grinned and shook his head. "We don't need no fuckin' second line."

He looked carefully around while I reached in my mind back to the video. Had he used only one line? And why hadn't I noticed that?

Conroy paced out a few distances, and settled on two thick oak trees about twelve feet apart. "This is a good stretch of ground. No dips, no rocks. It's pretty level. We need that."

Conroy's line was bright green. The one last spring had been red, but otherwise it was the same: about two inches wide and made of something dense, heavy, with a kind of woven texture to it. There was a short piece and a long piece. Conroy walked me through the process of how to set up the slack-line, which involved special sleeves to protect the trees, looped ends on the line pieces, and a ratchet.

"I'm setting this up at a height just below hip-level. When you get better, you could set it higher."

I looked down at my running shoes. "We did this barefoot that one time I've done this before."

He chuckled. "Okay, but with your frostbite? It's, what, forty-five degrees out, if that?" He shook his head. "Maybe next spring. No; the running shoes you're wearing will do fine. They're not too thick or heavy. You just need to be able to feel the line."

He moved to about the center of the taut line. "I know you've done this before, but I'm going to pretend you haven't. Humor me." He turned sideways to the line. "I'm going to walk through the process and talk while I do. Cool?"

I shrugged; whatever. He seemed to be in "leader" mode as though he were taking a group through something, or perhaps making one of his videos. But, hey, he knew a lot more about how to do this than I did.

As he talked, he performed the steps he described: how to get on and off the line; what to do if he felt himself falling; how he used his entire body to balance while keeping his head level; how he wasn't looking down, but keeping his eyes on the tree straight ahead ("You know, the wood."); how he felt for the line with his foot before placing his weight onto it.

Conroy seemed as confident on the slack line as in everything else he did. I watched as he walked all the way to one end of the line, where he rolled off, turned around and remounted, and walked back toward me on the line, where he rolled off again.

He smiled at me. "Your turn."

With one foot still on the ground, even though the foot on the line was placed well, my foot and the line moved back and forth. I looked at Conroy.

"Yeah, that's gonna happen initially. You won't be able to steady it until your whole weight is on it. So, back straight, bend the knee of the foot that's on the ground just enough, launch upward in a steady motion that's not fast and not slow, and let that foot hang. Keep the knee your weight is on flexed, just slightly bent."

I spent maybe ten minutes trying to balance on that green webbed line, which at least gave me practice rolling off of it. At first, I was good for maybe three or four seconds. But eventually I made it to ten.

Conroy clapped his hands three times slowly. "Well done! Now take a break; your knees and quads will probably be a little shaky for a few minutes."

He was right. He had me sit where I could lean my back against one of the trees. He lifted one of my legs and moved it enough to the side so that he could kneel between my knees, making me think something that had nothing to do with slack-lining was about to happen, making me *wish* something that had nothing to do with slack-lining was about to happen. But—no. He didn't look at my face. He placed both hands on my right leg just above the knee and massaged the muscle there, gently but deeply. After a minute or so he moved to my left leg. Then he sat back on his heels.

"Feel better?" His smile was genuine, but as much as I

wanted to take it personally, I had the feeling it was one he would have given anyone who'd signed up for one of his walks.

He didn't wait for me to respond. "Great, so now let's get you moving. Ready?" He extended a hand, I took it, and he pulled me to my feet.

I tried to remember everything he'd told me, but he had to remind me about looking ahead, not down. Every time I tried to shift weight, I had to roll off the line.

"Don't be discouraged, Nathan. You're not doing badly at all. Let's try a couple of minutes with training wheels." He had me get back onto the line while he stood beside me. "Now, with your hand, hold onto just the ends of my fingers. I'm here to help you balance, not to hold you on the line."

It was amazing how much more stable I felt, even though our hands were barely touching.

"Now, when you're ready, feel the line in front of you with your free foot."

Within a couple of minutes I was able to let go of Conroy as I stepped slowly forward. He kept his hand within reach and I grabbed on another couple of times, but together we made it all the way to the tree. As I rolled off, I turned to look at Conroy, who'd stopped following alongside me a few feet ago. He stood, hands on hips, an approving smile on his face.

He nodded once. "Nathan, that was great. If you keep working, you'll get really good at this."

I walked the line, as it were, twice more, mostly without Conroy's support, needing to roll off only a few times. I was thoroughly pleased with myself. And I was thrilled that Conroy seemed pleased with me as well.

I helped take down the slack line and pack it away into the bag Conroy used for it, and we started to walk around to the front of the dorm. On impulse, I stopped.

"There's, um, a back door. To the dorm." Back door, indeed.

Conroy tilted his head just slightly. "And?" His tone was gentle, maybe even insinuating. But he was waiting for me.

I trusted that we were thinking the same thing. "And my roommate's away for the weekend."

He nodded, squeezed his hand on my shoulder and released it. "Lead the way."

We passed a few other residents in the downstairs lounge. I nodded at them but didn't stop to introduce Conroy. For all they knew, he was just a friend. Right?

I led the way up the stairs, hoping there would be fewer people in the upstairs lounge, and in fact it was empty. I opened my door, held it open for Conroy, and shut it.

Immediately he pressed his body against mine, and mine against the door. With his hands flat on the door over my head, his tongue went into my mouth and took up residence, exploring everything it could reach and doing the rounds again. I grabbed his head with my hands, struggling to breathe but not wanting him to pull away even a fraction.

God! Fuck! I wanted this so bad. The feel of his hard, flat, male chest against mine, the mind-blowing sensation of his hips grinding as though trying to reach the door through my body made anything and everything else in the world go away.

Still deep into each other's mouths, I let my hands fall to his shoulders and on to his biceps—those firm, thick, hard muscles—and up to the forearms, squeezing and massaging almost frantically. He lowered his arms to clasp my hands in his and then pulled his head back. His eyes landed on mine and stayed there long enough to make me want to scream, long enough to make me want to make the next move.

So I did. "Fuck me."

I didn't think of myself as a bottom, at least not exclusively. Maybe not even mostly. But Conroy was older, stronger, and more assertive than any man I'd been with before. It felt exciting and wonderful. And scary.

Conroy grinned, stepped away, and began the process of undressing himself, and I did the same. Before removing his jeans, from some inner pocket he pulled a wrapped condom.

"Which bed?" he asked, the gravel in his voice revealing his state of arousal.

My eyes followed the condom as he flung it toward the bed I pointed to. I said, "You expected this, then?"

Another grin. "Not necessarily. That little piece of insurance is just something I don't leave home without." He stood beside my bed. "Lube?"

"Drawer. There."

He grabbed it and pushed me down onto my back. Holding my wrists down with his hands, knees on either side of my hips, he ran his lips and tongue over every inch of skin he could reach. Loving that, but not wanting to give in completely to helplessness, I bent my knees and pushed my legs against his until he had to shift his weight. In a flash, I wrapped my legs around his waist and lifted my erection up to meet his. He threw back his head and laughed.

"No prisoner, you," he growled. Then, somehow, he freed himself enough to bring his cock up to my face where I could tease it and nip it and suck the end. I wrapped a hand around the shaft against his body to shorten the length I'd take into my mouth; I wasn't convinced he wouldn't push too hard.

He flipped me onto my belly and sat on me, his face toward my ass, and pressed lube-covered fingers into me, teasing and stretching until my hands clenched around fistfuls of sheet and my eyes clenched shut. Then he repositioned himself. He pulled me onto my knees, I heard the condom wrapper tear, and the next thing I knew it felt like maybe my ass would tear. My eyes flew wide open.

Don't get me wrong. I was ready, and I was willing, and I wasn't inexperienced. But—wow. I nearly cried out, but I stifled that urge and turned it into a groan. I knew that if I held out, there would be payback.

There was. Conroy knew exactly what he was doing and how to give as much pleasure as he was getting. He lubed one of his hands and worked my dick as he pumped. His dick got at all the right places, and I came first. He pushed into me as deep as he could, and within seconds I heard him yell. It was a wild, wonderful, satisfying cry, all male, and completely sexual.

Conroy stayed inside me for several seconds, warm and throbbing, and then he rolled off, making me think (ridiculously) of rolling off the green slack line. We lay on that dorm-size bed, touching all down our sides, for several minutes. I don't know whether he dozed. I didn't, but I lay quietly in case he did.

The room was completely dark by the time I sat up and flipped on the lamp on my bedside table.

I picked up my wastebasket. "What did you do with...."

He sat up and located his discarded condom, dropping it into the basket I held toward him.

"I hate to fuck and run," he said as he climbed off the bed and onto his feet, "so instead, how about we go grab some dinner in town? Pizza? Something like that?"

"Sure."

"Bathroom?" He had dressed more quickly than seemed possible.

I handed him a clean washcloth and gave him directions, and then I finished dressing and grabbed my own washcloth. A little clean-up was definitely in order. It made me wince, but it was a price I was happy to pay.

Conroy was as casual after our carnal coupling as if it hadn't happened. I told myself I didn't really expect or even want anything else, but his level of detachment almost made it feel as though we were heading out directly from the slack-lining lesson.

At the restaurant, the only table open was the one where Alden had told me about his struggle with fentanyl. To be sure, I'd sat at this table many times since the fall of my freshman year, but the table would always be significant. I lowered myself very carefully onto the hard wooden chair.

Conroy and I both ordered a single pizza of our own and a pitcher of beer for the table. This was the first year I'd been able to order alcohol legally, and of course I got carded. I tried to act like it was ridiculous.

The waiter departed with our order, and Conroy said, "Nathan, you better get used to that." He leaned back in his chair and grinned at me. "With that baby face, that clear skin, and that firm, youthful body, you're gonna look younger than your years for a while."

I waved a hand. "Aw, shucks. You're just sayin' that." Conroy laughed out loud.

The beer pitcher arrived, and while we waited for our pizzas, Conroy pulled his phone out, located something on it, and handed it to me. It was a video he'd taken of me on the slack line.

"I'll send this to you. It'll help you improve your form." I watched it twice and handed the phone back. "Great."

As he tucked it into a pocket, he smiled at me. "You know, most people don't pick up the technique as quickly as you did. You're a natural athlete."

I raised my beer mug to cover my pleased embarrassment. "Thanks."

After a moment of silence, awkward for me and probably not for Conroy, I ventured, "Now that we've—you know—twice, can I ask you a personal question?" Nina's derision, that I hadn't known something about Conroy, was still poking at me.

"Shoot."

"Are you bi?"

One side of his mouth lifted in a half-smile. "Probably. Yeah. I guess so. Does it matter?"

I lifted a shoulder and dropped it. "Just wondered. I'm gay."

He nodded. "I figured."

I wasn't sure I wanted to know why he'd said that. What I did want to know, however, was something I'd been wondering about since Gram had told me Conroy had called her. So far, with every encounter he and I had had, he'd said or done something to leave me with the impression that anything between us was totally casual. Like, *super* casual. I felt like he'd been sending the message that he enjoyed my company, but only to a certain point. He didn't want affection. He didn't even want a real friendship, at least not the kind you'd have with a peer. He'd always been the one to contact me, and he'd never seemed to expect anything else.

Every time we were together was a one-off. It didn't feel like anything was building, or developing, or becoming any more important than a series of chance encounters. I wanted to know if the impression I was getting was the one he wanted to leave me with. Because if it was, then I needed to put on some internal brakes. I had to avoid falling, yet again, for someone who would hurt me.

And to find that out, I'd have to take a chance.

"Have you ever thought about putting down a few roots? That is, as opposed to moving from one house-sitting job to another."

He shook his head. "Roots. Not my thing."

"You never liked any place enough to stay there?"

"Trouble is, a lot of other stuff comes with the place. Otherwise I might still be on Kaua'i."

"Other stuff?"

He gave me an assessing look that lasted just long enough to feel like a warning. "Yeah. Like people. People who want to get a handle on you. Who want to make you a part of their lives, and want you to be a part of theirs."

"Okay, but even if you leave town tomorrow, aren't I a part of your life right now? A small part, maybe, and a temporary one, but still...."

"You're a part of my day, and I'm a part of yours. You might be part of another day." He shrugged. "If that's not enough, you should say so now."

One-off. Loud and clear.

In my head, an argument began.

Voice One: "Back-paddle, Nathan, fast, or this will be the last time you see this guy."

Voice Two: "And maybe not seeing him again would be the best thing you could do."

One: "What, you don't think you can handle yourself on Conroy's terms? Didn't you figure out how to deal with this after your relationship with Daniel?"

Two: "Said differently: Didn't you learn anything from that fiasco with Daniel?"

It was about at this point that an image came to me, and image of the snake biting its own tail. Someplace I'd learned it was meant to signify the infinity of life and death and life again, but right now it just felt like a nasty cycle repeating itself. I had to choose. And I decided to go with the first voice that had spoken. I back-paddled.

"Hey, I'm not looking for a boyfriend. I'm not trying to tie you down. It just seems to me that the way you live might get a little lonely."

Maybe I'd struck a nerve. Maybe he was tired of explaining his lifestyle to people like me who liked the idea of roots. Whatever the reason, my comment stopped him cold. He stared over my head for long enough that I began to wonder if he was thinking of walking out.

He smiled, and for once he couldn't make it look genuine. Or maybe it looked just the way he wanted it to. "That's my worry. Not yours."

"Okay. Sorry. I get it."

He waved a hand. "You're young." The pizzas arrived in time for a subject change. "What are you studying, anyway?" He lifted a triangle of pizza and bit the point off.

I took a second to get a perverse kick out of the fact that we'd met a number of times, had sex twice, and this topic had never come up. "Psych. Specifically around substance abuse and addiction."

He stopped chewing for a few seconds. When he could speak, he said, "Heavy. Any particular reason?"

I finished my own mouthful of pizza, taking my time, before responding. "There are a few particular reasons." I lifted my mug, waiting to see if he'd ask what they were.

"Look, if this is personal, just say so. Don't play games."

Was he mad at me because of my earlier questions? My tone had an edge. "Games?"

"*Are* they too personal? Your reasons?"

I let out a long breath to give myself time to think. "Maybe. They involve a friend of my roommate's, and another person I was involved with. Someone I loved."

He took another bite of pizza. Was I reading too much into his casual response? Was he relieved that I hadn't said it had been my own addiction? After another sip of beer, he asked, "Any particular substance?"

"Fentanyl."

"Wow."

"You know something about it?"

"I know how insidious it is. Just from what I've heard, I mean. I don't think I know anyone who's ever taken it recreationally."

I considered whether to change the subject or go deeper. I chose the latter. "It gets at you like nothing else ever could. Like nothing else ever can."

I watched his face. Did he want to know more? He seemed to be waiting, so I repeated, as well as I could remember, what Alden had told me. I watched Conroy's face as I talked to gauge whether I was going too far. It didn't seem like it.

When I stopped, Conroy echoed, "'A substitute for

hope in a hopeless situation.' Holy shit."

I added, "Depending on how it's cut, fentanyl is between fifty and a hundred times more powerful than morphine in terms of the high it gives you, the way it makes you feel. The first time is always the best, but people keep trying to get to that place again, and they get hooked. And then maybe they die."

He was still with me, so I rested my wrists on the table edge and gave him a glimpse into what my research in this field had helped me understand. "So many things in life, in society, make us feel like we're not quite enough by ourselves. Enough of what, isn't clear to us. Fentanyl can make you feel so great that you can convince yourself— temporarily—that you *are* great, that what you are is enough. And even though you know you got to that feeling only by using, you push that aside in favor of having the feeling again. Or, at least trying to get it back."

Conroy didn't speak, but his eyes were still on mine. So I threw one more layer at him. "People who know they're addicted have it the worst. Not only do they know they can't feel good without the drug, but also they feel bad about themselves for being addicts. This means they have an even deeper hole to pull themselves out of than they did when they started using."

Conroy's head moved slowly side to side a few times, more in amazement than disbelief, I was sure. "How the fuck does anyone climb out of that hole once they're in that deep?"

"That is truly the question. And there's no one answer. What I'm working on now, and what I want to specialize in, once I get to grad school, is how we can get a sense of what approaches might work better for which people. Not everyone does well on methadone, while for others it's a god-send. Some people respond to group counseling, some to private sessions, some to a combination, sometimes with methadone and sometimes without. Some people manage to turn themselves around after a good rehab treatment. Some go back for rehab several times and still can't recover their lives." I sat back. "My friend was like that. He'd been in an excellent rehab program before I met him. And then something happened, and he had to go back."

"Is he okay now?"

"I have no idea. I wasn't allowed to be in touch with him when he went back into rehab, and he hasn't reached out to me since then."

We stared at each other for a few seconds and then, his voice low and intimate, Conroy asked, "There's no way you blame yourself, right?"

I shook my head, but not too hard. Deliberately not too hard. I didn't want him to think I was, as the phrase goes, protesting too much. "No, you can't think like that. I don't know what sent him back to fentanyl. Different people have different reasons when that happens."

"Well." Conroy's voice had a tone of finality, like that was enough discussion of addiction. "God knows we need people like you. I keep hearing about it being an epidemic."

"It is."

After dinner we walked together until we came to the street light where my path toward the dorm veered off from his route back to his car. We stopped at the intersection for what I thought would be a quick "See you." But he stood still, looking at me.

"Nathan, I don't know whether we'll meet again, but I hope we do. You really impress me."

So this was his way of confirming what he'd said in the restaurant. I nodded my head once in his direction. "Thanks. I hope so, too."

We didn't touch, or kiss, or hold hands. Each of us turned in his own direction and walked on. I struggled to convince myself I had the same carefree attitude as Conroy. I'd fallen hard for Daniel, into that ill-fated and unrequited relationship with a guy Nina thought of as a loser. If she saw Conroy as similar, at least I wanted to be able to laugh and say, "Yeah, well, I'm not falling for this one."

Problem was, if I'd had to laugh about that right now, it would have been as fake as Conroy's smile when I'd mentioned loneliness. Maybe his loneliness wasn't my worry, but my attraction to him was. I needed to get a handle on that.

INTERLUDE IV: THE REAL NINA

Prickly. I think that's the best word to describe my relationship with my sister, at least before Neil died. I've always kind of worn my heart on my sleeve, as the saying goes, even though I don't mean to. She pretended she didn't have a heart at all.

Nina was two when a farm truck lost its brakes and demolished my grandfather's refurbished 1953 Studebaker. The truck driver died. So did my grandfather and both my parents, who were going with him to an antique car show. At two years old, maybe Nina couldn't actually remember our folks a whole lot better than I could, but it seems likely she would have been more directly affected by their deaths. In any case, six-year-old Neil must have taken his inherited role as the eldest sibling very seriously, because the older Nina and I got, the more he allowed us to depend on him. I think Nina saw him, sensibly, as a protective older brother. For me, he was the nearest thing I had to a father.

There were many times Neil took my part when Nina picked on me. Like the year I started high school. I'd always loved singing, but that year, thanks to Gram, I discovered torch songs. Think Judy Garland in her heyday. And I started singing them in the same vocal range as Judy.

Neil encouraged me to take voice lessons, so I did. But my practicing drove Nina crazy. She imitated me, making her voice harsh and ugly, and called my efforts stupid and a waste of time. Neil told her to knock it off, reminding her that no one was criticizing her interest in fashion design. Of course, we didn't really take that seriously at the time; now she's proving us wrong. But I still love singing, and I don't think doing something you love is a waste of time. Maybe Nina's ridicule wouldn't have made me stop, but Neil helped make sure that didn't happen.

Nina hid any vulnerability in many ways. Like the time Gram got really sick with the flu. Neil organized her care with a schedule and a list of tasks. He took the lion's share, but he conscripted Nina and me as well. She was only eight, but I was only seven, and although I was frightened and a little afraid of what Neil was asking me to do, I didn't protest. Nina made a real fuss about having to help with the nursing chores. It wasn't until she backed down from her high horse that I saw a look on her face that told me she was terrified. I think now that she had a better idea than I did just how sick Gram was, and what the ramifications might be if we lost the only adult in the house.

So it took me completely by surprise how efficiently, and how lovingly, she stepped into the breach right after Neil died. She'd been the one to tell Cotton Hazard, Neil's girlfriend (and probably about to be his fiancée) what had happened. Gram and I were both there, but Nina was the only one willing and able to take on the task. She was gentle and careful, and the tone in her voice was one I'd never heard before.

When Reverend Talby, who would officiate at the funeral, suggested that family members might want to say something at the church, Gram said she couldn't possibly, that she'd fall to bits. I just stared blankly and said nothing.

"I'll do it, Gram," Nina said, her voice soft but clear, no hint of the impatience or derision I might have expected from her. Her courage inspired me to prepare something as well, and when it was time for us to speak, Nina took my hand— something I can't remember ever happening before—and led the way to the front of the church.

All that was surprising enough. But what really stunned me was what she did for Mrs. Ford, Jeremy's mother.

Jeremy had been Neil's best friend since grade school. They joined the cub scouts together, and then the boy scouts, and when Neil started hiking, Jeremy was right there with him. I don't know whether Nina knew this or not, but Jeremy was gay. He was an only child. And his father had died years ago. So when he and Neil were caught in that fire-nado, Mrs. Ford had no one to lean on, no one to mourn with. Gram and I were the ones to tell her about Jeremy's death, and we did what we could to support her, but that wasn't much.

For anyone who's never had to organize a funeral, it's a long series of horrendous tasks. In one respect it's kind of like organizing a wedding: the venue, the officiant, the transportation, the wardrobe choices, the notifications, the ceremony, who will say what and when, and the reception. But for a funeral you have to do all this while fighting tears and often losing the battle. And afterward, all three of us went through Neil's room, his possessions, his life, and made decisions, each one as painful as the one before.

Mrs. Ford had no family to share her grief with. She had no one to help with any of these horrendous tasks. Or she wouldn't have, if not for Nina. Because even though she was pulling her weight in planning Neil's funeral, which would be the day before Jeremy's, Nina went to Mrs. Ford and helped her organize the funeral for her only child.

Nina didn't tell us she was doing this. Gram and I found out when we went to Jeremy's funeral. The three of us sat in the front pew with Mrs. Ford, who got up and did her best to say a few words about Jeremy, but she was so distressed she couldn't finish. The only thing I registered from her speech was when she thanked Nina. And then she broke down completely. The minister moved over to her, but almost immediately Nina was beside her. She put an arm around Mrs. Ford's shaking shoulders and walked her back to her seat. From her own handbag she pulled out a small bag and packet of tissues and handed the tissues, one at a time, to Mrs. Ford, placing the used ones into the spare bag. She never left Mrs. Ford's side as we left the church and went to the cemetery, or when we left the cemetery and went back to the church function hall for the reception, or at any time during that awful day.

Afterward, at home, Gram praised Nina. "That was a wonderful thing to do, sweetie." She seemed about to say more, but Nina interrupted her.

With a shrug, she said, "There was no one to help her."

But she didn't stop there. She spent the next three days with Mrs. Ford, helping her go through Jeremy's life, his possessions, making painful decisions. I know this, because I went with her. I'm not sure whether she inspired me or shamed me. Maybe both.

My sister might not want people to know this, but she is a trooper. She has a heart as big as the mountains Neil climbed. It took a tragedy for her to show it, and for me to see this. But see it, I do.

CHAPTER SEVEN

For the first three years of college, El Speed had left campus many weekends to be with Ellie. But when he'd been on campus, he'd been fully there. A few times, she'd come to UNH for a weekend, but only after El Speed and I had worked out a schedule that included me going home to Concord, leaving them the privacy of the room.

After El Speed had given Ellie that ring in October, though, things had shifted. It had happened so gradually that it had taken a while for me to notice that our conversations had started to be more about Ellie's parents this, Ellie's sister Nancy that, Ellie's cousin Donna something else. Then one Thursday evening sometime in February, with a snowstorm in full throttle outside, I kind of exploded. Quietly, but still.

I was at my desk, trying to finish an important paper for a psych class. El Speed was at his desk, supposedly working on classwork as well. But he kept leaning back, glancing at me, and talking.

"I don't think Nancy likes the dress she has to wear."

I tried to ignore him. Maybe that didn't register with him, because he kept talking.

"I guess the bride gets to choose the bridesmaid's outfit. I keep getting these emails from Nancy about—"

"Look," I said, not lifting my head from my work, "I need to finish this tonight. Okay?"

There were a few seconds of silence before he said, "Sure. Guess it's not reasonable to expect you to be interested."

"Not in dresses, no. I'm not."

More silence. And then, "Look, Nathan, this is my life now, y'know? This thing is using up all my chi." I looked up, not sure I'd heard him right. "Call me crazy, but I thought you'd care."

I stared at him, not sure what to say, where to start. Then I stood and gathered up everything I was working on. Snowstorm or no snowstorm, I was going to have to go to the library to get this work done.

El Speed watched as I shoved everything into a pack and pulled my parka out of the closet. Then, "Going someplace?"

Parka on, one strap of the pack slung onto my shoulder, one hand on the knob of the door I'd just opened, I turned toward him.

"I get it, okay? I get that right now your life is all about—well, all about the rest of your life, I guess. And yeah, I care. But Jesus, El Speed, it feels like there's nothing else we ever talk about these days. The wedding's not until June. It's fucking February. And right now, I gotta get some work done."

I walked out before he had time to respond, shutting the door rather pointedly behind me.

We didn't say much to each other Friday, and by two in the afternoon he was gone, on his way to Maine.

When he got back Monday, he had a plan.

"Ellie will be here this coming weekend. Taking a break from wedding stuff, I guess. But it'd be great if you hung around, too. Spend some time together, all three of us."

He sounded like a little kid who knew he'd done something Mommy or Daddy didn't like, and he was contrite but only to a point. I was sure he thought sharing Ellie with me for a weekend was a conciliatory gesture. I wasn't thrilled, but—hell, he was trying.

"Where's she gonna stay?"

He shuffled his feet, looked down at them, looked up at me. "Well, uh, I thought maybe we could find out if one of the guys here was going home for the weekend. And you could, y'know, bunk there."

A couple of thoughts went through my mind.

First: *This is a co-ed dorm. Ellie could "bunk" in one of the women's rooms.*

Second: *You spend every fucking weekend with Ellie. Are you telling me you don't "bunk" together all the time?*

Then it occurred to me that maybe they didn't sleep together at home. And I happened to know that one guy here would not be in his private room this weekend, and he'd probably let me stay there.

So Ellie stayed with El Speed in our room that weekend, and we did hang out together quite a bit. On the surface, it should have been a good thing. But there was something about the way they clung to each other that left me feeling like it was them and me, them and me. They were always holding hands, or if we were in line for anything—at the cafeteria, at the ice cream parlor, anywhere—El Speed would position himself behind Ellie and wrap his arms around her while we stood. And over meals, or anytime there was conversation, there were so many little gestures, and code phrases that meant something only to them, and moments of private understanding, that I felt excluded. That is, I didn't know what the code was for. They reminisced about something that I hadn't been part of. They talked about people I didn't know. They seemed so happy together that I hated how irritated I was feeling, and I did my best to hide it or push it away. But it kept coming back.

The truth was, El Speed and I had been growing apart to some extent since after our climb up Madison. It wasn't because we wanted to. It was just a natural by-product, an artifact left like a fossilized impression by the retreating closeness we'd known.

I didn't hear from Conroy again, or even see him anywhere around town, until March. Three months. Three fucking months. Despite his comment that he hoped we'd run into each other again, I wondered if my questions over pizza and beer had scared him off.

Several times I'd come close to calling him, or texting him. I even composed a number of text messages on my phone that I never sent. Several times I wandered past the house on Garden Lane, sometimes after dark so I might be able to peek inside, but the drapes were always drawn. Somehow I knew that if I contacted him, while I might be able to convince him it was super casual, I knew that for me, it wouldn't be.

But in March, serendipity stepped in, just as it had on Cannon. We met up by accident. In fact, there was an omen that coincided with that meeting. The omen: My right little toenail had just fallen off.

This toenail had fallen off for the first time a month or so after St. Patrick's Day my freshman year. Escaping the absurdity of that particular holiday—green hats, green carnations, green foil decorations, students over-indulging in green beer—had inspired Daniel to invite/conscript me for the climb up Mount Chocorua. The frostbite my feet had endured after that event had left me unable to walk for a couple of weeks. My ankles had swelled so much that I couldn't see the bones. And after the swelling subsided, that little toenail began to wobble in its bed. I wrapped it in soft tape for maybe a week, and then one day it just came off. Well, all right, there was a little skin holding it in place, but I gritted my teeth and pulled, and off it came. Several days later I could see the beginnings of a new nail, and finally the whole thing grew back. I thought that would be the end of it.

My sophomore year, on the anniversary—and I mean the exact date—of that climb, that nail fell off again. I hadn't even noticed that it was getting loose. It hadn't hurt. It just fell off. And it grew back, and stayed. Nothing happened in March of my junior year, so I thought that really *would* be the end of it.

Anyway, my senior year, that toenail fell off yet again, a few days before St. Patrick's Day, which fell on a Sunday. The weekend of that fateful anniversary, El Speed was in Maine, as usual. I'd considered going home to Concord, but I'd just been there the weekend before. So I was left to socialize with the few students in Hall House who either hadn't gone home for the weekend (UNH is an empty place on weekends) or who hadn't gone to the mountains for long walks in snowy woods, sometimes using snowshoes. They'd rented a large cabin off the Kancamagus Highway to serve as home base from which they planned a number of outings.

I knew the Kancamagus pretty well. The trail for my second climb up Chocorua, the Champney Falls Trail, starts along that east-west road which runs across the northern part of the state. It cuts through the White Mountain National Forest, and there are mountains and trails all along its fifty-six-plus mile stretch. In autumn foliage season, it's a leaf-peeper magnet. But this time of year I knew there would be lots of snow, and the description of the cabin left me with the distinct impression that it was rustic enough to be a challenging place to keep my feet warm or to warm them up when they got cold.

I would love to have gone. I liked the house members who were going, I loved the area, I loved being out in the woods (even in the cold), I loved the activity, and I really hated the idea of being someone who wouldn't be able to hack it—whatever "it" was—for any reason whatsoever.

So that's where my head was that Sunday afternoon as I tramped around campus, not wanting to be in the dorm when the hikers returned, knowing they'd be vociferously celebrating when they got back. To pacify my sulky self just a little, I found my way over to the trails in College Woods, which I knew would be a little snowy but manageable, where I knew I could keep moving (which would keep my feet warm), and from where, if necessary, I could get back to the dorm fairly quickly and warm my traitor feet up again.

It was just before two o'clock when I made it to where the trails begin on the west side of campus. The snow cover was about what I'd predicted, so I turned off my phone—I didn't want my sulk interrupted—and started my trek. The trails here are quite varied in terms of twists and turns, flat sections, and short, steep grades up and down. I deliberately took turns I'd never taken before, knowing that I could get only so lost in two hundred and fifty acres, many of which I was already familiar with; if I kept going in any direction, I'd come to a section I knew.

So I got delightfully lost. I actually enjoy getting lost, as long as conditions aren't severe and I don't have a time limit, or I'm not about to lose light. After maybe an hour I followed a narrow path that almost wasn't a path, and it led me down a slope I knew I had been on in my Nordic skis just last year. I kept going, remembering that it had eventually led to the banks of the Oyster River, which followed the southern edge of the woods.

As I approached the river, which was moving just fast enough to be heard and was frozen just enough to have icy edges, I saw there was someone sitting on a fallen tree, his back to me, gazing at the water. And it was a tree, not a log. The tree had fallen parallel to the river bank, and it was fairly level, just over two feet off the ground. A white pine, I was pretty sure. The man was sitting on a section of trunk between a couple of branches that pointed up toward the sky.

I stood still, knowing he wouldn't hear me over the sounds of the river. I could just turn around and go back. I wasn't really in the mood to make small talk; I'd come here to sulk. But a branch under the snow my foot was on gave way with a crack loud enough to make the guy turn around.

Conroy.

My guts did a somersault.

"Nathan!" He sounded glad to see me. "Pull up a tree and join me."

I felt torn. Did I want to talk to Conroy? Hell yes.

But—three months.... And in those three months I'd gone back and forth between "Fuck Conroy; I don't need him," and "Why hasn't he called? Why haven't I called him? Why the fuck can't I just be satisfied with what he can give me and leave it at that?"

Finally I decided the only alternative to accepting his offer of company was to be totally rude, and I didn't want to do that.

When he saw I was moving forward, he turned back to the river and waited for me to hoist myself up on the other side of one of the branches that flanked his seat. No slaps on the back. No shaking of hands. No "How've ya been, guy?" We just both stared at the river.

Finally, he spoke. "I love this place. Gonna miss it next year."

"Moving on to another house sitting job?"

"Yup. I'll be gone by July. Going to Texas, actually. Austin." I let that hang in the air. Then he said, "Just got back from leading a trip. Arizona. Painted Desert and the Petrified Forest National Park."

He probably wanted me to ask questions, to sound impressed with what he did for a living, to be impressed by him. I wasn't in the mood. We sat in silence disturbed only by the river for a couple of minutes, and then Conroy looked my way.

"You okay, Nathan?"

"Sure. Why not?'

"You seem kind of down."

I considered telling him why I was in this mood, rejected the idea, and said nothing.

"What you need is a hike." He didn't know how right he was.

"Probably."

"D'you remember me talking about the Kalalau Trail? On the island of Kaua'i?"

"More than once, as I recall."

He turned back to the river. "It's magical, Nathan. I know I went on a bit at Thanksgiving, and you were all very polite to listen to me."

"Except Nina."

He laughed in that familiar way that pulled at something deep inside me, and I realized with a slight shock that I had missed it. He said, "Yeah, except Nina. She's okay. She just didn't know what to make of me, so she didn't trust me. She's the type who needs to figure people out quickly."

Again, he was so right; but this time, I think he knew it.

"Anyway, I'm planning a Kalalau hike, and I'd love for you to join it."

Not join *me*. Join *it*.

"I doubt I'll have the money for something like that. College has been expensive, and I've got to figure out grad school. I'm already behind on that chore."

To say "already behind" was putting it mildly. It seemed like every few days I wracked my brain trying to figure out why I was dragging my feet. Didn't I want to go on in school? Yes, I did. Didn't I want to continue in psychology? Yes, I did. Wasn't I still determined to work in the area of substance abuse? Yes, I was. Then, what?

Finally my "what," sent out into the universe like some kind of plaintive cry, had a response. It was not a response I would have expected. And yet I was not surprised.

Gram.

Neil had gone to grad school in Colorado, and then he'd died. Nina had moved to New York and would certainly not come back to New Hampshire when she was ready for more schooling in fashion design. That left me. The youngest child. The baby. The final fledgling.

Of course—really obviously—this was the way of things. My studies had confirmed what I would have guessed: the youngest child is very likely to feel the greatest guilt when the time came to leave that nest. In my case, I'd lived in that nest, that house in Concord, all my life. I'd known no other home. I'd known no other parent, just Gram. And she was alone.

Sure, she'd been alone ever since I'd started at UNH, but I'd gone home a lot, especially during my sophomore year, the first school year after Neil had died. To her credit, Gram never made me feel obliged to spend time with her, never did anything to indicate that it was my responsibility to keep her from being lonely. She wouldn't have done that. And she wasn't alone, really. She had her church, where she had lots of friends, and she had her volunteer activities, the number of which had increased gradually over the last five years or so.

Still.

So the idea of grad school, which would most likely be someplace other than UNH because I might want to be in a big-city environment, carried with it the idea of deserting Gram. Leaving her truly alone.

So I'd had trouble focusing on what it would take even to apply to grad schools.

I sighed audibly.

Conroy picked up where he'd left off: the Kalalau Trail. "Well, think about it. I've already got some stuff up on my website. And you should google images of the Na Pali Coast." He swung his legs back and forth a few times under the tree. "Ever heard of the Kalalau outlaws?"

That made me turn to look at him. "The what?"

"Kalalau outlaws. People who came to the Na Pali Coast and either couldn't leave, or couldn't stay away, and they spend all or part of their time actually living in the valleys between those knife-edge peaks that plunge down into the Pacific."

"What do they eat?"

He shrugged. "They fish, they find berries and fruits, they might kill a wild pig or a goat. Some of them have set themselves up with living quarters that—well, okay, they're extremely rudimentary, but they're functional. We might or might not see any of them, because they hide."

"Why are they outlaws?"

"They're not supposed to be there. You need a permit, good for only a few days, to hike farther than two miles down from Ke'e Beach, and especially if you're planning to camp out. I'll have to get special permits to stay in the area for my walk. Anyway, every so often the park service goes in to try and roust them. But, see, the landscape is so wild and crazy, it's nearly impossible to find them. So they catch a few, but there are others. And some of the outlaws live someplace else for most or part of the year, and then they come back to the Kalalau."

"Why?"

"Why do they come back?" He shook his head. "Like I said, some of them never leave. They can't bring themselves to leave." He shifted on the tree to turn a little toward me. "Nathan, you gotta see this place to believe it. I wasn't exaggerating at Thanksgiving. The place really does affect me like that. And my guess is that it affects the outlaws like that, too."

He turned back toward the river. "In fact, I've got myself so psyched up now, I think I'll plan to go stay on the island for a week or so ahead of the hike. Just hang out. Pretend I'm an islander. I kind of am, in spirit." He sighed. "Yeah. That's what I'll do."

He went on for a little while about the island itself—the Waimea Canyon, the road called the Kuhio Highway that's the only road around the island, a "highway" that on the north shore is too narrow for two vehicles in some places. "You can't drive across the island. The mountains, and especially the canyon, prevent it."

"No road through the mountains?"

He laughed. "Nathan, the terrain is so impossible that even helicopters can't land there, except in the few places where there's enough flat ground. There are signs that say, 'No camping. Helicopter landing pad.' Pad! That's a riot. It's just the only flat piece of ground for miles around large enough to land on."

We stared at the river for a few minutes, and then he jumped down. "Well, think I'll head back. Got some planning to do. You?"

I shook my head. I knew I should go back; my feet were complaining loudly. But I didn't want to walk with anyone. "Not yet."

"Check out my website. See you, Nathan."

And he was gone.

It was almost dark when I left College Woods behind. When I got back to what was official campus, with buildings and paved roads, I pulled out my phone to turn it on.

Five calls from Nina? Two had voicemails to call her immediately. I nearly dropped the phone trying to hit the right button to call her back.

When she picked up, her voice sounded strangled. "I'm on my way home. Rented a car. I'll be in Durham in about thirty minutes to pick you up. Nathan...."

She paused, and I couldn't tell why. I nearly shouted "What?"

"It's Gram. She's gone."

"What? Gone where?" My heart pounded. I was having trouble breathing.

"She's dead, Nathan."

CHAPTER EIGHT

Friday night, Gram had been doing something—it wasn't entirely clear what—in one of the upper cupboards, which meant she'd been standing on the top step of a folding ladder she kept for this purpose. The medical examiner decided that the most likely sequence of events was that she had a stroke, fell off the ladder, hit her head and broke her hip, and lay there unconscious until she died, sometime on Saturday. He said the stroke was massive, which was probably why he didn't dwell on the possibility that she might have been conscious for at least part of those many hours, helpless, in pain, unable to call for help, and—worst of all—with no one to help even if she cried out. When she didn't show up for church on Sunday, her neighbor and another friend came to see if she was all right. She was not.

If I'd been there, I would have gotten her to the hospital, probably in time to save her life. I'd said as much to Nina on the drive home, after she'd picked me the Sunday I'd been walking through College Woods.

"Don't be an idiot, Nathan. Neither of us could be there all the time. Besides, the last thing I think she'd have wanted would have been to wake up in some kind of debilitated state, unable to speak maybe, and live out whatever time she had left like that."

"But she died alone!"

"Nathan, everyone dies alone." I stared at her in stunned silence until she added, "Look, I'm trying not to cry, all right? I need to see the road. Either talk to me about something else, or don't talk at all."

Between her words I could hear something she'd said to me a number of times over the years: "This isn't about you, Nathan."

And yet, it was. Because it was about my love for the woman who'd raised me, who'd loved me, who'd done her best to accept me for who I was even though she couldn't understand it. Maybe feeling guilty was a little self-centered, but everything Nina and I would do for the next several days—the funeral, the will, deciding what to do with the house, all that stuff—wouldn't be for Gram. It would be for us, about us. Even the funeral wasn't for Gram. I almost quoted aloud a verse from a song Neil used to play all the time: *Gravestones cheer the living, dear; they're no use to the dead.*

Gram's funeral was even bigger than Neil's had been. Everyone who'd known Neil had loved him, or at least liked him, but practically everyone in Concord had known Gram. She'd been involved in community efforts for all kinds of things from cleaning litter from parks to raising money for the local library.

After Nina and I had each said something to the crowd in the church (a task that required a microphone because of the size of the congregation), other people came up to speak. I lost track of how many there were. I paid attention to the first two or three, but after that my mind went back to where it had been, on and off, since Nina had told me Gram had died: If I'd gone home that weekend, she might still be alive.

I'd never given much thought to Gram's religion. Each of us kids had stopped going to church at some point in our respective childhoods, and she'd never tried to insist that we keep going. It occurred to me, working through the list of hymns, that there might be a whole lot of stuff about Gram that I'd always taken for granted, or had never given any thought to.

For example, if I had given any thought to why she

kept going to church, I'd probably have figured it was for the sense of community, the connections, the friendships. But some of the things the minister and a few of the other parishioners said before the funeral, during the funeral, and at the reception made me realize she'd been pretty serious about the religion part. For a brief moment, I considered taking on the role of observant Christian worship, picking up her practice as I'd picked up Neil's mountain climbing. But it was a very brief moment. I also considered asking Nina if she'd been aware of that part of Gram's life, but the truth was that if she had, I didn't want to know.

El Speed and Ellie sat beside me during the funeral, which had probably kept me from bawling my eyes out—although I was pretty cried-out by then, anyway. They spent the night in Neil's room and left the next morning.

I was glad to see them leave; for the past couple of months, any time I spent with them had made me feel like a third wheel. So when I was with El Speed, now, even when Ellie wasn't around, I wasn't with *him*. I was with *them*. My friendship with El Speed had been the best of my life, the only close friendship I'd had since I'd realized I was gay. It felt like I was losing my grandmother and my best friend more or less at the same time.

As soon as they left, though, Nina and I had to begin the task of going through things. I knew this would be a dreadful task. It had been bad enough after Neil had died, but now the whole house—essentially my whole life—would be pulled apart. I would be in limbo.

Soon after the funeral, Nina and I met with Gram's attorney. I hadn't even known she'd had an attorney, but evidently she'd decided to have her will drawn up officially at some point without mentioning it to me. Nina had known, which bothered me a little.

I took in Ms. Landry's short salt-and-pepper hair, neat

maroon suit, cream blouse with a soft bow tied at the neck, creamy pearls in her earlobes, and wondered what Gram's will would say. She'd always been so careful with money, so there wasn't likely to be much in the way of cash.

There was the house, of course, owned outright, and all its contents, which Gram's will said went to Nina and me jointly, leaving us to decide what to do with everything. In some families this might have been awkward, but I had a feeling the unsentimental Nina would want to keep very little for herself. We'd have to get the house assessed to know what it was worth; I had no clue, and I doubted Nina did, either.

There was some money in Gram's checking account, maybe seven thousand, which was legally Nina's because she had signatory power on the account. The savings account, roughly sixty thousand, went jointly to Nina and me. Then there were a few certificates of deposit, which she willed to the church. Then came the big surprise.

"Your grandmother had taken out a life insurance policy not long after the accident that took your parents and her husband," Ms. Landry told us. "She told me it had made her painfully aware of how fragile life can be, and it convinced her that unpredictable events can turn one's life upside down. It was not a term policy, but a whole-life, which means its value continued to increase. It was not a small policy when she opened it, and now its value is quite high. In addition, she had opened an annuity in both your names, to be shared equally. The total of the annuity and the insurance together, the amount to be divided equally between you, amounts to just under a million dollars, at roughly nine hundred eight thousand dollars."

I heard Nina's sharp intake of breath as my jaw fell nearly to my chest. My first thought (I've come to realize that first thoughts after a shock are almost never rational) was that at least Nina had not known that.

Ms. Landry waited for that news to sink in and then went on. "The way your grandmother structured her invested assets lets you avoid probate for most of it. The insurance and annuity will come to you almost immediately. The house, however, will need to go through probate. And its value will be in addition to the total I mentioned already."

She paused to see whether we were still following, and I think she wasn't sure. I wasn't, either. She spoke slowly. "We can go over all this at a later date. For now, I'll just say that probate shouldn't take long, but it can be a little unpredictable. We'll talk further about that. For now, though, I understand you both have student loans. You'll probably want to pay those off; they aren't the sort of loan that would benefit you to keep on the books. And if each of you hasn't yet got your own credit card, I'd advise you to get one."

She paused once more and then said, "I can help you with references to a couple of estate liquidators I trust, when you're ready to take that step. They would handle the sale of the house itself, if you decide not to keep it, as well as any contents you don't keep."

There was silence in the room for several seconds. I had no words, and evidently Nina didn't either, which was remarkable.

Ms. Landry reached into a drawer. "In this envelope, which your grandmother sealed herself, is a key to a safe deposit box. She had the other key, of course, but I wouldn't know where it is, and you might not either. I'm sure the box holds things like the deed to the house, the title to her car, things like that. Obviously you'll need those things."

There was a little more discussion, and then Nina and I left. I felt decidedly unstable on my feet; Nina seemed lost in thought but otherwise not as stunned as I was.

There were no major surprises in the safe deposit box; we left everything there for the time being and began the job of going through Gram's paperwork so we could pay off anything outstanding.

ON THE KALALAUA TRAIL

"You can take the car," Nina told me. "I certainly don't need it. I'll take care of the last payments, using her checking account, and that should balance things out financially."

I had no problem with this arrangement. In fact, I liked it a lot. When El Speed had come for Neil's funeral, Gram had asked him about his Forester. She'd been thinking of getting an all-wheel-drive. He'd raved about Subaru, and she'd decided to get a new Outback, dark blue. This was now my car.

Over the next few weekends, Nina and I worked through what was in the house, giving clothes and a lot of paraphernalia to various charities. One day I was getting started on the sifting-and-sorting chore of going through Gram's stuff before Nina arrived. I had pulled out a bunch of music CDs, and I had examined and set aside for giveaway most of them when I picked up one with a cover image that looked like Hawai'i. It was the soundtrack from the movie *South Pacific*. On a whim, I played it.

Most of the tunes seemed kind of sexist and outdated. But there were a couple that really grabbed me. One was "Bali Ha'i," which brought to mind the intensity with which Conroy had talked about Kaua'i. It said the wind and sea would whisper "Come to me." It said my hopes and dreams shone in the waters. It promised I'd find "my special island."

The other tune was "Some Enchanted Evening."

It was gushy and sentimental and implied a belief in something like destiny. I rejected all those things. And yet there was one verse I couldn't get out of my head. "Someone may be laughing. The sound of that laughter will sing in your dreams." There was no way I felt gushy or romantic about Conroy. But his voice, his laughter... the effect that had on me was something I couldn't deny.

But why? Why would the way someone's voice sounded, the way he laughed, be enough to make me keep wanting to be with him when I knew it wasn't love? The song's lyrics had the answer to that, too: "Fools give you reasons. Wise men never try."

Maybe I was a fool to look for a reason. But a voice in my head kept asking that question: Why?

Conroy texted me a few times for coffee, but I kept putting him off. Did I want to see him? Yes. No. Maybe.... Yes. I also knew he didn't want to see me in the same way. And right now, as vulnerable as I felt, the pull to be with someone who would hold me—even if it was more for sex than out of affection—was massive. Did I love him? No, that wasn't it. But he made me feel special. He made me feel like I belonged someplace, which was ironic and distressing, because he seemed to think he belonged no place. And it was that juxtaposition, that contradiction that helped me keep him at a distance, even if it was only a slight distance.

El Speed wasn't on campus any more than he had to be, no doubt preparing for his wedding, which he and Ellie had decided was going to be outdoors after all, in the park where they'd gone for their first date. They hadn't liked the look of the hall they'd been promised. They also pushed the date into July.

All in all, I felt pretty alone.

There were two decisions that troubled both Nina and me, equally, I think. One was the house itself.

"I'll never live here again," Nina said over takeout Chinese one Saturday evening after we'd piled a lot of things together for giving away. "I haven't actually lived here for a while. What about you?"

I'd given this a lot of thought, and I was ready to talk about it. "You have an apartment, a place to live. After graduation, I'll have no place else to go."

"You'll need a place of your own, though, sooner than later. You're graduating this year, and you've said you'll be going to grad school. Once probate is finalized, don't you agree we should sell the house?"

As I'd told Conroy, my plans for grad school had been going slowly. Since Gram had died, the plans had stalled completely. "I'll need to take a gap year," I told Nina.

"Okay, but where?" Good question. "Wouldn't you rather do that in an apartment someplace near your first choice of school? Someplace you could find a half-decent job? You wouldn't want to live here all by yourself, would you?"

She was right. I'd thought about that and, rather foolishly, had decided it would be fine. But as soon as she said it, I knew it was a crazy idea. This was a large house, with a yard, and a garden, all of which would need maintenance. The rooms would echo with any sounds I made as well as with the ghosts of dead family members. "No. I guess not."

We decided to talk more about it later, to give me some time to think about where I'd live. But then there was the other question.

I stabbed a Peking ravioli with a chopstick. I didn't look at Nina. "What about Neil's things?"

She exhaled slowly, not quite a sigh. "I don't know."

I looked up. "Maybe put them into a rented storage unit for now?"

She blinked. "What a good idea. I mean, there might be some stuff that we wouldn't keep any longer. I haven't been downstairs in three years to look at what we did keep. Have you?"

I shook my head. "There might be some things. But let's plan on a small rented space, yeah?"

"Yeah. Okay."

"It's weird," I offered, thinking aloud, not quite sure what was going to come out of my head. "Most of Gram's things will go. Most of Neil's things…. Why are they harder to let go?"

She sat back in her chair. "Maybe it's just that Gram lived a pretty full life. Neil died so young."

Sunday morning we visited Gram's and Neil's graves, as we'd done every time we'd both been home. For a reason I couldn't have described, as we stood at Gram's new headstone, next to her late husband's, I reached for Nina's hand. She welcomed the touch and even squeezed my hand a little before letting go.

Nina headed back to New York after lunch. I'd planned to leave then as well, but something was teasing at the back of my brain. It was the line from that song about gravestones, the one that had occurred to me during the grief-stricken drive to Concord weeks ago, as it had sunk in that Gram would not be there for the first time in my life.

It was a song Neil had played enough times that he'd memorized the lyrics. I'd been in my torch song days, and a song like that had felt beneath me somehow. But I remembered that the tune and the harmonies were somewhat compelling. I decided to see if I could figure out what it was, which meant going through Neil's PC, searching through his music collection.

Neil's musical tastes had been all over the place. He'd bought albums from lots of bands famous during his own teens, but he'd also collected many other kinds of music—so many that these other categories didn't qualify as outliers. At his funeral, his girlfriend Cotton had played a bluegrass piece by a group called Cherryholmes. The essential line, which Cotton had said exemplified Neil's life philosophy, was, "Go grab your life and live it." At the time it had surprised me that Neil had been into bluegrass. So I wasn't sure where to start looking for the gravestone song.

Gram had been using Neil's PC for the last few years, and she'd shared the password with Nina and me. I sat with it at the kitchen table, sifting through the collection, getting more frustrated as the hours passed. I didn't know the name of the song, whether it would be in an album, listed alone, or included in a playlist, and it was hard to know what approach to take.

I was just thinking that I'd either have to go get something for dinner or leave and head back to campus when it occurred to me to search for just that line on the internet.

Eureka. The song was "Buy for Me the Rain" by a group who'd called themselves the Nitty Gritty Dirt Band. As soon as I saw that name, I could hear Neil's voice in my head: "This is the only song they did worth anything, but it's really great."

Talk about ghosts.

The music itself was as compelling as I expected, and the singer's voice was so clear I didn't need to follow the lyrics online. I let it play through five, maybe six times.

The singer asked someone—his "darling"—to buy rain, sun, and bird for him, and he'd reciprocate with rainbows and gold, sheltering shadows, and trees for nests. All of it needed to happen before he grew too old, before the years got away from them. It was uncannily reminiscent of Cherryholmes' "Live It." I could almost hear Neil summarize the sentiment for me: Life is happening now; don't waste a minute of it.

But then there was a fourth verse. The singer couldn't buy happiness, couldn't buy time, couldn't keep tears away. But he could buy a gravestone. The last line was the one I had remembered: "Gravestones cheer the living, dear; they're no use to the dead."

Don't waste your time on the inevitability of death. Don't waste your time in the graveyard when it's not your turn to be there.

So the Nitty Gritty Dirt Band couldn't keep the tears away. Gram couldn't keep the tears away, and she couldn't buy more time for herself or for Neil. And Neil—

Shaking off the negativity coming over me, I looked the group up on the internet. They're listed in the category bluegrass. Like Cherryholmes—a style of music I'd never associated with Neil.

I was getting the feeling that I hadn't known either my brother or my grandmother very well at all. Sure, I'd known Neil played this song a lot, but I'd never listened carefully to it. I'd been clueless about the song Cotton had played at his funeral reception. Both these songs described a deeply-held philosophy about Neil I hadn't recognized. And Gram? It turned out her Christian religion had played a much bigger part in her life than I'd ever suspected.

What kind of selfish, self-centered, self-absorbed person had I turned out to be? And did that have anything to do with how very alone I'd felt for most of my life?

Christ! I wanted to belong somewhere. To someone. Almost anyone, at this point.

Gravestones cheered me up not a bit. Alone in the house, with no one but the ghosts to witness, I lay my arms on the table and my head on my arms, and I wept.

CHAPTER NINE

The last Friday in April, Ms. Landry called me late in the afternoon—after El Speed had left—to tell me probate was moving quickly enough that Nina and I could sell the house by the fall if we wanted to do that. She said she'd already spoken to Nina.

Nina called not long after that. "I know we're nearly ready to turn the house over to the liquidators, at least in terms of probate. And I'll come help you get the place ready as often as I can. But Fashion Week is in September, and everyone is going crazy getting ready. Still, it would be great not to miss the summer selling season entirely if we don't need to. D'you think, between us, we could get it ready by, say, mid-August?"

I'd done precious little to figure out where the hell I was going to live. Maybe a deadline would be motivating. I said, "That's fine. Do you want me to go ahead with a storage place for Neil's things?"

"Sure. That would be great."

I was tempted to add another thought that had been nagging at me: What should I do with all the money in my bank account? She had the same question, perhaps, so it would have been something we could talk about. But she seemed a little rushed, so I kept it to myself.

I hung up with Nina and hadn't put my phone down before I got a text from Conroy.

Okay guy I'm starting to think you're avoiding me. <Slight sarcasm> How about if I treat you to some Ethiopian yirgacheffes?

I couldn't help chuckling. I replied, *You can spell it, but can you say it?*

His reply: *Come find out. Fifteen minutes?*

Why not? It was about time I pulled myself out of this funk.

Conroy had already nabbed a table, and there were two steaming cups of coffee on it.

"I haven't had a sip," he told me, grinning. "Waiting for you."

I grinned back. "Thanks. Sorry to be such a wet blanket lately. My Gram died in March. It's been kind of crazy."

"Oh, man, I'm sorry. I really liked her. She was a sweetheart."

"She was." That was the perfect word for her.

We sat there for a few minutes, hands wrapped around our cups. Conroy was silent, but he didn't seem to feel awkward. It was more of a respectful silence, even a memorial moment of silence for Gram, perhaps. It encouraged me to tell him more.

"I've been feeling really weird. It's like—well, after my brother died, there were a few things that came to light that made me think I hadn't known him as well as I'd thought. And the same thing is happening now. I feel like there was a side to Gram I didn't know." I rubbed my face before going on. "I grew up with her. She was like my mom since I was a baby. How could I not have known her?"

Conroy took a sip of his coffee. "That's the kind of existential question I don't think anyone can answer. But think about it this way, Nathan. You were a kid for most of that time. It's kind of a kid's job to be all about themself. Kids are trying to figure out the entire world, and the only way they have to do that is to think about it from their own point of view. I'm not sure we can blame ourselves for not being adult enough to have the kind of empathy you're expecting of yourself at this point in your life."

I blinked, trying to decide if I bought what he was saying, or if I liked it only because it got me off the hook.

He asked, "What's something about your Gram you didn't know?"

"She went to the same church all her life, I think. Certainly all of mine. She kept going after none of us kids would go with her anymore. I always thought it was just to stay connected with other adults, to make friends, that sort of thing. But after she died," I took a sip of coffee to give myself a few seconds to think, "after she died people who'd known her said things about her Christian spirit, and they said things that made me think she took the whole religious thing much more seriously than she ever let on. At least, to me."

He thought about that for a bit and then said, "Okay, but given what Christianity is supposed to be all about, if it was the religion itself—the doctrine—that was important to her, don't you think she would have tried to get you kids to go? Wouldn't she have made more of an effort to—y'know, save your souls, or whatever? Not in an obnoxious way, I don't mean that. But wouldn't she have at least suggested it a few times?"

"I never thought of that."

"You know what I think?" He sat back in his chair, one arm resting on the seat back. "I think she was more spiritual than religious. Remember at Thanksgiving? When I was babbling on about Kaua'i? I think if she'd been, like, super Christian, she wouldn't have been comfortable with what I said. But she was fascinated, man. Did you see the look on her face?"

I had not; I'd been watching the look on Conroy's face. I shook my head.

He leaned forward, arms flat on the table on either side of his coffee cup. "I'm going to suggest something, here, but before I do I want you understand that it's not something I would have said if you weren't feeling like this. Because I already said it once, and I wasn't going to mention it again. But, Nathan, I think you need to do something spiritual. I think you need to celebrate the best part of your grandmother in a way that's respectful to her and enlightening to you."

He watched my face as though waiting for me to ask what he was talking about. But I didn't. My mind was going in circles at the concept of what spirituality meant, and what it meant to me. So he spoke again.

"What I said before, and what I'm going to say now for the last time ever, is this: Come experience a place where the physical and the spiritual are one, a place where you just might be able to connect with her again. Not in a creepy kind of way. Not that. But in a way you can't do in a place where all the memories are, because there are bad ones as well as good ones. You can't do it in a place where you don't feel good about yourself." He paused. "Nathan. Come to Kaua'i."

Something in my mind yelled, *Yes!* I picked up my cup and took a few consecutive sips to prevent that yell from getting out. Was it Conroy or Kaua'i I wanted?

Conroy said, "I'm getting the sense that you're more ambivalent than negative. So this isn't me putting pressure on you, but I have to know by the end of this week, because the Kalalau requires me to get a permit by then, stating how many people are in my group."

"How many do you have so far?"

"Four."

So it was real. Actual people had been putting their money down for this trip.

"Tell you what, Nathan. Let's drink up here and head over to my place. I have photos of my last Kalalau hike on my computer. You can see what it looks like. I'll play some Hawaiian slack-key guitar music. Maybe the gestalt will call to you."

I almost said something aloud about how I certainly didn't have the same financial constraints I'd had last time he'd brought this up. I also nearly said something like *Okay, but no sex this time.* I didn't. But I did drain my cup.

On our way out, I noticed the barista for the first time. It wasn't Janice today. It was a young man, very likely a student—and by the way he eyed Conroy, very likely gay. I felt a surge of something like jealousy. And I hated it.

At the house, Conroy was all business. He went right for his computer, which was set up in a kind of alcove at one end of the living room.

"I almost left this on before I went to meet you for coffee," he told me. "I was working on my website earlier today."

Waiting for the computer to boot, I gazed around at the simple furnishing, the modest decor of this small ranch-style house. I'd heard college professors, even tenured ones, didn't make a lot of money. For sure there wasn't a lot of money here. Conroy was not living in luxury's lap.

Even so, what was here had been thoughtfully put together. Whoever decorated the place, I liked their taste. As I looked around I noticed several small pieces of art. There was an intricately carved wooden box on the mantel over the small fireplace, and beside it was a large glass orb with multicolored swirls and designs worked into it. Perched on one of the end tables was a small, exquisite little bird carved from what looked like jade. And on one of the book shelves was—could it be? Really?

I stepped over to the awkward-looking carving, about five inches tall, that resembled a collection of grey stones shot with something white. As I expected, it was all one piece. I picked it up carefully, and a wave of sadness welled up inside me.

An inukshuk.

I had seen only one before in my entire life, in Alden's living room. His had been maybe an inch taller, and the stone had been dark green with pale green veins running through it. At the time I'd thought it resembled that rock monster, Gorignak, from the film *Galaxy Quest*.

Conroy's voice interrupted my reminiscence. "Isn't that

cool? It's an inukshuk."

I almost said, "I know." But I wasn't sure of my voice.

He got up from the computer desk and came over to where I was standing. "In northern Canada and Alaska, the Inuit people would stack rocks into these shapes, human-size and sometimes human-like, and the arm pieces would point the way along some trail or track. Or maybe they pointed toward hunting areas, or food caches." He shrugged. "It's a little vague, now. But they were important markers to the Inuit. I mean, finding your way around arctic tundra, with few landmarks and snow covering everything, these things would have been pretty important."

"How do you know this?"

He shrugged again. "They're not a secret. I think the inukshuk is kind of a national symbol in Canada."

I set it back carefully. Canada. Canada reminded me of Alden. Canada, where Alden had retreated when he'd deserted me.

"Anyway, I've got things set up over here. Come take a look at the Na Pali Coast."

Conroy had one of those portable Bluetooth speakers near the computer. When he connected the speaker, what started to play was a sweet, relaxing, almost swaying melody on an acoustic guitar that didn't sound quite like a regular one. The melody was prominent, but the player supported it with a lot of additional finger work. None of it sounded rushed. It was more like gentle winds blowing through palm trees.

Conroy let it play for a minute before saying, "Keola Beamer."

"Sorry?"

"The guitarist. Lives on Maui. He's an icon in this genre." He opened a computer folder. "Here. Take a look." Conroy got up and stood behind the chair. I sat and clicked where he told me to, and an image appeared, then faded to reveal another image, and another, all while that sweet, swaying music played.

The images were very much as he had described them. The colors were intense: greens, browns, rusty reds, deep blues, turquoise greens. At first there were no people, just a narrow red-dirt trail leading along what looked almost like the side of a cliff, but not a dangerous one. In front of the camera, steep edges of lush green plunged down from the left, starting someplace out of sight and cutting downward toward the right and into the ocean. Somehow I could tell the steep slope of the land continued far below the waves.

The next set of images included shots of a tiny beach, with a gentle slope up to the left that was covered in separate piles of rocks, cairns really, that had been deliberately set. There were probably hundreds of them.

I heard Conroy behind me say, "Hanakapi'ai Beach."

Suddenly the image changed to a dense jungle of bamboo, which gave way to a tropical forest of sunlit green leaves and a sparkling stream. Several images later the view opened up to a magnificent waterfall.

"Hanakapi'ai Falls."

Maybe it was the music. Maybe it was the surreal landscape. Maybe it was the magical sound of those exotic names. Whatever it was, I felt mesmerized.

The images kept coming. I kept watching. Conroy's rich voice spoke magical words from time to time, and I nearly shivered with each one of them.

"Ho'olulu."

"Waiahuakua."

"Hanakoa."

"Waimakemake."

And then came an image of turquoise water hundreds of very steep feet down on the right, a rim of white lace where sparkling water met brown rock. Directly in front of the camera was the back of a hiker, fully-loaded frame pack on his back. He was slightly bent to his left, a hand held out to steady himself against the nearly vertical, reddish-brown rock face, his head down to watch his feet as they did their best to stay on the narrow trail and avoid tumbling down to that turquoise water below. His right hand was wrapped tightly around the handle of a trekking pole, which he'd stabbed into the tiny bit of level ground between his right boot and oblivion.

"Crawler's Ledge. There must be a Hawaiian name for it, but I've never known what it is.

"Anybody ever fall?"

"No one who lived to tell about it."

I turned in the chair to look at him. "You said this was paradise."

"I also said it was the place where there's no bridge between life and death, because they're both right there." He nodded toward the screen. "The kind of beauty that makes you glad to be alive. The kind of danger that makes you acutely aware of being alive. And the chance, almost any second, that you'll pass into another plane of existence."

He stepped up to the computer and brought up a few images of bubbling liquid earth the color of fire, the results of the Kilauea eruption last year on the big island, Hawai'i.

"Pele. The Hawaiian goddess of fire. She has another, formal name. Ka wahine'ai honua. Roughly, that's 'she who devours the world.' She sleeps for some time, and when she wakes up, liquid fire overruns and destroys anything in its path. When the fire leaves and she sleeps again, there is more land than there was before. She both destroys and creates. Death. Life. Death. Life. It's all there."

I knew the islands had been formed by volcanic activity. I'd even heard of Pele before. But the way Conroy put it all together made it sound mythical, romantic. Even compelling. I was torn between looking at the beautiful images on the screen and gazing into Conroy's eyes, which were looking not at me but at something very far away with a kind of love I'd never experienced. It was a kind of love I'd never believed in, never believed anyone in real life would feel.

There it was, in Conroy. Yet it was like he wasn't there. He was somewhere else, somewhere he called paradise, a paradise unlike any I'd ever imagined.

What would pull someone so powerfully, so profoundly? What would pull me?

As I pondered the rapt expression on Conroy's face, it came to me. It was the one place he belonged. I wanted that sense of belonging. I wanted it desperately.

"I'll go."

Conroy blinked slowly and almost seemed to shake himself. He looked at me and smiled. "Good. I'm glad. You can afford it after all?"

"Now I can. Gram's insurance." I didn't go into details.

"Yes." He said, but what that meant wasn't clear until he followed it with, "This is what I meant. Your wonderful grandmother has made it possible for you to take this spiritual journey. It's both homage to her and a rite of passage for you, right at the end of your undergrad college days." He smiled, almost sweetly. "Perfect."

He reached for my hands with his and pulled me to my feet with a gentleness I wouldn't have associated with him. Without a word, without asking me for permission, without explanation, he led me into a bedroom.

I almost pulled back. I hadn't wanted sex today. I really hadn't. But Conroy was behaving in a way so unlike either of the times we'd had sex that I wasn't at all sure what was happening. So I said nothing as he slowly, almost painstakingly undressed me, and then undressed himself. My dick had started to react; his was soft.

He took my hand and moved to the bed, pulling me down to sit next to him. With one hand he caressed the side of my face, and his gaze moved slowly from my eyes to one ear, to my chin, to my mouth, and then to my hair as his hand pulled softly, teasing my scalp with gentle movements. Then he lay slowly back onto the bed, bringing me with him. I could feel my pulse increasing, and my breaths were following each other more quickly than before. Conroy seemed perfectly calm.

Somehow I knew he was in control, and not only was that not a problem, but also it was perfect. I felt myself calming under his touch as he ran one hand across my body—not so softly as to be teasing and not so firmly that it implied anything immediate or intense. If there was an inch of skin he didn't caress, I couldn't have said where it was.

I almost wished it would go on forever, that he would never stop. But at some point he rolled me onto my side to face him, and he held me close to his body. We lay there, still, silent, and it felt for all the world as though we were becoming one being.

As I left the house later, Conroy gave me one kiss, a sweet and chaste kiss. Neither of us had spoken a word since he had declared my trip to the Kalalau, as homage to Gram, to be "perfect." Leaving Garden Lane, my mind jumped back and forth between two conflicting ideas.

Would Conroy have treated me like that—sweetly, tenderly—if he didn't feel more for me than if this were just a casual relationship? Was that gentle stroking something that held real emotion in it? Would he have been so sensitive about the feelings I'd expressed, and so thoughtful about what I might do about them, if he didn't care? And care a lot?

On the other hand, Conroy had told me in as many words that he was not the kind guy to get romantically involved, and his lifestyle validated that statement. He moved from place to place, no roots, no real home, unless Kaua'i counted. Was I projecting emotion onto Conroy that *I* wanted? Emotion he couldn't give?

And what would this mean for me, for us, on this trip? Would he show me this tenderness there? Or would I be just another hiker in the group?

Fuck.

But did it matter? After all, it was the place that called

to me. Conroy had been the messenger. Kaua'i was the message.

Back at the dorm, before even thinking about dinner, I brought up the site for Finnegan's Walks, opened the page for the Kalalau, signed up for the hike—July twenty-one through twenty-six—and paid for the whole thing with my brand new credit card.

CHAPTER TEN

When El Speed got back to the dorm Sunday evening, I was tempted to tell him about Conroy, about my decision to hike the Kalalau, but his excited chatter about his weekend knocked all the verbal wind out of my sails. I listened politely to him, interested and yet not involved in anything he had to tell me. And I didn't want another confrontation like the one where he'd tried to tell me about Nancy's objections to her bridesmaid's dress.

He said he was exhausted, and he went to sleep fairly early. I sat at my desk for a while, listening as his silent breathing changed to a gentle snore while I browsed online images of Kaua'i. Even without Keola Beamer's music, I found myself close to the physical experience of feeling gentle trade winds on my face, nearly able to feel the exchange of energy where waves met land, almost blinded by the intensity of the greens and blues, enjoying the feel of red, rusty earth working its way slowly between my toes.

Once in bed, I didn't fall asleep right away. Instead of images of Kaua'i, what haunted the space behind my closed eyes was an inukshuk. Alden's inukshuk. And then there was Alden himself.

Did I still miss Alden? Maybe not with the intensity I'd felt at first. But I wondered if I'd ever meet anyone else like him. He was intelligent, thoughtful, considerate, honest, just good-looking enough, and generous. He was talented, too; he'd really shone in acting class. For the final project, the two of us had done the first act of a play he'd suggested, *Eastern Standard*, written by Richard Greenberg.

Stephen, a straight guy, is having lunch with his gay friend, Drew. Drew (my part) has all these really fun, zingy lines, but Alden coached me to deliver them so that they were

136

hiding an underlying insecurity. He played Stephen, and the way he played the part left the audience wondering just how straight Stephen really was. Alden walked us through rehearsal techniques I would never have thought of, techniques we hadn't learned in class. I wouldn't have been surprised if he'd gone into acting, or writing plays, or both.

Except for the fentanyl.

Every once in a while I googled his name just to see if he was doing anything, but none of the results looked like the same Alden. At least I never saw an obituary.

If only Alden hadn't gone back to fentanyl! We would have been together for both of my freshman semesters and maybe longer, and I wouldn't have gone looking for love/attention/whatever from Daniel.

Nina had compared Conroy to Daniel. She had to be wrong. Sure, Conroy was a charmer, a wanderer, and he was definitely capable of keeping things superficial. But that didn't make him like Daniel. And Daniel had led me on two misguided trails: one up Chocorua in winter, and one that made me think it could lead to him, when it couldn't. Conroy wouldn't get me lost; his job was leading people safely on hikes. Conroy, unlike Daniel, wasn't afraid to let me know he wanted me, but also he was clear about no attachment. And Conroy, unlike Alden, wouldn't disappear into the fog of substance abuse, leaving me wondering what the fuck I'd really meant to him. Maybe it wasn't what I wished I meant to him, but at least he'd been clear.

By the following weekend, when of course El Speed headed to Maine again, I had not yet mentioned my plans to him. I also hadn't mentioned the small fortune Gram had left me. There were a couple of times when I came close, but either something happened to distract me, or this weird feeling came over me. At first I didn't want to admit what that feeling was, but when I got back to the room after a Friday morning class and El Speed was already gone, I had to face it.

It wasn't just one feeling, actually. There was jealousy, because not only had he found the person he wanted to spend the rest of his life with, but also he had less and less time for me. And there was resentment, because the whole world—or all of his world, anyway—supported him, encouraged him, celebrated with him. He was a straight, white man marrying a straight, white woman and they were setting themselves up for a normal life in which they would probably raise some number of (presumably) straight, white children, meeting all the expectations and hopes of family and friends.

I could expect none of that.

While I'd encountered little or nothing so far in my life that had to do with people resenting or hating me because of my vague but fairly obvious Chinese heritage, I'd definitely felt animosity and worse because I'm gay. And right now, with El Speed's wedding approaching, I was feeling a direct line between that event and the resentment I'd felt since high school, when my supposed peers, rather than feeling like they had to hide their attractions for each other, talked about them. Bragged about them.

And it wasn't just the other kids. You know those required school films with the dire warnings about what will happen if you engage in certain activities and behaviors? It made sense for the pregnancy warnings to involve girl-boy pairings. But whenever they showed kids at parties, or driving and drinking, or when they talked about where STDs came from, it was all based on girl-boy relationships.

Where was my place in the world? Was there some secret pact in society that said "Don't depict gay people?" Except that it wasn't secret. It just wasn't often talked about. And when it was talked about, there was a message— sometimes as subtext, sometimes direct—that being gay was at best not desirable, and at worst it was condemnable. It should stay hidden.

Social media didn't help. I'd notice headlines saying

things like one in five queer young people will attempt suicide every year, and others saying some elected officials are calling for the execution of LGBTQ people. Laws were cropping up that allow medical professionals to refuse to treat gay people. But it seemed like anytime I'd mention any of these things to a straight person, they wouldn't know what I was talking about.

Even El Speed wasn't exempt. He and I were in Candy Bar the first week of May getting an ice cream. He was a big fan of the place, and he knew a couple of the staff well enough to chat with them like old friends. I'd decided what I wanted, but El Speed was chatting away with some guy behind the counter who was evidently from someplace in the Midwest where they were having all kinds of floods. There was another staff person waiting on someone else, and there were a few other people kind of milling around.

I listened to El Speed and his buddy for a bit, feeling bad about how terrible things were for the guy's family, but when the two of them started going on and on about what was causing the weather I got a little impatient.

"Oh, it's no secret," I said loudly enough to be heard over their ramblings. "Just blame it on the gays."

Dead. Silence. Total Silence. Everyone, even El Speed, stopped whatever they were doing and turned to stare at me as though I had bragged about drowning a puppy.

I looked around, trying to understand what had just happened. "What?" I said into the silence. And then it hit me.

No one there, no one but me, was aware of how many times "the gays" get blamed for things that have nothing to do with us. Hurricane Sandy was our fault. So was Hurricane Katrina. We're responsible for the war in Iraq. The attacks on September 11. The list goes on.

"Kidding!" I shouted, hoping that would be the end of it. But—no. Still staring. Still silent. "Hey, guys, I'm gay, all right?"

I barely heard El Speed say to his buddy, "Maybe later.

Take care." And he put a hand on my shoulder and tried to steer me toward the door.

I shook his hand off. To the strangers staring at me I yelled, "Are you really all that ignorant? Do you really not know that gay people get blamed for everything?"

El Speed's quiet voice came from behind me. "Nathan, give it a rest. Come on."

I wheeled toward him, furious, glaring, and pushed past him and out of the store. I didn't care what direction I walked in; I just needed to walk hard and fast. With his long legs, El Speed caught up with me quickly.

"What's with you?" I ignored him. "Nathan, will you talk to me?"

I didn't stop walking. "And what, exactly, would you like to talk about?"

"Oh, how about why you went ballistic in there."

I stopped suddenly and he was a few feet past me before he halted.

"Tell me this," I challenged him. "Why was I the only one in there who seemed to know that September Eleven is my fault?"

El Speed's face was blank. He lifted his arms out sideways and dropped them.

"Dead birds falling from the sky. Fish going belly-up in rivers. Tsunamis. Fires, floods, earthquakes, tornadoes. Is this ringing any bells for you? Because it sure as fuck does for me." I stopped, but he didn't look any more on board. "Do you think I'm making this shit up?"

He said nothing, so I turned and headed in another direction, once again walking fast. And again, he caught up with me.

"Nathan—"

I froze again. "Can you tell me why it didn't occur to anyone in that shop, on a relatively progressive college campus, in the year twenty-nineteen, that I was being facetious? I'll bet you can't. But *I* can tell *you*. It's because they haven't paid any fucking attention to all the shit that gets thrown in the direction of 'the gays.'" I took a deep breath. "That includes you."

El Speed is famous for his calm demeanor. He talks a little slowly, he moves a little slowly. I've seen him angry to the point of danger, but only once. We were freshman, and Ellie's friend Gordon Wellington, who was gay, had been horribly hazed by a frat he was pledging.

I could tell he was getting angry now.

"Look, Nathan, when have I ever given you the slightest reason to believe that I give a shit that you're gay? When have I done or said anything against being gay? You've got no right to yell at me about this. None."

He was breathing hard through his nose. So was I.

"Bully for you," I threw at him. "You haven't called me names or short-sheeted my bed. But you also haven't paid any attention to people who do worse than call me names. You must have heard at least a few news reports where some idiot says gays should be executed, or where some asshole says 'Gays are more of a threat to America than terrorism and Islam.'"

"Islam is not a threat to America."

"That's not the point!" I heaved an exasperated breath. "Do you think I don't know that? So you focus on that, which is fine, of course it's not a threat. But you completely overlook the horrible things people say about *me!* And— Jesus, there are so many! This church, that pastor, this organization, that politician…. Did you know the Westboro Baptist Church went to Orlando to picket the funerals of the people shot by that asshole at the Pulse nightclub three years ago?"

I waited a few seconds before I heard his subdued, "What's the Westboro Baptist Church?"

I nodded. "That's what I mean. That's exactly what I mean. Does the name 'Pulse Nightclub' even mean anything to you?" We stared at each other for several seconds. Then I said, "Don't follow me." And I headed up over the hill in the direction of Newmarket, not knowing how far I'd walk or whether I'd ever stop.

I'd guess it was half a mile later that it dawned on me to take at least a little comfort in the fact that everyone in Candy Bar had looked at me like I'd said I eat baby brains for breakfast. It was a problem for them that it seemed like I was saying something bad about gay people. That was something. That was good, actually. But I expected more from El Speed.

How was I going to tell him that it wasn't enough for my best friend to accept me, if it stopped there? I wanted acceptance from everyone. From *him* I wanted more. I wanted him to understand. And that would have meant that when he heard someone blame gay people for something—for *anything*—that he'd not only remember it, but also that he'd fight against it. I wanted him to be an ally. From him I wanted the United Kingdom, not friggin' Switzerland.

Now it seemed like he didn't even notice any of the shit that got said about gay people.

About a mile later a voice in my head asked, *Are you being fair?*

Another voice answered. *This isn't about fair. This is about how much he cares.*

I stopped and turned around, waiting to see if my feet would move forward and take me back to campus. Standing there, hearing the swish of cars go by, cars I wasn't really seeing, I whispered, "I've lost my brother. I've lost Gram. And now I'm losing my best friend."

I went to a dining hall for dinner in a part of campus where I knew I wouldn't run into El Speed. When I finally made it back to the dorm, he as in bed and snoring lightly.

Four years. El Speed and I had been roommates for

four years, and best friends for most of that time. It seemed all wrong that it now felt like our relationship had soured. And over what?

We were both to blame, really. Okay, I'd had that meltdown about expecting more from him over blaming gays for everything. And okay, he'd been at Gram's funeral. But that had been the end of any comfort from him. He'd been absent every weekend after that and preoccupied during the week, between the wedding and preparing for finals and graduation. We didn't talk much anymore. I would have thought our connection could have survived these problems. But I was beginning to doubt.

The Monday before final exams ended, with commencement at the end of the week, Nina called.

"Just want to make sure we can find each other after the ceremony. I don't think I can get there much before it starts, so I'll need to find you later. Where's the best place to meet up?"

Ceremony? Oh! She meant commencement. "I, uh, I was thinking maybe I'd just go home—I mean, to Concord—Friday." There would be no Gram at my graduation. There would be no Neil. I figured Nina would be in New York. El Speed would be with his family. And anyway, maybe he and I weren't enemies, but we hadn't fallen back into our old comfortable ways, by any means. Why would I go to some ceremony all alone?

There was silence for maybe one second. "Bullshit, Nathan. You've worked for this. You've earned it. You came to my graduation, and I'm coming to yours. Now, what's the plan?"

What I heard in her tone was, Stop the pity-party. But she didn't say it. We settled on a plan, and then she gave me her news.

"I was going to wait until I saw you to tell you this,

but—well, Nathan, I've moved in with my boyfriend."

"You—I didn't know you had a boyfriend."

"I haven't said anything, because I met him last winter, and I knew Gram wouldn't approve. He's thirty-two."

"Wow. Um, what about Isabella and—what's your other roommate's name again?"

"Darlene. I helped them find another roommate." There was a pause. "Is that all you're going to ask me?"

"Well, I—okay, what's his name? What does he do for a living? Is he married?"

"Don't be absurd. Of course he's not married. His name is Luc Beaumont. He's a photographer. He's divorced, and—"

"You're sure?"

"Sure what?"

"That he's divorced?"

I heard an exasperated sigh. "Yes, Nathan. But it doesn't matter. It's not like I'm going to marry him. Where was I? Oh, yes, he and his ex-wife have a five-year-old daughter who lives with her mother in New Jersey. Luc travels a lot. He's a fashion photographer, and sometimes he goes back to France to visit his parents and his brother."

"Back to France?"

"He grew up in Bernay, in Normandy."

I was trying to take all this in, and I was having some difficulty. Nina had never referred to anyone as her boyfriend in the past. She'd dated, sure, but she wasn't one to get tied down. It didn't sound like she was tying herself to this guy. But she had moved in with him....

"So your address is different now?"

"It's a loft on Broome Street. I'll text you the address."

"A loft."

"Yeah. Listen, I have to ring off. I'll see you soon, okay?"

So that was all I got out of her. Maybe I'd learn more when I saw her.

Seating for graduating seniors was organized according to the students' program or school. This relieved me of any worry about whether El Speed and I would sit together. His academic area was food chemistry.

Saturday was sunny and warm, and I had to wonder about the wisdom of making a huge crowd of people sit in the sun wearing long, heavy robes. The speaker was David Brooks, this political journalist. Pundit. Whatever. I wasn't expecting much. Even I knew that these things are pretty formulaic, having been to both Neil's and Nina's commencements. But Brooks surprised me.

Two things he said stuck with me. The first was when he pointed out something obvious, but something I hadn't given much thought to. He said that as students, our lives so far had been essentially very much point-to-point, with expectations—as well as the next point—pretty well laid out. That predictability was now behind us. I was just wrapping my brain around that when he asked us what *kind* of lives we were going to live. This was not the question I had expected. *What are you going to do with your life* is different from *What kind of life will you live*.

The second thing that hit me was a topic he spent most of his speaking time on: connection. Relationships. He said to ignore what we'd heard about life being an individual journey, that the real meaning, the real meat in life (not his words) were the bonds we weave with other people. He said we should accomplish these bonds with something he referred to as aggressive friendship (his words that time).

Aggressive friendship. It stuck in my brain like a stick trying to go sideways down my throat. I've never been aggressively anything when it came to other people. Once, the biggest thing stopping me had been the need I felt to hide who I was, to keep other people from finding out that I was gay.

Now? What's my reason now? I shrugged mentally. It

just isn't how I see myself. It isn't how I feel. But he had a point about relationships, and friendships, and the tapestry that we make when we weave those bonds. We create for ourselves a place to belong.

As soon as the formalities were over, I pulled out my phone and texted El Speed. I figured he'd have his phone on so he could contact his folks. I was right.

I texted, *Where are you?*

He replied almost immediately. I worked my way through the crowd, sweating under my robe, moving past laughing, shouting students, ignoring all the wacky writing and decorations some of them had put on their caps. He saw me weaving—there's that word again—through the mob and waved his cap over his head. Then he headed in my direction.

We both stopped with about three feet between us, eyes to eyes, and then we nearly threw our bodies together. Neither of us said a word. All the communication was in that embrace, which went on and on.

CHAPTER ELEVEN

So my undergrad days were over, and I had nothing lined up for grad school. I had done some research to see which schools offered what programs, and I knew what I'd have to do to apply. I just hadn't taken any action.

El Speed was back in Maine, and all the other students I had known had left for their respective homes or summer jobs. I kept expecting to feel the kind of nostalgia (or worse) that ought to come with leaving a part of my life and a number of friends behind, but it didn't come. Or it didn't hit very hard. Or maybe it couldn't find its way through the shitty feeling of leaving Gram to die all alone.

Nina was far away in Manhattan and completely absorbed in her work and her new life with Luc. She'd told me a little more about him when she'd come up for my graduation, even showed me a picture. Handsome fellow, in a European kind of way. Great clothes, of course. But she didn't gush, she didn't say anything about my meeting him, and she didn't seem as though she was in love. I put it down to the relationship being very French and left it at that.

As for me, the only place I had to lay my head was my old room in Gram's house (I no longer thought of it as my house at all). To say that it was lonely is like saying there's only one trail up Mount Chocorua: a massive understatement.

My way forward was a blank. David Brooks had been right.

In an attempt to maintain some kind of equilibrium, some kind of connection with the rest of the world, I texted El Speed a number of times.

My first message: *Hey, hope wedding plans are going well. Chat?*

His response came a few hours later: *I'll get back to*

you.

Hearing nothing more, I waited a few days before trying again. *Got time for a chat today?*

That time the response took a full day. *Will let you know.*

A week later I tried one more time. *Kinda quiet here. I think the place is haunted.*

If my phone hadn't let me know the message had been delivered, I might have suspected it had gone astray. I never heard back.

I spent a lot of time in the mountains. One week I rented a cabin in Bartlett, of all places. Summer is far from my favorite time to hike; it's hot, and then there are the bugs. But I put four more notches on my boots.

The only bright spot, in terms of people, was Conroy. If memory serves, I didn't contact him; he contacted me, maybe about every ten days or so, which was much more than during the school year. Maybe his own pickings were slimmer over the summer, with people like Janice and the other baristas—who were, no doubt, students—gone. Or maybe he felt more for me than he wanted to admit. Whatever the case, I was determined not to open the door to my heart and contact him. At least, I wouldn't open it wide.

When Conroy and I got together, it almost always included sex. He was insatiable, and I was lonely and desperate for connection. If there was a downside for me, it was that whenever things went anal, he always wanted to be top, and he didn't seem even to register that I might sometimes want that role. A few times I tried, physically rather than verbally, to get things to go that way, and each time he seemed to take it as a fun challenge, like wrestling for "top." If that had really been what was happening, I'm sure I could have held my own at least some of the time; he wasn't that much bigger than me. But something in me always held me back, kept me from making the challenge real. Looking back, I think I wasn't willing to risk losing my connection with Conroy—the only connection available to me at that point—by challenging him in that way. He'd made it evident, in so many ways, that he wanted to be in control. I felt rather than knew that changing that dynamic could bring the relationship, such as it was, to an end. And, such as it was, I needed it. At least, I needed what I could get.

So I decided this was a concession I was willing to make. Sex was sex, I told myself, and it wasn't like I didn't enjoy everything we did.

I think it was the first day of July that he texted, *Let's get you ready.*

For?

Kalalau. Equipment. Today good?

Equipment. One of the areas where Daniel had badly— very badly—fallen down on the job for our Chocorua hike. *See, Nina? Conroy is not like Daniel.*

When he arrived, Conroy had me bring everything I had for the trip into the living room so he could take inventory. As he looked things over, I started a playlist I had prepared. It included a large selection of slack-key guitar numbers, including some by Keola Beamer. At the end I had tacked on "Buy for me the Rain" and then Cherryholmes' "Live It."

As "Live It" played, Conroy looked up at me. "I wouldn't have pegged you for bluegrass, Nathan."

"It was a favorite song of Neil's."

He nodded and turned back to my gear.

"Great tent," he said, fingering the material and examining the zipper. He deemed my frame pack adequate. Rain gear, he wasn't so happy about.

"This poncho will fly up and around with the wind. And I don't see any rain pants."

"Rain pants?"

"Nylon leg pieces you pull up and tie onto your belt loops. Did you even read the equipment list on my website?"

"Of course I did." I just hadn't believed I'd need them.

He examined my boots. "These are great for mountains, Nathan. But you need something lighter. You might still want ankle support—you know your own ankle strength best. And you still want waterproof. But these," he let one boot fall to the floor where it made a resounding thunk, "will be hot and heavy. And not in a good way."

I already had a lot of things from his online list, but not everything. And some of my equipment were a little more battered than was ideal.

Conroy wanted to help me fill gaps. "You up for a field trip?"

"There's an Eastern Mountain Sports here in Concord."

"There's also an EMS in Portsmouth."

"That's an hour away."

"I'll drive. We could get your gear, then drive into town and wander around the waterfront. And you can treat me to dinner." He grinned like he knew I'd agree.

At EMS, Conroy convinced me to spend quite a bit of money. Besides hiking shoes, I bought more socks, a new fancy headlamp, some water sanitizer to augment the little I had at home, fresh bug spray, sunscreen and soap that wouldn't harm marine life, hand sanitizer, batteries, a solar charger for my phone that collects power as it hangs off of your pack while you hike, and a really expensive pair of sunglasses that looked totally fabulous on me.

I thought we were done, but he headed toward the trekking poles.

"I don't want those," I told Conroy. "I hate it when I'm hiking and someone is using them. All I can hear is tick-tick-tick-tick-tick—"

He laughed. "I hear ya. And for a lot of hikes, I agree. But if you don't have one of these babies on Crawler's Ledge, you might not need your return plane ticket."

He didn't exactly tell me which pole to buy, but he

selected only a few for me to choose from. "You don't need to use two poles. In fact, on the ledge, two would be a problem. So just get one, but get a really good one that can withstand you leaning hard on it. These all have special tips that are less likely to slip if the surface is wet."

Each of the ones he selected cost more than a hundred dollars. For one pole. I wouldn't have guessed. But—hell, it wasn't like I didn't have the money. I chose one with a cork handle and bright red locking clamps.

Conroy bought a few things for himself as well, and then we headed into town.

Over dinner we talked about hiking, hiking equipment, and the upcoming trip.

"Just so you know," he told me, "I've talked, emailed, whatever, with each of the other people who've signed up, to make sure they're up for the hike. Especially for Crawler's Ledge."

"Do people really die on that part of the trail?"

"Oh, yes. More than a few."

"I remember you said you wouldn't lead a hike up the Precipice Trail in Maine. But you'll lead this one?"

"The ledge takes experienced hikers between ten and fifteen minutes. The Precipice is a longer trail, and it's practically straight up, so there are a lot more places things can go wrong. So the risk there is much greater. Besides," and here he waved his fork for emphasis, "the idea of falling off the Precipice and dying feels like tragedy to me. If I died on Crawler's Ledge... let's just say I can't image a better place to die, or a better way to do it."

I couldn't help wondering if the other hikers on this trip felt the same. "So who else has signed up? Anything you can tell me about them?"

"I can tell you there's only one woman. Women are usually scarce on my more ambitious hikes. Mind you, I've met many women who could handle anything I ask of them, but I don't get a lot signing up for hikes like this one."

"How many other guys?"

"Besides you, three. One of them had signed up for my Katahdin hike last year but had to cancel."

Katahdin. A hike Neil and Jeremy had done. My phone still had a photo of them on the summit, taken after they'd crossed the knife edge.

On the drive home, Conroy asked if I'd reserved my plane tickets yet. I had not.

"I'm giving myself a little extra island time. Leaving here on the sixteenth, coming back the thirtieth. The hike starts on the twenty-second, with the meet-up dinner Sunday, on the twenty-first, when you and the other hikers will arrive, so I'll have five days to finish up any prep for the hike, plus some time to hang out and enjoy the island."

"Like what? What will you enjoy?"

"Probably spend a day in the Waimea Canyon, which I think I described at Thanksgiving. Maybe kayak into caves along the coast. Maybe take a catamaran trip."

"Sounds like paradise."

He chuckled. "It is. You've signed up for your room, right?"

And there it was: confirmation of my suspicion that on the hike, I would be just another member of the group. I did my best to disguise my sigh as nothing more than a deep breath.

"I was going to do that this week. There are still rooms available." His website had recommended a place that had just reopened after last year's floods, a collection of buildings on the north shore, not far from the Kalalau trailhead. I had checked the place out online, kind of hoping that I wouldn't need my own room. So much for that hope.

"Don't put it off, though. Seriously."

"I'll do it tonight. Plane tickets, too."

Conroy dropped me off in front of the house. "Gotta get

back," he told me. "Still got some administrivia to take care of for the hike."

As soon as he was gone, I went online and reserved a "premium ocean view" suite. The place didn't have any rooms directly on the ocean; maybe that wasn't allowed. But from the website pictures, the porch on my room was as close as you could get. If I couldn't have Conroy, then I'd have the next best thing.

Next I reserved my plane tickets. It would be quite a haul, time-wise. I hovered my cursor over a flight that would take almost sixteen hours, with a stop in the San Francisco airport. That appealed to me more than flights that stopped in other cities, because… well, San Francisco. Someday I would go there for real, but—one kind of paradise at a time. But at least I'd get near it.

My cursor was in position to finalize the itinerary, but there was something nagging at me.

Experimentally, I said, "What if," to the empty house, and waited to see if any of the ghosts had anything to say. And there was a response, though I'm pretty sure it came from inside me.

What if you went out early? You and Conroy would be there together, with no other hikers crowding the scene.

On impulse, I backed out and chose a more expensive reservation, one that allowed for changes, in case I thought better of my new plan after I finalized it. After all, Conroy had practically told me not to show up before Sunday. I set my flight dates to arrive on the eighteenth instead of the twenty-first.

There was an odd sense of accomplishment that washed over me. It wasn't just that I'd finalized my plans. Or, they were at least conditionally final. No; it was that I'd just done something I'd never done before, something I'd always seen as firmly in the camp of "adult" things. Making hotel arrangements, reserving flights, and paying for them were all things other people did. They were things adults did.

Was I an adult now?

A lot of things had hit me hard after Gram had died. But one thing that was just hitting me now was that there was no one still alive above my generation. Nina and I were now at the top of that ladder. This had the benefit of meaning that I didn't have to look to anyone else for permission or agreement for what I would or wouldn't do. But what came with it was a feeling that made my entire body tingle unpleasantly.

When there's no generation above you, it means you're the next to die.

Don't get me wrong; I wasn't thinking my turn was coming soon, and I wasn't getting paranoid. But up until now, I'd been in that head, largely a teen-age phenomenon, when "it wouldn't happen to me," whatever "it" was. Car accidents, addiction, dread diseases—they're out there, sure. But me? No. There was something of an "I'm immortal" feel to it. Or maybe it was more like an ignorant innocence, a lack of appreciation for what life really is. It was something like what Daniel had said at the start of our fateful hike: "It's a good day to die."

Suddenly the risk of Crawler's Ledge had more meaning. I wasn't backing out; I still believed I had the chops to handle that threat and handle it well. But I admit, it gave me a moment's pause.

In bed that night, I had a hard time falling asleep. I'd shaken off the mortality issue; I still saw that as in the far, far distant future. But something else was nagging at me. Was my new itinerary a bad idea? Was I worried about whether I should let Conroy know in advance that I'd get there on Thursday instead of Sunday? Well, yeah, I'd need to decide about that. But it felt like there was something else trying to rise to the surface. My mind bounced around and around, from one subject to another no matter how unrelated they seemed, until finally it hit me.

I sat bolt upright in bed.

ON THE KALALAUA TRAIL

El Speed and Ellie were getting married on Saturday, July twenty-seven. I would be somewhere over the Pacific Ocean, on a fifteen-hour flight back from Kaua'i.

CHAPTER TWELVE

I got a text from Conroy two days after our Portsmouth field trip.

On my way out. Austin, here I come! See you in paradise.

Austin? Shit! I'd forgotten he was leaving in July. And was this all I'd get by way of goodbye?

But I didn't need to ask that question. I couldn't pretend to be surprised. If I'd been hoping that seeing more of Conroy after school had ended meant he was changing the way he felt, I'd have been an idiot. Everything he'd said, every way he'd acted toward me had supported his rolling-stone persona. It was all he had to give. Or all he was willing to give. And this text was a seal on that message.

I felt like I'd been left in the dust, even though I didn't really think Conroy saw it like that. He'd been clear to me. I hadn't been honest with him. That might not be his fault, but it still hurt. A lot.

I gave myself a minute or so to recover before texting back. I knew my reply had to be equally empty of expectations. I could show no weakness, if for no other reason than to hide how much his message had hurt. I saw no benefit in suddenly telling him something he didn't want to hear. I wanted to keep some pride intact, even if it was a façade.

I texted, *Bon voyage. Hope you like Austin.*

I'd just sent Conroy's reply, still feeling something between angry and hurt, when my phone rang. Nina.

"Hey, just thought I'd let you know things are going smoothly enough here that I can escape for a few days. How about if I drive up July twenty-fourth? We can get the house ready for sale and get it on the market before the summer selling season is all gone."

"Uh, well, I mean—"

She didn't give me a chance to get my verbal feet under me. "Nathan? What's up?"

"I, uh, I won't be here."

"School visits?"

"Not exactly."

"Nathan, spit it out."

Deep breath. "I'll be on Kaua'i, hiking the Kalalau Trail."

Long pause. "What?"

"Kaua'i. It's one of the Hawaiian islands. You should google the Kalalau Trail. Unbelievably gorgeous scenery—"

Her voice was louder now. "By yourself?"

"I signed up with a small group of hikers."

Another, longer pause. "Conroy." Her tone would have burnt asbestos.

I ignored her. "I've moved most of Neil's stuff into the storage unit, along with most of the stuff I want to keep. I didn't want to mess with yours, so you could come up and take care of that while I'm away. There's a key to the storage unit in the drawer of the drop-leaf table, and—"

And again she didn't let me finish. "Nathan, are you out of your mind?"

I took a breath and held it for a couple of seconds. "No, Nina, I am decidedly not out of my mind. I've already decided to take a gap year, and—"

"You're supposed to be looking at schools. You're supposed to be decided where you'll *live*, not where you'll *hike*." When I didn't reply immediately, she added, "You haven't figured out yet that he's a hammer, and you're the nail. He just needs you so he has something to hit."

This was so close to the bone that I had to bat it away as quickly as possible, however I could. "My mother died many years ago. Who do you think *you* are?"

Silence. Stunned silence. I could feel it right through the phone. I hated what she'd said. I hated I'd said. I bit my lip and then started to say, "I'm sorry." I didn't get it out before I heard the line disconnect.

In the two-and-a-half weeks before my scheduled departure, I had two very uncomfortable conversations to face. One was to apologize to Nina. I planned to give her a couple of days, text a short apology, and follow that by asking if it was a good time for me to call. I concluded that Nina would forgive me; we were family, and my apology would be sincere. So I started there, and that's pretty much how it went, though she did take the opportunity to suggest I get cracking on my future plans as soon as I got back from the hike.

The other conversation was with El Speed. This one scared me.

Despite our graduation-day hug, I wasn't at all sure of my current standing with him, especially in light of his lack of response to my messages a few weeks ago. I was even less sure of getting his forgiveness for the transgression of missing his wedding.

Ellie and I had gotten off to a bad start three years ago, what with that awkward stay in El Speed's Maine cabin right before Neil died. She'd redeemed herself quite a bit by finding out the details about Neil's funeral on her own and showing up with El Speed.

I didn't dislike her, and I don't think she disliked me, but we'd never really clicked. I didn't suspect her of deliberately inserting a wedge between El Speed and me. Still, I couldn't help thinking that my lukewarm connection with her would factor into the friendship. At the very least, I was sure it had reduced the time El Speed and I spent together.

Imaginary conversations with El Speed filled my head for the next couple of days. I had to weigh being with my best friend on his wedding day against a once-in-a-lifetime trip to paradise that just might turn out to be a kind of vision quest. I could be with El Speed on a very, very important day in his life, a day that—all things working out well—would never be repeated, a day that the people who care about him would share with him and with each other. Or I could go where I could stand beneath the swaying palm trees that Keola Beamer's music made me picture in my mind. I could walk along the top of a red-dirt ridge, with nothing between my shoes and the crashing ocean other than hundreds of feet of space that would be empty if it weren't sparkling with excitement and the promise of connection with something bigger than me, connection with the spirits of Gram and Neil.

Ever since Conroy had talked about Gram and spirituality, I'd felt compelled to see if being in a place where the physical and the spiritual meet—as Conroy had described it—would eradicate the guilt I'd felt since Gram's death, a guilt born of knowing she might have survived if I'd just gone home that weekend, instead of hanging around campus for no good reason, sulking because I couldn't go with my housemates on a trek into the winter mountains, sulking because my best friend—the same one whose marriage was now on the scales being weighed—wasn't spending time with me anymore.

There would be a very large number of people at El Speed's wedding, most of whom I wouldn't know; he'd already told me so. And he wouldn't have more than a couple of minutes to spend with me there. So it would be no better, for me, than it had been for the past several months.

In Kaua'i, I might come to some reconciliation, some absolution I didn't know where else to look for.

That sense of belonging I wanted so badly would be far less likely at a gathering where I knew almost no one than in a place where magic might reconnect me with my family. I didn't just *want* to go to Kaua'i. I *needed* to go.

The first couple of times I called El Speed, he didn't answer.

When he picked up, on my third attempt, he said he was "in the middle of something" and asked if he could call me back. I waited a couple of days, alternately fuming from being ignored and terrified because of what I had to say. Then I tried again and got the same put-off. He couldn't already be mad at me, because he didn't yet know what I had to tell him.

By this point I was feeling not nearly as much guilt—regret—call it what you will—about going to Kaua'i instead of Maine. But I still needed to let him know. I gave up calling and resorted to a text.

I really need to talk to you. When's a good time to call?
It was half a day before I got, *Now good for you?*
It was.

"Hey, guy," I opened.

"Sorry I've been so hard to reach. Things are mad crazy around here." His voice sounded distant—the kind of distant that you hear when someone was hoping to avoid talking to you. Was I imagining this?

To give him the benefit of the doubt I asked, "Wedding plans?"

"Mostly. Part of it, though, is that Ellie's grandparents are already here. They live in Arizona now. They came for a long visit, and they have all these special needs. He's on an oxygen tank constantly; has to pull it around with him. Her arthritis won't let her stand for more than a few minutes at a time. They both have special diets, and there are medical appointments.... Sorry; I'll stop. It's just that Ellie and her mom are heads-down with the wedding planning, so I've been helping out with the grandparents."

I wasn't sure I bought that excuse. I'd been trying to reach him for weeks. But I did my best to set that aside.

"Bet you'll be glad when it's over and you can escape to Nova Scotia."

"You have no idea! Listen, when you come up—"

"Uh, well, that's kind of why I called."

"Whad'ya mean? You don't know what I was gonna

say."

"I can't come."

"What?" His tone sounded like he genuinely wasn't sure he'd heard me right.

"When the date got moved, it landed right in the middle of the time when I'll be away."

"Away?" It was like he was exploring the word, trying to figure out what it meant by the way it sounded.

"I'll be in Hawai'i. On Kaua'i, actually. I had already signed up for the trip. Non-refundable." I hadn't actually paid attention to the financial arrangement; maybe Conroy would have given me credit toward a different hike. But it wouldn't have been Kaua'i.

"Kaua'i." It was like he wasn't quite getting it.

"It's… it's kind of like a spiritual quest. I have some demons I have to toss into the ocean."

"But—*Kaua'i?*"

Yeah, I said to him in my head. *And if you'd been around since, like, January, you'd have known about it before now.*

"Nathan, you could toss any demons you want into the ocean off the coast of Maine. You don't have to go to fucking Kaua'i."

I let out a long breath, willing myself to hold my temper. "I can't explain things in a few minutes over the phone. I'm thinking that once you're back from your honeymoon, I could drive up and stay for a few days. Give us a chance to catch up." Silence. So I added, "We wouldn't exactly have a chance to do that at the wedding."

"Nathan, this is very important to me."

"I get that. I'll be with you in spirit. But Kaua'i is very important to me." More silence. "I can explain it when I come up in August."

The line nearly crackled with silence. Then, "Does this have anything to do with you not being my best man?"

"What?" *Did he really say that?* An angry, trembling

burn shot through my gut. "No! How petty d'you think I am?"

"Whatever."

He disconnected. I sat staring at the phone in my hand for nearly a minute. It was everything I could do not to throw it against the wall.

One of the last things I did before leaving for Kaua'i was to move the last of Neil's things from the basement to the storage unit I'd rented. I would have expected to feel overwhelmed by this task, but I think I was too angry at both El Speed and Nina for sentimentality to overtake me.

CHAPTER THIRTEEN

As soon as I stepped off the plane at Lihue Airport, I knew I was not in Kansas anymore, as the saying goes. I had a few clues. For one thing, the very small airport had photographs on the walls depicting native Hawaiians doing what appeared to be ritual dancing. People all around me were wearing that garment choice known as the "Hawaiian shirt," regardless of how pale the wearer's skin was, or how light their hair. When I stepped outside to walk over to the car rental area, I had to navigate my way around a chicken. That made me laugh.

But I think the real giveaway was the air. At about eight thirty in the evening, it was still warm, with temperatures in the seventies, and it was moist. But it wasn't oppressive. And it wasn't still. The air had a freshness to it that moved around my body and into my lungs in a way I'd never experienced before. Gram had once splurged and taken us three kids to Florida's Daytona Beach, the summer I was nine. I remember palm trees, and sandy beaches, and very hot air, whether it was moving or still. This was nothing like that.

I was delighted that the car rental place actually had the vehicle I had requested. I know these places are notorious for giving you the keys to a Lincoln Continental or a Mini Cooper when you asked for a mid-sized Toyota sedan. But they had my Jeep! I was thrilled. It was a bright red Jeep Wrangler Sport. Two doors. Removable cover on the back.

Throwing my luggage into the back felt so fucking good. This was perfect. This was me, being my own person, doing whatever the fuck I wanted to do, and having the goddamn money to do it. Conroy had said there would be a shuttle at the airport to pick up anyone who arrived Sunday and didn't want to rent a car, but of course I couldn't take advantage of that. I didn't want to. I was arriving on my own schedule. And I'd be driving a Jeep.

The universe seemed to have forgiven me for disappointing El Speed. I'd worry about his forgiveness when I returned from paradise.

The drive to where I was staying, on the far west end of the north shore, was over an hour away. I had scoped this all out days ago. Conroy had been right; there was, literally, no way to drive across the island. You just had to go around.

The airport is about two-thirds of the way down the east coast, and in one of my conversations with Conroy he had spoken disparagingly of this area as the "coconut coast." He'd said there were lots of coconut trees, and if I multiplied the number of trees by about fifty thousand I'd get the number of tourists there on any given day. I had no doubt he'd exaggerated; even so, I didn't intend to stop anyplace along here, especially given the late hour.

In some ways, the Kuhio highway looked like any other highway in a rural, south-coastal area of the U.S., at least from what I'd seen on TV and in films. There were stretches with lots of greenery, a small, single-story house on one side or the other of the road, and other sections where there were more houses than trees. I passed commercial strips with little stores selling beach chairs or beer, the sorts of things Conroy's denigrated tourists might want. Sometimes the ocean, to my right, would stretch out into infinity. But proof of exactly what coastline this was came from the left side of the road.

Perhaps there are other areas of the world where the landscape looks like Kaua'i, but I don't know where they would be. I'd left the little houses and tourist shops behind when I started to see peaks. It was after sunset by now, but there was still enough light for me to see jagged, irregular points of land, rising up steeply and apparently out of nowhere. Mostly they were very dark and had a kind of fuzzy look, which I knew meant they were covered in plant growth: trees, grasses, whatever—it was hard to tell in this light. But sometimes there were jagged, barren rocky formations.

As I say this, I realize my description doesn't go very far to portray the extraordinary experience. Maybe it was the air, or my solo adventure in a far-away place, or the mystery of not knowing what the next several days would bring. Or maybe words can't do the experience justice.

Once I hit the eastern end of the north shore, it was tempting to stop at a few places: Anini Beach; Queens Bath; the Hanalei Valley Lookout; Waiola Beach Park. But it was dark, and getting late. I'd already had to tell the resort where I was staying that I'd need a late check-in.

About an hour from Lihue, I got to the little town of Hanalei. On the map, it's positioned in a curve of land surrounding Hanalei Bay. The words were so sweet! I mumbled "Hanalei Bay" to myself several times as I cruised the few streets, looking for a place to get something that would pass for my dinner.

Hanalei has its share of little shops, too, but the vibe here was totally different from the coconut coast. The sandal-shod waiter who brought me an outrageously expensive burger and fries (something I'd been warned about—that is, the expense of getting supplies shipped out here) was so laid back, he might have been on something. But really I think he was just high from the air. I was beginning to feel like that, myself. As he walked away, I noticed a circlet of pastel colored beads or shells—some were cream, but most were pale shades of green or blue or pink or yellow—around one of his ankles. I couldn't say why, but I found it very appealing.

Half-way through my meal it occurred to me that I couldn't remember ever having eaten alone in a restaurant before. The dining hall at school didn't count.

At the counter by the cash register, where I paid for my meal, there were a few items placed for impulse buying. My gaze landed on one of those little metal tree-like things designed to hold cheap bracelets and such. One of the arms had a selection of anklets, just like the one on my waiter's ankle. A label read "Puka Shell." I bought one.

I don't recommend traveling the northwestern part of the Kuhio Highway in the dark. In most places it's barely big enough for two cars, and along the road are several short bridges wide enough for only one vehicle. There wasn't a lot of traffic, to be sure; still, as unfamiliar as I was with the place, it was a little unnerving. And then, of course, there was evidence all around of flood damage from last year's inundation. There was still a lot of work going on to repair the road and some of the bridges.

It took nearly half an hour to get from Hanalei to my resort. A sign on the office door had a number to call. It took about five minutes for someone to come, and I don't think she was thrilled at how late it was, but I had no control over the airline schedule.

Alone in my "premium oceanfront suite," luggage at my feet, ceiling fan turning slowly overhead, I felt suddenly overwhelmed at what I was doing. I'd never been the sort of person who has to have a group of people around them at all times. I've hiked alone, I've driven alone, I've done all kinds of things alone. But all of a sudden I was on the far side of the world, on a piece of volcanic rock in the middle of a vast and powerful ocean, with no one anywhere around me whose name I knew, or who knew who I was. I had decided not to let Conroy know I was arriving early. Maybe I'd run into him. Maybe I wouldn't.

Fuck him. And I don't mean literally, not this time. Maybe never again.

So I stood there in my temporary living room, all the lights on, the front window revealing little other than a few pale lights of other suites off to the right or the left. The rooms in my suite, the furnishings, were not luxurious, but everything was clean and perfectly serviceable. The decor was decidedly "island casual." This place was all about the location, really. I switched off all the lights other than the bathroom and stepped out onto my porch.

Out here the feeling was very different. Nothing inside mattered. The air wafted in from the ocean, which was directly in front of me. I could see the white edges of the waves as they approached land, and I could hear the surf, its sighing sound rolling over me and almost making me sway with it. It wasn't a whisper, that sound. It was deep and powerful. It was compelling. Very compelling.

Almost in slow motion, I went to my bags and pulled out some sandals I had bought for the trip. I changed into shorts and a T shirt. I fastened my puka beads around my left ankle. And I walked off of my porch.

I couldn't tell where the tide was at that moment. I just knew I had to get to the water. As I moved forward, the grass in front of my suite gave way to sand and then to a hard surface, irregular and lumpy. I squatted down to feel it with my hand. The surface was very dark, and it revealed nothing else about itself, and yet I knew it was volcanic rock.

I stepped carefully a little farther out until the white lace of the waves washed over my feet, and I stood there.

In my research about Kaua'i, which I'd done at night alone in Gram's house while playing slack-key guitar music to keep the ghosts at bay, I'd learned that there are some beaches on the island not considered safe for swimming. After daybreak, I expected to see signs that read, "DO NOT TURN YOUR BACK ON THE OCEAN." I'd learned that the little beach I'd seen on Conroy's computer, the one with all the cairns on it, was an especially deadly spot. The knife edges of land really do plunge endlessly down into the ocean, and when a wave hits the beach it follows the land underwater, down down down to unknowable depths, and it just might pull with it anyone foolish enough to wade there. Not swim. Wade.

This beach promised to be not quite so treacherous. And yet as I stood there, my feet washed in Pacific Ocean water, my face peering into the dark distance, I was fully aware of how very puny I was, how very insignificant. Neil had told me that if he'd died on a mountain, it wouldn't care. I realized the same was true for the ocean. For the little cairn beach. For the entire island of Kaua'i.

Friday I woke up very early. It was around five thirty. The overhead fan, rotating lazily, had kept me comfortable all night. I turned over and tried to go back to sleep. But the ocean was calling, and that confused me. That ocean that didn't care about me. How could it both call to me and not care about me? Perhaps its very objectivity was the appeal. Perhaps I felt compelled by something I couldn't influence, something I couldn't hurt, something that had no opinion of me at all and would, therefore, not judge me. I pulled on my swim trunks and walked out onto my porch.

In the early morning light, beneath a soft blue sky decorated with clouds ready for the sunrise that was not quite brightening them, the sea was dark and yet somehow not threatening. Neither was it friendly. It just *was*.

Barefoot, almost in a trance, I walked across the grassy strip of land and then over sand, coming to a halt on the smooth, uneven layer of water-worn rock. I glanced along the beach in both directions. The only other person I saw was someone quite a distance up the beach to my right. The form, while obviously human, looked almost fuzzy in the pre-dawn light.

I'm not sure how long I stood there watching sea water flow in and out of depressions and holes in the rock, occasionally covering my feet and wetting my puka bead anklet. I wondered if the beads, which were from the sea originally, longed to return to it. From time to time I glanced up to see how different the clouds looked as the sun's rays approached, how their color changed from blue-grey to the palest yellow to white. I was not aware of any thoughts. Like the sea, I just *was*.

"Nathan?"

It was as though I'd heard my name called from a great distance, and not in a way that required my attention. Slowly, I turned my head toward the sound. I was not surprised to see Conroy, and in fact no emotions of any kind registered with me. I nodded once in acknowledgement, and he stepped closer.

"What are you doing here?" I couldn't interpret his tone. Maybe the sound of the waves rendered it neutral.

I blinked. It was a silly question. I pointed to my suite, but I didn't speak.

"It's Friday. You're not due here until Sunday."

"I know."

"So—"

"Is there a problem?"

"Well, I... I mean, I'll be busy arranging things. The shuttle bus, supplies, all that kind of thing." With a certain emotional remove, I noted that there was no mention of the fun things he'd told me he'd be doing with some of his extra time.

I said, "Okay." He looked exasperated. I smiled a gentle smile that, as I think back on it, probably appeared somewhat cryptic. "I'm not here to see you."

"Oh. Well." I couldn't read the expression on his face.

I turned away from Conroy and walked slowly to my right, moving into the water so that the waves lapped up to my knees before retreating again. After about fifty yards I stopped and watched the sea for some amount of time. The interaction between the sea and the land here did not seem dangerous. The land apparently descended gradually under the waves, unlike what I'd seen in images of the western coast. Still, it seemed likely that at some point, if I went far enough into the water, the land would plunge suddenly, creating a powerful undertow. And at any moment, a large wave might arise out of seemingly nowhere. I would not turn my back on the ocean.

As I returned to my suite, I didn't see Conroy. Perhaps he'd stayed just long enough for a quick dip in the ocean before heading out on his errands. Or his island "fun."

A quiet sense of something like glee rolled over me. He'd been so dismissive of me—or that's how it had felt— with his farewell text, and just now, I'd been dismissive of him. It hadn't been deliberate, or planned, or even considered. It had just happened.

Perhaps I was over him as much as he was over me.

The town of Hanalei looked different in daylight, as most things do. After a leisurely restaurant breakfast I strolled around, bought some postcards and stamps, and picked up some groceries for the next couple of days. Hanalei was cute, but I didn't want to have to come here for all my meals, and my suite had a functional kitchen. The resort had a restaurant, but my encounter with Conroy had left me feeling like I wanted to be on my own, and he might take meals there. I was relishing a feeling that was unfamiliar to me: joyful independence. The loneliness I'd felt back in Concord, in Gram's haunted house, was—literally and figuratively— worlds away from being alone here. I had thought I'd understood the difference between lonely and alone. I hadn't. Not until now.

In my research, knowing I'd have a couple of days to explore, I'd collected information about things I might want to do. I could visit caves. I could go on a catamaran cruise. I could try kayaking, which I'd never done. All of this had sounded very appealing, before I'd arrived. That is, before I knew how affected I would be by just—well, by just *being* here.

That afternoon, sitting on my porch with a cold beer,

feet up on the railing, eyes trained on the sea that seemed both completely empty and also fully alive, I let my mind wander in all kinds of directions. I thought about Gram and religion. I thought about Neil and his "live life now" philosophy. At one point I laughed aloud; the way I was experiencing Kaua'i, all that existed was "now."

While going through Neil's music collection weeks ago, I had encountered another song that had surprised me. It was a two-part song by James Taylor, "Before This World / Jolly Springtime." There was a line that came to my mind as I watched the empty, living sea: *Thin, thin, the moment is thin. Ever so narrow the now.* Here, on my porch, with only the sea for company, "now" seemed not just wide, but bigger than massive. "Now" was all-encompassing.

I woke very early again on Saturday. After another communion with the sea, watching the water reach for my anklet and retreat, and reach again and retreat, I decided a catamaran trip along the Na Pali Coast would be perfect. I would almost certainly see the caves, the sea animals, and the full coast—part of which I'd be hiking—all in one activity. And I was lucky; it was too late for the morning cruise, but there was one seat left on the afternoon cruise. And no rain was predicted.

The boat was crowded, as I'd expected. But it wasn't long before I gave up my seat and went to stand in the bow. The captain said the water was only slightly rough, but even so the bow rose and fell over and over, sending spray in all directions, including on me. I loved it.

As soon as we rounded the northwest part of the island and passed Ke'e Beach, the Na Pali Coast came into sight. Words can't do justice, either to the view or to the feeling it gave me. But I will try.

Steep triangles, one after the other, marched their way down the coast. The closer ones were covered in dense greenery of varying hues, and the ones farther away were sharp lines of greenish blue, then blueish grey, disappearing out of sight into the misty distance. The water near the land was a sparkling, pale turquoise that grew intense as it got deeper. The farther down the coast I looked, the less turquoise there was close to shore, replaced by deep marine blue, even very close to the land. I knew this spoke to the steepness of the land as it met the water and descended beneath it.

I'd seen this view on my computer screen. I'd thought, *Wow, that's gorgeous*. Now that I was here, "gorgeous" didn't come close. During the ride, one after another, the stunning views seemed like they were trying to outdo each other. Sheer lava rock face, tropical trees, distant misty hills and turquoise ocean—and not a human structure in sight. It just didn't stop. I kept having to back away from the bow and the sea spray so I could take pictures without getting water on my phone. After maybe fifteen or twenty shots, I gave up; there was no way to capture this digitally. I would have to store it deep inside me and bring it home that way.

Going into the sea cave was a riot. The captain positioned the boat directly under a waterfall, and the passengers squealed with delight. I just closed my eyes and allowed the experience to have its way with me.

Turtles and dolphins swam around the boat, and I saw a few goats high up on the hillsides. Once, maybe a hundred feet from the boat, a large ray leapt completely out of the water and splashed its way back below the surface.

It was a perfect afternoon, a perfect prelude to following this same enchanted coastline on foot.

After that odd encounter on the beach Friday morning, I hadn't seen Conroy again. Saturday evening, I finished my dinner of tuna sandwiches and green salad and beer, and I took cookies and sparkling water out to the porch. As I sat there I let my mind wander wherever it wanted to; this had become a familiar pattern, one I liked very much. This time it went to a rather esoteric place, after contemplating the difference between the sea here and the sea along the Na Pali Coast, beneath the Kalalau Trail. Geographically, the two coastlines were very close to each other. They were more or less around the corner on the same small island. But that was deceptive.

Here in the north, the coast—the ocean—was benign, even aloof, as long as I didn't challenge its depths, as long as I stayed in my place, as it were. Here, it was live-and-let-live. There, however, just a few miles away, it was treacherous, and capricious, even deadly. And yet both were the same ocean, the same sea, the same water. The difference was not the water. The difference was how the water interacted with the land.

How different was I, I wondered, as I moved through life, interacting with one person, or one situation, and then with another? Was I as changeable as the sea? And were the changes not actually a part of who I was, but more directly related to who and what I encountered?

It was at about that point in my mental wanderings that I heard someone walking through the grass in my direction, and Conroy appeared. Hands in his pockets, he strolled up onto my deck and sat in the chair on the opposite side of the round table from me. I hadn't wanted to see him, but I was feeling so "now," so live-and-let-live, that I didn't care one way or another. He nodded once, I nodded, and we both stared out at the sea.

After a few minutes he pulled something out of one of his pockets. I wasn't watching, but I heard the strike of a match, and from the corner of eye I caught the flash of a small flame. Almost immediately the odor of marijuana floated toward me. Still, I watched the sea, until Conroy held the joint in my direction. I took it rather automatically. Unafraid of addiction from this substance, I'd enjoyed the occasional use of weed during my years at college, so although I was no pot-head, I was familiar enough with smoking to take the joint from Conroy without hesitation.

We shared the joint without speaking until it was gone and we had finished the bag of corn chips I'd fetched from the kitchen, and then we stared at the sea as the light gradually faded, the water darkened, and the white surf stood out in stark contrast.

I became vaguely aware that Conroy had stood. He reached for my hand, pulled me slowly to my feet, and led me into the bedroom.

It was as though I was sleep-walking. Between the porch and the bed so many thoughts went through my head I felt dizzy.

1. I've given in to the idea of just being while I'm here, relinquishing control to the fates. It might ruin that easy go-with-the-flow attitude to refuse Conroy.

2. I don't care that he was honest with me. I don't like the way he's treating me, taking control again, taking me for granted. I should pull away. I should *say* "Fuck you" rather than do it.

3. Maybe there's a middle path. Maybe I can turn the tables.

I went with number three. Call it the deep power of the ocean. Call it the exhilarating independence I'd discovered. Call it whatever you want.

As he placed the condom wrapper between his teeth so he could undress himself, I took the condom from his mouth and tore it open.

Our dicks were ready, pointing eagerly toward each other, yearning for touch and yet enjoying the anticipation. I knew Conroy expected me to put the condom onto his dick. I didn't. I put it on mine.

He spoke for the first time since he had appeared on my porch. "What the fuck—"

"My turn, I think." My voice faltered, just a little.

"Oh no," he said, a hand held up toward me, fingers

splayed apart to create as large a barrier as possible. "I don't do that."

I wanted to argue with him. I wanted to live up to this new-found independence I'd felt the last couple of days. But—and I hated to admit this—I also wanted Conroy. I stood there in the twilight of the room, the nubs of a cotton rag rug poking at the bottoms of my feet, my dick sheathed in its protective covering, and I couldn't speak. I couldn't move.

Conroy stepped close enough to embrace me, but he didn't. "I hear ya, kid. I just can't go there." There was something final in his smile. He caressed the back of my head, turned, collected his clothes, and left.

I stared at the space he had occupied, listening to his retreating footfalls until the only sound was the ocean's constant surging. Then I ripped the condom off my retreating dick and threw myself face-down onto the bed. I wanted to scream. I wanted to cry *and* scream. Finally I did let out one growling yell smothered by my pillow.

Underwear the only clothing I put back on, I grabbed another beer and another bag of corn chips and resumed my position on the porch, feet up on the railing, eyes on the black sea decorated with white foam. I was still a little high from Conroy's weed, feeling the munchies, but also feeling like—well, like someone else. I barely recognized myself.

Things had been going so well! I had felt like I was coming into my own, becoming a man at last rather than the little kid who'd waddled after big brother Neil, and then wannabe mountain man Daniel, and then true mountain man Conroy. As I sat there, I tried telling myself that the position a man takes in sex is not a measure of his manhood. I knew that was true, and yet I felt as if Conroy had dismissed me the way someone might dismiss a person they'd outgrown. I felt like my belief in my progress toward manhood had been deflated.

I fought that feeling. "He couldn't let me fuck him because his own manhood is so fragile he was afraid it would shatter," I said aloud into the darkness.

An answering voice, almost audible, said, *So guess how he sees someone who lets someone fuck them. That would be you.*

Kid. He'd called me "kid." I was not a man to him. Fuck him.

Why did I care so much? He didn't love me, I was sure of that. I wasn't in love with him. Was I?

No. But I was captivated by the feeling I got when I heard him speak, when I heard him laugh. Something in that resonance pulled at my gut. It didn't sound like the voice of anyone else I'd known, as far as I could remember.

Suddenly it hit me that the deep resonance in Conroy's voice, paired with his self-assured independence, spoke of undeniable masculinity, a masculinity I didn't sense within myself, a masculinity I'd been searching for all my life.

It wasn't Conroy I wanted. It was Man.

What was happening to me here, in paradise, in this nexus between one thing and another? Between a man and his voice? Between life and death? Between what was and what will be? Who was I? Was I becoming a man, capable of being a leader, or was I realizing I'd always be a follower? Who had I been, and who was I becoming? I had no answers, just this feeling of otherness. Other-world-ness. Other-me-ness.

Before going to sleep that night, I masturbated with a ferocity I couldn't remember ever feeling before. It wasn't anger. It wasn't frustration. It just was.

CHAPTER FOURTEEN

Sunday morning I didn't wake up until nine, which surprised me; both Friday and Saturday I'd been up before dawn. I spent the day feeling low on energy, with my only excursion being to wander through the Limahuly Gardens and gaze sightlessly at the different plant species found on the island, many of them endangered. According to their website, the garden "honors the connection between nature and humanity." That was something I'd felt powerfully my first couple of days here, something Conroy had punctured last night, and I wanted to get it back.

I almost succeeded.

I didn't see Conroy all day, and that suited me just fine.

All the hikers were to meet in the resort's dining room for dinner, compliments of Finnegan's Walks. When I got there, I saw a large table off to one side of the dining room, and Conroy was there, along with three other guys. I wasn't entirely sure of my welcome, after what had—or, rather hadn't—happened Saturday night, but I'd paid for this trip. I refused to be intimidated. So I wandered over.

Conroy, looking very native in a green and blue shirt with large, stylized turtles all over it, glanced up and gave me an impersonal smile. "Here's Nathan Bartlett, another hiker in our group. Have a seat, Nathan."

So that was how we were going to do this.

Standing so that I could easily shake hands, I looked at each of the others as Conroy introduced me to them. First he pointed to the man seated across from him, Erik Buxton. Erik seemed older than the others, maybe in his forties. His brownish hair was thinning and pulling back from his freckled forehead, and the skin around his eyes had the look of someone who'd spent a lot of time squinting against the sun. The rest of his face was a little patchy, some suntan and some freckles that had melded together. His blue eyes were pale but intense, like he was really taking in whatever he looked at. He wore a pale blue cotton shirt, sleeves rolled up to his elbows, which contrasted nicely with his tan.

Owen Palmer, probably in his mid-thirties, had hair nearly as black as mine, with a grey patch on the left side of his head over his ear. His tan wasn't like Erik's. I was sure he had paid for it. He wore a cotton knit polo, mostly navy, but with red-and-white bands of color around the bottoms of the short sleeves, a red collar with white trim, and two bright yellow circular bands of color that went all the way around the sleeves at the shoulder. There was a bee embroidered over the left pec area. He was in the chair on Conroy's left.

Hugh Campion had the chair on the other side of Conroy. He looked a few years older than me, unless the strong jaw and deep tan made him look older than he was. His hair was short and very blond, and he had rolled up the sleeves of his navy-and-white pinstripe shirt. A heavy, gold chain with an intricate design showed beneath the open collar.

As I took the chair beside Erik and across from Hugh, whose whole body was turned slightly toward Conroy, something caught in my chest. I did my best to ignore it, but I knew what color it was. It was green. It was green jealousy. And it was there because—I couldn't have said why—because I knew Hugh was gay. And because something either was going on or had been going on between him and Conroy.

Doesn't matter to me, I told myself. *Conroy and I were never an item, never going to be an item*, I said. *We're both free agents*, I said.

Erik and Owen looked like the sort of people who would sign up for a challenging hike in an exotic location. Hugh didn't give me that impression; he looked like he'd be more at home in a gym than on a hiking trail. I wondered if he'd been specifically, and very personally, invited by Conroy. You know, like I had been.

As the meal progressed, Hugh's voice, which seemed a little high for his bulk, began to grate on me. He laughed rather too much and a little too loudly, usually at something Conroy had said. Still working at not caring, I told myself that if Conroy had personally invited not just me but also Hugh, so what? I already knew Conroy hardly limited himself to one intimate partner. Hell, he didn't even limit himself to one sex. But I was still seeing an ugly green haze when I looked at either of them.

To distract myself, I focused on something that wasn't there, rather than something that was. "Wasn't there also a woman who signed up for this hike?" I kept my facial expression as bland as possible as I looked at Conroy.

"Margot Truman," he said, glancing at the empty chair across from Owen. "Yes. She decided to stay somewhere else. She's having dinner there."

Hugh turned to Conroy to ask something. I don't remember what. But the look on his face had an eagerness, a puppy-dog attitude, and he started to lay a hand on Conroy's forearm. He pulled back just in time, just before Conroy noticed; I was sure it was not a gesture Conroy would have tolerated. Not here. Not now. Maybe not ever. The point, though, was that this was obviously not the first time the two of them had met. And it made me determined that I was going to act as though I did not have any idea what it felt like to hold Conroy's dick in my hand, or my mouth, or my ass. I was not going to say anything—at least not right away—to let on that we'd ever met before. I did not want Erik, Owen, or the not-yet-present Margot to see me the way I saw Hugh.

At one point Erik turned to me. "What line are you in, Nathan?"

Line? It took me a second to realize he either thought I was older than I was, or he was paying me the courtesy of assuming it. It took me another second to wonder what his accent said about him.

"Still working on that," I told him. "I'll be going to grad school in a year. Psychology. Just taking some time to explore the world a little." Whatever that meant. "You have an interesting accent."

"Christchurch," he said, smiling, revealing yet more wrinkles in his weathered face. "New Zealand. Maybe you'll make it out there on your world tour."

I smiled back at him. "Maybe I will." What a provincial idiot I was! It hadn't occurred to me that there would be anyone on this trip who wasn't from the U.S. But Conroy's website went everywhere, so of course his clients could come from anywhere. "How about you? Your line, that is?"

"Airline pilot."

I nodded. He sure looked the part.

By the time the meal ended, I'd learned that Owen was a CPA from Hartford, Connecticut, and Hugh worked for his father, who owned a company somewhere in Pennsylvania where they designed furniture. Owen's wife was a golf pro associated with a country club. He passed around his phone with a shot of his fourteen-year-old twins, a boy and a girl, who were learning to golf.

"See this grey patch on the side of my head?" He turned so everyone could see. "It grew that way after I used my head to stop a golf ball my son sent in the wrong direction." He laughed at his own humor, such as it was, and the rest of us chuckled or smiled obligingly.

Other than Hugh's father I learned nothing more about his family. No one asked Erik or me about family, and neither of us said anything, though I noticed he wore a gold wedding band.

I listened more than I talked during the meal; I wanted to get a sense of who these people were. Hugh, whose motives I figured I knew, seemed not to be getting quite the response from Conroy he might have wanted. Owen spoke frequently, always quite fast, and not always in line with what had just been said by someone else. There was something slightly manic about him that I couldn't put my finger on.

I decided I liked Erik. I enjoyed his accent, sure, but he seemed like the sort of guy who takes things as they come and people for who they are. There was an easy grace about him I wished I could emulate.

Everyone had dessert, and when most of the food was gone from our plates, Conroy said, "Anyone want anything else?"

"I'm chocka," Erik said, patting his belly. Somehow I knew what he meant, but Hugh didn't.

"Chocka?"

"Sorry. Full."

Conroy laughed and said, "Then I suggest we all turn in. Get lots of sleep. We'll work hard from this point on!"

Conroy's instructions for the group were to meet in front of the restaurant at nine a.m., so I figured I'd get myself ready, eat at the restaurant, and wander outside in time to meet up with everyone. But just like last night, when I got into the dining room everyone else was already there. Again, except for Margot. We ate pretty quickly, which suited me; I wanted to get on the trail, not only because of the trial, but also because in this enclosed space it was hard to pretend not to know Conroy and not to care about Hugh.

At one point I glanced at my watch: eight forty-five. Conroy's phone rang, and he got up and walked a little away from the table to answer it. That call ended, and then he called someone, obviously unhappy over something. When he approached us again, I could tell he was making an effort to appear unruffled.

"That was Margot," Conroy told us. "It seems she's having some trouble getting here." He glanced around the table at each of us. "Nathan, you must have rented a car, right? You're the only person the shuttle didn't pick up at the airport."

I blinked. He knew damn well I had a car. But this was pertinent how? "Yeah."

"The bus that's taking us from here to the trailhead is already here, and the driver refuses to go back and pick her up. I can't leave the group. So can you hop over to where she is and get her? I'll text you the address." He didn't wait for me to agree or argue; he tapped on his phone, evidently sending me her location.

I had two choices. I could say, *It's not my job to corral your clients.* Or I could just go and get the troublemaker.

On the road, not sorry for another reason to drive my red Jeep, I wondered how long Hugh and Conroy had known each other, and how they had met. Conroy had been in Wolfboro, New Hampshire before his stay in Durham. Hugh lived in Pennsylvania. Had Conroy been there before Wolfboro? If so, Hugh had known Conroy longer than I had. If not, where was it they had met, and how?

Not that I care, I told myself. *I don't care at all,* I said. *Makes no difference to me,* I said.

Margot was at a place on the Kuhio Highway, about a mile east of the resort. I nearly drove past it; the place looked more like a glorified shack than anything else. But it was directly across from Waineha Bay Park, where the ocean comes within a few hundred yards of the road.

As soon as I turned into the driveway, I noticed a young woman standing under a tree, a frame pack and a suitcase at her feet. She smiled as I pulled up beside her. I got out to help load her things.

"Nathan?" she said, holding out her right hand.

"And you're Margot," I replied as we shook hands.

She seemed about my age. Her face was a beautiful combination of sparking green eyes, lots of freckles, and arched eyebrows a few shades darker then the strawberry-blond, shoulder-length hair. A bright green headband held her hair back from her face, giving the impression that she was even younger than she must have been. She gave off a vibe somewhere between a sheltered, innocent teenager and a model from an ad for health food products. Her resemblance to El Speed's girlfriend Ellie was slight, but it was enough to cause a sense of guilt to wash over me. I pushed it away; it was not my fault they had rescheduled their wedding for the middle of my trip.

Margot settled quite naturally into the Jeep, as though it was just same-old, same-old to her. "Thank you so much for coming to get me. I'm sorry to be so much trouble."

"Not a problem." I was tempted to add, *Just an annoyance.*

"I can't wait to see the trail. I hope I don't feel too out of place. I know I'm the only girl on the hike." She laughed prettily. "I assured Conroy I've done my share of hiking."

"Where are you from?"

She spoke quickly, as though needing to get a lot of information out in very little time. Or maybe she wasn't sure how long she could retain my interest. "Idaho. Lots of mountains in Idaho. Plus I've hiked in Alaska and western Canada. This won't be my first trip away from the comforts of home."

I didn't doubt her. Not exactly. But there was something fragile about her, which took her in the opposite direction from Ellie. "And when you're not hiking?"

"What—oh, you mean—I've just completed my MSW at Idaho State. Social work. Now I'm giving myself a bit of a break before diving into job hunting. What about you?"

So she was older than she looked, or she was a prodigy. I let a beat go by. I was feeling a little rushed by her speaking pace, and that contrasted unpleasantly with the "in the now" feeling I'd been enjoying on the island, a feeling Conroy had destroyed and one I wanted to resurrect. "Taking a gap year," I said, drawing the words out a little. "Then grad school.

Psychology."

"Really? Do you want to be a therapist?"

Another beat. "Addiction fascinates me." I think she wasn't quite sure what to make of that, because she didn't say anything else for several seconds, which for her was probably an eternity.

She recovered. "Have you had a chance to talk to the others?"

"We had dinner last night, and breakfast together just now." I stopped, not wanting to talk the whole trip back.

She asked, "What's your take on Conroy?"

"He's very self-assured." It came out quickly, and almost as though someone else had said it. And it was probably the most charitable thing I could have said about him at that moment. I said, "We're here," and immediately wished I had asked for *her* take on Conroy.

There was a small shuttle bus in the parking lot, motor running, obviously waiting for us. Conroy was the only person not on it. He called us over.

"I've checked everyone else's stuff," he said. "Your turn. I have a list."

He went through a checklist to be sure we'd brought everything we were supposed to have. We had.

I went to fetch the belongings I wouldn't be taking on the trail to move them into the storage room Conroy had arranged for us. Conroy was there with Margot's suitcase.

He gave me a quick glance and then dropped his eyes to the luggage. "You okay?"

A number of responses flew into my head and disappeared. What I said was, "Why do you ask?" And, taking my time, I left.

On the bus, Conroy addressed the group as we drove toward the road. "There's no overnight parking near the trailhead, which is one reason we need the bus. Theoretically we could have walked from here, but it's over two miles, and walking along this narrow road might just get you to the wrong paradise." He grinned, and I heard chuckles. "As you know, the trail has only recently been opened again after last year's floods. So we all need to watch carefully for any unstable areas. If you go over the side, there ain't no comin' back."

The bus passed a long line of cars parked along the road, and then I saw a sign for the Kalalau Trail. We drove on a little farther, and the driver dropped us off at the southern-most section of Ke'e Beach. Packs on, we all followed Conroy out onto the sand as the bus did its best to navigate an about-face and drive away. I couldn't help noticing that Hugh wore a beige T-shirt—no logo or any other design—that was one or two sizes too small, presumably so that his biceps and pecs could be appropriately admired.

Owen had another polo shirt on, similar to the one he'd worn at dinner. This one was white.

Margot noticed it and said, "How cute! A little bee."

Owen looked at her as though she should know the significance of the bee. "Gucci puts it on some of their shirts."

"Oh. So that's a Gucci shirt?" Owen gave her a glance as though her comment didn't deserve a response.

Erik eyed the shirt. "Isn't that the same one you wore to dinner last night?" And he winked at me.

Owen evidently didn't know when he was being teased. "It is not! That one was a completely different color!"

"Hmmm. Guess the bee fooled me." And Erik turned away from Owen to follow Conroy onto the sand.

Conroy had an empty plastic jug fixed to the top of his pack. It looked like the sort of container Gram used to buy ammonia in. I considered asking what it was for, but Margot beat me to it. Conroy's response was, "You'll see!"

As we stepped onto the sand, Margot laughed. "Oh my goodness! Chickens!" They were all around us.

"Yeah. You'll see them running free almost everywhere on the island," Conroy said. "Shouldn't be any on the trail, though. Anyway, I want you all to see this."

He walked almost to where the waves were crashing onto the sand, turned to face south, and extended his right arm. "The Na Pali Coast."

I decided against saying anything about having seen this view already, from the water. It was irrelevant. I barely heard the exclamations from others in the group.

Standing on that beach, I felt like an integral part of the island. Conroy didn't matter. Nothing mattered but here, right now, this moment.

There was magic here. Something in my chest, something mysterious and nearly overwhelming, expanded and expanded until I thought I would burst. I felt light-headed, nearly dizzy with a kind of euphoria I had never experienced. It was as though of all the places on earth, this was where I belonged. This was where I was meant to be.

CHAPTER FIFTEEN

There was no mistaking the Kalalau trailhead. A tall metal post held three different signs, brown with yellow borders, that admonished us to pack out what we packed in, that gave distances, and that prohibited all animals but service animals. Propped beneath these, on the ground and leaning against the post, was a small whiteboard with handwritten letters that read, "Hanakapi'ai Beach / WARNING / Strong Currents / Do Not Enter The Ocean."

Conroy stood beside the post, facing us. Hands loosely gripping his pack's shoulder straps, he told us, "All these cars tell me there are a lot of people here today, some on the beach and more on the trail. But the cars can't stay overnight. So that means almost anyone on the trail is here only for the day. So we'll see people along the first two-mile stretch, but most of them won't go beyond that."

He turned toward the post and gazed down at the whiteboard. Then he looked back at us. "Hanakapi'ai Beach is no joke." He looked from one of us to the next. "No one who hikes with me will even take your boots off when we get there. The tide should be low when we arrive, so we can step into a small cave for a few minutes. But *no one is wading*. I don't care how hot your feet are. Is everyone clear?"

He waited until we had each acknowledged his instructions.

"Ready?" He grinned.

"Yes!" Margot. Of course.

On the first part of the trail, as Conroy had predicted, there were quite a few people, and the sheer number of them punched a hole in that euphoria I'd felt on the beach.

Everyone in our group had a heavy frame pack, but I didn't see anyone else wearing anything heavier than a light pack that would probably contain a couple of water bottles and a sandwich. Conroy, Owen, and I all had portable solar collectors dangling off the sides of our packs so we could charge our cell phones. There wasn't any coverage on the trail, but the phones could be useful in other ways. For one thing, mine would be my camera.

Before we'd gone a hundred feet, Owen—directly in front of me—pulled two telescoping trekking poles from where they protruded through the top of his pack. I bit my tongue, wondering if I dared say anything. But Conroy, who was in front of Owen, must have heard the sound they made as they extended. He stopped, which meant everyone stopped.

"Put those away," he said. His mouth was smiling, but I knew him well enough to know his eyes were not. I also knew we weren't moving forward until Owen obeyed. "You won't need a pole until tomorrow. And when you do, you'll use only one."

Owen hesitated, as though he either didn't believe Conroy or was going to mutiny, but he collapsed them again, took his pack off, and returned them to their place. I barely heard him mutter, "These things cost me a fortune."

As Owen was hefting his pack again, a young woman with long, dark hair, apparently of Hawaiian heritage, passed us on her way back to the trail head. On her slim, tanned body she wore a sky blue sleeveless blouse, navy shorts, and nothing on her feet. No kidding; she was barefoot. And she stepped along the trail as casually as if it were the path between her bedroom and her bathroom.

Behind me, I heard Erik's voice. "A Hawaiian princess. Sweet as."

I looked at him. "Sweet as what?"

He laughed. "Sorry. Kiwi expression. Just means really, really nice." He grinned. And I grinned back; even if she might attract him more than she would appeal to me, she had been strikingly beautiful. In a quick feat of mental gymnastics, I figured out that "Kiwi expression" meant something a New Zealander would say.

As I was about to turn back to the trail, I noticed Margot behind Erik. She smiled cheerfully as our eyes met, but I couldn't help wondering how she felt about her position in the line, bring up the rear. Someone had to be in that spot, of course, but she had already told me she was afraid of feeling out of place. And then it occurred to me that I didn't see Hugh ahead of me. So I looked behind Margot.

There he was. I would have expected him to be at the front of the group, as close to Conroy as possible. Hugh didn't look happy, and I wondered if Conroy had asked him to take that spot, the "sweep" position at the back. The sweep's job is to make sure no one in the group lags too far behind the others and to notify the leader if there's a problem. I wouldn't have thought it would be a necessary role with such a small group. In any case, someone in that role has assumed some level of responsibility. Was that Hugh? And if he'd accepted that responsibility, was Conroy paying him, taking advantage of Hugh's infatuation, or—and this gave me a rush of something like unholy glee—was he trying to keep Hugh at a distance?

The two-mile stretch of trail to Hanakapi'ai Beach was not especially rugged, though it would have been muddy and slippery in the rain. In its own way, though, it held danger. Scattered here and there in the hard-packed red dirt were stones and rocks and nubby roots. It wasn't that they made the trail particularly hard to navigate. It was that I might not see them because I didn't want to take my eyes off of the incredible vistas that appeared between palm-like trees as we climbed gradually along the sides of the cliffs. From the catamaran, I'd been able to see some sections of the trail and some of the people on it, and I'd assumed it would be less glorious as a hike than it had been as a sea tour. I was wrong. The two were different, but they were equally glorious.

Margot kept saying she'd never seen anything so beautiful. And a few minutes later she'd say it again. I might have been annoyed at all the times we had to slow our pace because of someone going slowly on a narrow stretch of trail ahead of us, except that it gave me a chance to take picture after picture, despite my conviction (from the boat yesterday) that it was pointless. It was irresistible.

In a few places the trail felt rather narrow, with an impossibly steep uphill incline to my left, and on my right a plunge of a hundred or more feet to the pounding surf below. If I'd tripped badly on one of those obstacles, I might—as Conroy had warned—find myself in an unintended paradise. I knew this was nothing compared to what awaited us on Crawler's Ledge.

As we approached the little cairn beach whose coming had been foretold to us in dire tones, I saw one sign after another—wooden, unofficial-looking—with unambiguous warnings. One had the hand-painted heading, "Hanakapi'ai Beach WARNING! Currents have killed many visitors!" As if to prove the point, there were at least fifteen of those groups of four vertical lines and a fifth line diagonally through them. That was one sign. Fifteen times five visitors. Seventy-five-plus dead people. I didn't know whether to believe the sign or not. There were other signs, similarly worded, some adding, "They were only WADING!" It was impossible to know whether the hashed numbers on one sign represented the same people another sign indicated, but I figured it didn't really matter. The point was made.

The trail sloped a little steeply down to the beach, and as soon as I could see beyond Owen and Conroy, I saw the cairns. As with the view of the Na Pali Coast, I'd seen this image on a computer screen. And as with the first, the screen didn't do it justice.

I'm going to say there were nearly a thousand of them.

Some consisted of little rocks piled directly on top of each other with a large rock at the bottom. Others were rocks of decreasing sizes as the pile got higher. Some were a foot tall. Others were higher than my knees. The cairns were packed so closely together I'm not sure I could have walked among them.

Conroy came to a stop at the edge of the cairn field and moved to the right a few feet so we could all take in the sight. Even Margot, who'd kept up an on-and-off conversation with Erik for much of the trail so far, was silent. I was thinking Conroy might tell us if they stood for anything. The number of waders taken by the ocean, perhaps? But he said nothing.

Owen broke the spell. "Holy shit." And as soon as he did, Conroy turned toward the water. He moved carefully around the cairn field, staying conspicuously away from where water met sand, and led the way to the opposite side of the cairn field, around a rocky outcropping, and into a sand-bottomed cave. It was obvious what would happen at high tide: any air-breathing beings would drown.

Back at the cairns, we took a few minutes for a water break, and then Conroy led us inland, more or less following a stream. "Two miles to the waterfall!"

We climbed past the giant bamboo trees I'd seen on Conroy's computer screen, and we laughed at the tiny area of flat, grassy land marked as a helicopter landing pad. From there the trail, such as it was, grew extremely challenging, especially with heavy packs. We crawled through dense greenery, over rocks slick with water and something green and slimy, while fallen branches and small trees did their best to make footing even more difficult. Owen, behind me now, swore a string of obscenities that must have left a blue streak behind us. Hugh was still in sweep position, but Margot was in front of me, with Erik and then Conroy ahead.

Between Owen's epithets, I heard an occasional gasp or grunt or small cry from Margot, who was struggling quite a bit. At one point she lost her balance on a slippery boulder and nearly fell. I caught her before she hit the rocks all around me.

"I'm so sorry, Nathan!" She looked near tears.

"Don't worry about it," I said, smiling, hoping to ease her discomfort. "I'll bet it's very different from hiking in Idaho. Not so lush and slippery there."

"You're right about that!" And she turned back to the rock that had nearly done her in, navigating it very carefully and succeeding this time.

Behind me I heard, first, Owen panting, and then Hugh's irritated, "What's the hold-up?"

"Sorry!" Margot called without looking around.

I glared at Hugh and followed Margot over the boulder.

The trail went on like that until we came to a clear pool of water surrounded by rocks big enough to sit on. We sat, and we all took off our packs and then our shoes or boots to dangle our hot feet into the coolness.

"Good time for lunch?" Conroy asked.

No one argued, so we all pulled out whatever we'd brought for our first meal on the trail. Conroy's website had listed a selection of food items we should pack. Mostly it suggested freeze-dried items for dinner, which would be light and could be reconstituted with purified water, but bread and cheese were great for the trek out, at least. I'd augmented my supply for the first day with sliced turkey.

"Where'd you get that?" Hugh wanted to know.

I looked at him while I chewed and then swallowed. "I've been on the island for a few days." I took another large bite and gazed into the thick forest across the pool.

"So have I."

He'd been here. Had he been here with Conroy? If so, why had Conroy showed up at my suite Saturday night? If not, then....? I decided to ignore his comment.

Margot, beside me, looked a little done-in. I was feeling hot and unpleasantly sticky, but she looked like she felt even worse.

"You okay?" I asked, quietly.

She let out a long breath. "I will be. It's just so humid in here. I guess I'm not used to that."

"Everyone?" Conroy called. "I want to be sure you drink enough water. This pool is a great place to collect water for purification. Just don't drink it without purifying it. Remember the goats!"

His website had warned about animals, especially goats, that pee in the water inland, causing bacterial contamination. This wasn't news to me; I always purified water, wherever I hiked, anytime I couldn't bring enough with me.

Conroy declared the lunch break over. "I hope you noticed that we didn't meet anyone else on our way here from the beach. If you'll follow me just a little while longer, you'll see why trekking through that jungle was worth it."

Erik laughed. "Okay, but what about trekking back out through it again?"

Conroy grinned at Erik. "Troublemaker. Okay, everyone, onward."

It really was just a little farther, and around a rock face, and the Hanakapi'ai Falls were before us. The tumbling water fell from a tremendous height, straight down and into a pool, where there were five people swimming and splashing around. Hugh moved forward to stand beside Conroy. Owen nearly knocked Margot over trying to get a better view.

Hugh stared at the swimmers. "Now that looks like a great idea."

Conroy thought not. "Sure, but they'd better hope they don't swallow any water, and that they don't have any cuts anywhere on them."

I could barely make out Owen's words, he spoke so softly. "And they'll need a pretty tight asshole. Not a good idea for Hugh, I think."

I stared at him, trying to figure out whether I wanted to say anything and, if so, what.

Erik, who was standing closer to Owen, beat me to it. Also quietly, looking at the falls, he said, "That's enough of that, Palmer."

I decided to get to know Erik a little better.

CHAPTER SIXTEEN

The journey back through the jungle wasn't quite as onerous as the trek in had been, but going downhill over slippery rocks presents its own hazards, so progress was slow. Conroy allowed us a fifteen-minute breather when we got back to the beach, but then he led a punishing pace on the trail. We'd passed the two-mile limit for anyone without a permit, so we no longer shared the trail with day-hikers.

After leaving the beach, the trail climbed eight hundred feet in the first mile. And then it went downhill again, and with heavy packs, this was the usual trial for hips and knees. Sometimes the trail pinched its way between steep rock faces, and at other times we followed switchbacks where the trail went up and over those knife edges we'd seen in the distance, and then back down into the valleys between them.

In the weeks before the trip, alone at home, I'd done a lot of conditioning, and this trail was making me glad I had. I kept an eye on Margot for a little while, but she was doing great; I figured it had just been the humid, slippery jungle that had gotten to her.

At one of the places where the trail widened out and we weren't forced into single file, I pretend to make an adjustment to my shoe so that I could fall back to where Hugh was still bringing up the rear. I'd decided to find out who the guy was, and who he was to Conroy.

I stepped beside him, nodding as I did. He was taller than me. Taller than Conroy. He glanced at me but that was all.

Eyes forward, I asked, "So are you the official sweep?"

He took several seconds to answer. "Not what I signed up for."

I gave that some space, and then said, "If you'd like a

break, I can stand in for you for the afternoon."

That got his attention. He turned his head briefly to look at me. "Probably should check with Conroy."

More space. "Sounds like he asked you to do this. You must know him pretty well."

I heard a sound somewhere between a chuckle and a snort, followed by, "You could say that." He let a beat go by and then added, "Conroy trusts me."

"Known him for a long time, then?"

"On and off, a couple of years."

"Hiked with him before?"

"No. Look, if you're serious, I'll leave you to it."

He glanced at me, nodded, and moved forward, excusing himself to pass the other hikers and find his way to where Conroy led the charge. I lost sight of him around a bend, so I didn't see Conroy's reaction to Hugh's appearance. What I did see was Erik, behind Conroy, turn and look at me, and then move to the side so others could pass him. In the brief span of time before I got to where he stood, I decided I knew everything about Hugh and Conroy I needed to know. What I didn't know was why Conroy had come to me Saturday night.

Erik fell into step beside me when I got to him. Neither of us said anything right away. Maybe twenty paces went by before he said, "Any ideas about the dynamics of this group?"

I feigned confusion. "Dynamics?"

"Is Hugh a co-leader?"

"I don't think so."

"He seemed like the assigned sweep."

I chuckled. "He did, yes. And he didn't seem too happy about it. I told him I'd take over for a bit."

"Generous of you."

"Generous, or scheming."

"Eh?"

"Kidding. But I confess I'm a little curious about the dynamics, myself."

"You done a Finnegan's walk before?" My own question, back to me.

"Nope. You?" I didn't want him asking any of the other questions I'd asked Hugh.

"Almost went with him up Katahdin last year. Had to cancel." So it was Erik that Conroy had referred to over our dinner in Portsmouth. Then he said, "Really wants us rattlin' our dags through here, eh?"

I nearly stopped walking. "Sorry?"

He smiled in an almost conspiratorial way. "Thought you'd enjoy that. Dags are the clumps of shit that stick to the fleece on the backside of a sheep. If the sheep moves fast, it's like the dags rattle."

I couldn't help but laugh.

He changed the subject. "Margot's a trooper."

"She is."

"Standard tramping guidelines say the average woman, based on height and physical build, should carry about half of what the average man carries. But that never seems to happen."

Tramping, I figured, meant trekking, in "Kiwi." Hiking. I laughed again, remembering what Margot had said about convincing Conroy she was up to the trip. "I don't know her well, but I think she'd be unlikely to give up one pound of her pack for anyone else to carry." This was another way she reminded me of Ellie.

"I like that in a woman. It isn't fair, but I like it. Mind you, I'd take some of those pounds if she'd let me."

It seemed unlikely that Erik was gay. And, after all, there were already two gay and one bi men on this trip, a statistic way higher than the population as a whole. So I asked, "I see you have a wedding band. Family at home?"

He was silent for so long I thought that either he hadn't heard me, or he was ignoring the question. Finally, he said, "Wife just died. Cancer. No kids."

Man, talk about stepping in it.

Before I could decide on the best response, he added, "It's why I canceled Katahdin. This trip is a way to distract myself."

"Is it working?"

More silence. "Not much."

The trail narrowed, so we could no longer walk side-by-side. That conversation needed stopping, anyway.

Every once in a while, Conroy waited by the side and let everyone pass, no doubt checking to be sure no one had any serious issues, and then he'd work his way to the front again. One of the times he did this, he waited for me to catch up.

"You volunteered to sweep, Nathan?"

"For the afternoon. Not looking for a permanent position."

"Any particular reason?"

There were a few replies I might have given. For starters: *So you take him as much for granted as you took me, eh?* Instead, all I said was, "Hugh didn't seem happy in the role." I hadn't intended to put an edge into my voice, but I heard it.

He looked at me as though trying to figure something out but said nothing more, and then he made his way back to the front of the group.

Right after we had forded what Conroy called the Ho'olulu Stream, he halted the group to make camp.

"I knew we wouldn't make it to the half-way point at Hanakoa, what with that detour in to see the falls. But anyone else overnighting probably aimed for Hanakoa, so I didn't think we'd want to be there anyway. If we go inland here," and he pointed up a slightly open slope, "we'll come to a spot in about five minutes where I've camped in the past." He waited to see if anyone had questions and led the way uphill.

The spot he led us to was probably the most level spot we could have found close to the trail. It had obviously been used before for exactly this purpose, but there was no one else there now. With the stream nearby, we could collect and purify enough water to make dinner. I watched to see whether Hugh had his own tent. I figured he would, because I doubted Conroy would do anything to call attention to his relationship with any one hiker. As it turned out, not only was I correct, but also Conroy waited for everyone else to set up their tents before selecting a spot that was as far away from the rest of us as possible. I supposed he could have deliberately let others take the more comfortable spots first. Or maybe he was waiting to see if anyone needed help. But I was prepared to be only so generous toward him.

Fortunately everyone had taken seriously Conroy's instruction that we bring our own camp stoves. His website had said that other than the fire pits at campsites, no open fires were allowed.

We all sat around in a circle to eat our dinners. I noticed Hugh maneuvered himself so that he was next to Conroy, who seemed not to notice.

Margot was next to me, enjoying her reconstituted lentils and rice. I asked if she was a vegetarian.

"Nope. Just like to eat various things."

I'd felt the need for meat, so I'd chosen my freeze-dried beef stroganoff with wild mushrooms. It advertised itself as a package to serve two, but I didn't care. I ate the whole thing.

Addressing the group, Conroy asked, "Any impressions you'd like to share about today's hike?"

After a few seconds of silence, Margot said, "The falls were lovely. But that trail!"

Conroy chuckled. "Kaua'i doesn't make it easy. But I couldn't send you away without showing you the falls. And fair warning: When we get to the Hanakoa area tomorrow, we'll be following the Hanakoa Stream to *those* falls, as well." He grinned at Margot. "The trail is shorter than the one today, and the terrain is different, but it offers its own challenges. For one thing, we'll have to watch out for falling rocks. They don't fall often, but—as the saying goes—it only takes once. Any more general impressions?"

Erik offered, "This is a trail worth getting knackered over. We have an expression in New Zealand for being in the middle of nowhere. Wop-wops. That's where we are, and that's where I wanted to be."

Conroy laughed. "Glad to hear it. Yeah, this is a special place for me. I hope that by the time we're finished, you'll call it special, too."

There were a few more comments back and forth, though Hugh said nothing. Neither did I, until Conroy asked me what I thought.

I looked directly at him, let a beat or two go by, and said, "If I were a god, I would live here."

Nina had said Conroy was adept at dealing with people in different situations. He'd have to be, with this job. But even in the gathering darkness, as he heard his own words from that Thanksgiving meal echoed back to him, I saw his expression change. It went from congenial host to mild shock to something like quiet fear, and I wondered if he might be afraid I'd let the cat out of the bag and reveal what he and I shared. Let him worry, I thought.

He recovered quickly, and at first I didn't think anyone else had noticed anything. But then I caught sight of Hugh's face. His expression was somewhere between puzzled and worried. *Stupid*, I thought. *It's not worth getting Conroy's goat if Hugh figures out that I've known Conroy in the biblical sense.*

Conroy kept going around the circle. "Owen? How are you enjoying the trail so far?"

I have to say I hadn't warmed up to Owen. At Sunday's dinner, and again today at breakfast, he'd seemed a little too eager to impress. I'd heard his voice a number of times in the beginning of the hike, asking Conroy questions, offering tales of his own experiences, always in that slightly-too-fast, slightly-too-intense manner of speech. But since lunch I couldn't recall hearing him say much of anything. And now he was not just quiet. Now he seemed like an odd combination of anxious and sleepy. His gaze was either down at his food or flicking nervously around, though not at anything in particular that I could tell. With dinner over and nothing specific to hold onto, his fingers looked twitchy as though at a loss for what to do.

To Conroy's question, he responded, "Yeah. Wonderful. Really gorgeous. I'm, uh, feeling kind of tired now, though. Think I'll turn in, if that's okay."

I glanced at my watch: eight-fifteen.

"Whatever you like," Conroy replied. "Keep your backpack and tent fully zipped. You don't want to invite centipedes, or spiders, or scorpions." To the rest of us, he said, "We can't have a fire, but I have the next best thing." He disappeared into his tent, his headlamp lighting the way, and came back with that large, empty plastic bottle. He tied a spare headlamp onto it, the light facing toward the bottle, and switched on the lamp. "Instant campfire!"

Margot laughed delightedly, which made Conroy look at her, and then at her leg.

"Margot, is your leg bleeding?"

Everyone looked at Margot's leg.

"Oh, no, not anymore. That happened on the way to the falls.

"Did you get it wet?"

She shook her head.

He disappeared into his tent again and came back with a first-aid kit. "Turn your headlamp on," he told her, "and hold it to help me see what I'm doing."

He used some purified water and gauze to wipe the wound, which didn't look too bad to me. He sterilized the blade of a folding knife with a lighter and cut open a small piece of plastic.

"What's that?" Hugh wanted to know. His question surprised me; I'd seen it on the website.

"A piece of a plastic straw. You seal one end with a match or lighter, fill the piece with antibiotic cream, which this is, and seal the other end. You can use them for toothpaste or anything similar. Salt, pepper, even hot sauce."

"I have my own, actually," Margot told Conroy. "I saw that on your website."

Conroy looked up at her. "But you didn't use it?"

She shrugged. "I guess I didn't think the wound was that bad."

As Conroy finished his ministrations and covered the wound with a band-aid, he said, "This is a bacteria-rich environment, and it's humid, which the little buggers love. I don't recommend taking chances."

Whatever else I might have thought of Conroy, I couldn't say he didn't take care of his hikers. I couldn't say he didn't know his stuff.

And was I imagining things, or did Conroy seem a little pissed at Hugh for not having read the information on his website?

Alone in my tent, I went back over the day. Thinking about my conversation with Erik, I wanted to find a conversational topic for tomorrow that was on safer ground than his grief. As for Margot, it seemed she was an interesting contrast of sweet, home-town girl and adventure woman. I liked her. Owen was beginning to worry me—though, again, I couldn't have said why. And Hugh… there was nothing more to say. And "nothing more" is what I should say to anyone else, or I might give myself away.

Other than that one indiscreet comment, I wondered whether Conroy appreciated that I'd done nothing, and had said nothing to indicate that we'd ever fucked. Or that we'd ever even met. Very likely he did, but that didn't mean I'd ever know it from him. I went back mentally to Saturday night at the resort, when he'd showed up unannounced, shared a joint, and come on to me. He said he'd made sure everyone who'd signed up was a competent hiker, so even if he hadn't seen Hugh in a while he must have known who he was. If Conroy was trying to avoid him that night, would he merely have wanted to be somewhere other than his own suite, and I was handy? That seemed the most likely. But then there was the sex, almost. And couldn't Conroy have refused to allow Hugh to sign up? Or was it that with so few hikers, Conroy needed the money?

I fell asleep with that puzzle unsolved.

And then I woke up to the sound of my tent zipper opening very slowly. There was just enough moonlight that I could see a shape, a person, opening the flap. I sat up.

"Nathan." I barely heard Conroy's voice. "It's me. Don't speak."

When he was fully inside, he zipped the flap as slowly and quietly as he had unzipped it. WTF!? He couldn't possibly be here for sex, so—what?

"I need to talk to you." I waited while he took a breath or two. "You're being really cool about this, so I'm just letting you know that I had to talk to Hugh. It can't come out that you and I have—you know."

"I get that. Anything else?"

"Hugh didn't get it. I'm pretty sure you've noticed how he is around me, so I wanted you to know I've talked to him."

And, I thought, *maybe you wanted to make sure I behave, especially after my comment earlier.* Whatever. But—here was my chance. "Does he know about me?"

"Not as far as I know."

"So why did you invite two guys you've fucked to go on the same trip?" That time the edge in my voice was intentional. And it was a hard edge.

I heard him breathe out through his nose. "Here's the thing. I didn't invite him. When I met him, over a year ago now, he was going by his first name, which is David. When he signed up—email—I didn't know it was the same guy.

And as you've seen, he's not exactly being discreet. That's why I asked him to be sweep on the trail."

I almost laughed aloud. "So he snuck up on you?"

"That's about it."

Hysterical. This was hysterical. The sure-of-himself, confidant, man-of-the world Conroy Finnegan had been bested by a fawning former fuck!

Conroy could tell I was practically hysterical with laughter, and I'm sure he heard my strangled, "Jesus Fucking Christ!" from behind the hand I was pressing against my mouth.

He said, "It's not funny."

I couldn't speak for smothering my laughter.

"Well…," he admitted at last, "I guess it kind of is." And then we were both rolling with laughter around my small tent, struggling to keep from making noise. To no avail.

My tent flap unzipped again, noisily this time.

"What's so funny?"

OMG! It was Hugh. David. Whoever the hell he was. His voice wasn't loud, but it was loud enough to be heard over the sounds made by whatever critters were awake in this tropical paradise. Everyone in the group must have heard not only Conroy and me, but also Hugh.

Even in the darkness I could tell Conroy was trying hard to get himself under control so he could fabricate some response, but Hugh appearing like that made the entire situation even funnier. If I could have stopped laughing, I would have shouted, "David Hugh Campion, you've been punk'd!"

Finally, Conroy mumbled, "I'll tell you later." And he managed to sit up and then crawl out of the tent. He zipped it back up from the outside, and I interpreted the next sounds I heard to be Conroy leading Hugh back to his tent before heading for his own.

I lay there in the dark, chuckling softly, for several minutes. The next-to-last thing I remember thinking before falling back to sleep was that it seemed likely Hugh would figure out that there was history of some kind between Conroy and me. And I'd have been willing to bet that Hugh wouldn't take it nearly as well as I had. Hugh obviously wasn't through with Conroy. I was.

The last thing I thought was that I couldn't wait to describe this scene Nina. I couldn't wait to tell her she'd been right. I was ready to give her that, now.

CHAPTER SEVENTEEN

The next morning's hike was more of the same: magnificent views, crazy switchbacks on the trail, ups and downs and ups again. We forded another stream and kept going until we came to the campsites at Hanakoa. It was evident someone had been here last night, so I guessed Conroy had been right to camp where we'd been.

Just past the campsite was another stream, the Hanakoa. I watched as Conroy and then Owen in front of me forded it. Hugh was in sweep position again today.

Suddenly Conroy turned left and disappeared. When I got to the spot where he'd turned, I couldn't figure out how he'd known where to go into the overgrown plant life, but soon I noticed the occasional bright pink ribbon tied to a twig.

I had to assume we were headed inland for the Hanakoa Falls.

Conroy had been right; the trail here was very different from the trail to yesterday's waterfall. We hugged eroded ledges that overlooked the stream below, or we pushed our way through densely shadowed overgrowth in directions that would have confounded me, but Conroy seemed certain of the way.

For the first part of the trail I kept half my attention on Margot, who was right behind me. But she seemed fine today. I forced myself to stop worrying about her; because of the ways she reminded me of Ellie, whose wedding I was going to miss, I put it down to misplaced guilt.

I was getting annoyed with Owen, and I imagined Conroy was as well. He kept talking and talking, commenting about everything. Sometimes he'd see something that reminded him, inexplicably to me, of something in his personal life, and out would pour two or three stories about people only Owen knew. Evidently he was back to his manic phase.

Was he manic-depressive, I wondered? But he hadn't seemed depressed last night, just anxious and withdrawn. And usually the moods of manic-depressives didn't vacillate that quickly. And oh, yes—sleepy. That's how he'd looked. Not just anxious, but also sleepy.

As I followed behind Owen, doing my best to ignore his chatter, it hit me. He was taking drugs. I couldn't be sure about it, but he must have taken something yesterday morning and again today to perk himself up, and at some point yesterday evening he'd taken something to bring himself down again.

I'd never seen Alden when he was using. I'd had only a glimpse into how Ellie's friend Gordon had been when he was using. Was I assuming facts not in evidence, to borrow a courtroom term? Was I over-sensitive because of how much Alden's disappearance had hurt me?

I couldn't be completely sure about Owen, but my gut was churning. Should I tell Conroy? What could he do? Would the "up" drug Owen had taken mean that Crawler's Ledge, which we'd get to after this trek to the falls, would be more dangerous for him?

I watched Owen closely for several minutes to see if his footing seemed sure, and I didn't see any signs of instability or of misjudging distances. Still….

I heard the falls, and then I saw a sign warning of falling rocks, and then the falls came into view. Hanakoa Falls looked much like those at Hanakapi'ai: a long ribbon of white falling from a great height between vertical ridges of green, splashing hard and fast into a pool of water surrounded by boulders.

Conroy came to a stop, and there was no room to go around him, so everyone stopped.

He had to raise his voice to be heard. "This is as close as we'll go. The falls start way beyond where we can see," and he pointed up and toward the top of the falls, "way up the slope. So we're seeing only the final portion." Grinning, he glanced at each of us in turn. "I hope you agree it was worth it."

Each of us gazed obediently up at the top of the falls. As my eyes followed the descent of one lacy, scalloped shape after another, I waited for something, some feeling, some sense of awe, to warm my chest or crowd into my brain or stir my guts. I was impressed with the beauty of the exotic environment, but nothing else came to me. Where, I wondered, was the magic I'd felt at Ke'e Beach? Why was I less overwhelmed by this than I'd been by the magnificent views of the first morning's hike, or the glorious scenery from the boat?

Conroy called out to Hugh, the last in line. "Hugh, do you think you can lead us out, or should I work my way back there?"

I watched Hugh's face carefully, and I was pretty sure he looked even more unhappy than he had yesterday. "I'll be fine," he shouted, but he didn't look fine.

At the first opportunity I stepped to one side, pretending I wanted one last look, and Owen passed me, chatting away to Margot, who was now ahead of him.

I gave Conroy a glance full of meaning so he'd pay attention to me, and I waited for Owen to get a little ahead.

"I can't be sure," I told Conroy in as quiet a voice as I could with the falls in the background, "but I think Owen is self-medicating."

Conroy's head pulled back a little in surprise. "For what?"

"That, I can't tell you. But I think he's taking some kind of amphetamine in the mornings and a barbiturate after dinner."

I saw something like recognition flash across Conroy's face. "Okay, well you're the expert on drugs. What do you think I should do? Will this be a problem on the Ledge?"

"I've been watching him. His balance seems fine, and he's not making bad choices for where he steps. But even if I knew what he'd taken, I couldn't tell you for sure that he'll be okay. He's kind of manic right now. If he calms down a little, he might be fine."

"Okay, but I don't need him thinking he can conquer the world when he's a step away from certain death."

"I get that. And I don't know what to tell you."

Conroy gestured for me to move forward. Behind me, he said, "Maybe I should ask him if he's okay. I wouldn't have to say I thought he was on something, and really I can't even be sure he is. But if I stress the dangers to him in private, maybe he'll be more careful."

We walked in silence for a few minutes. Then, "Nathan, will you help me assess him? Will you walk right behind him and keep an eye out?"

"I'll do my best." It wasn't my job. It wasn't my responsibility. But even though I resented being put into this position, I didn't want anyone plunging hundreds of feet into the surf crashing onto volcanic rock.

Back on the main part of the trail, Conroy took over the lead again, and I stepped in behind Owen. Almost immediately we came to another campsite area.

"Water break," Conroy called. He approached Owen and said something to him, and the two of them moved a little off to the side.

I tried not to watch, but I kind of wanted to know what Conroy was saying, and how Owen would respond.

Erik moved to stand beside me. He didn't look toward Conroy, but he said, "What d'you suppose that's about?"

I wasn't going to tell Erik I thought Owen was taking drugs. "I hope he's telling Owen not to talk quite so much."

Erik chuckled. "Hard out." He took a swig of water. "Sorry. What d'you Yanks say? 'For sure?'" After a moment of companionable silence he said, "Wonder if the bloke will pack a sad again tonight."

I turned toward Erik. "You're doing this deliberately, aren't you?"

"Eh?"

"Throwing all these Kiwi terms at me."

He laughed aloud. "Just trying to educate you, is all."

"So, 'pack a sad?'"

"Go all moody. Downer."

So Erik had noticed, too. Maybe he was no expert, no more than I was, but his comment made me glad I'd said something to Conroy. For whatever that was worth.

His pack on the ground at his feet, Conroy called everyone to attention, and we gathered around him.

"Couple of Hawaiian terms for you. Mauka is how you refer to the mountain side of a trail. Makai is the ocean side. There's a good reason the language has terms for these relative positions, as you might have realized already. Not too much farther ahead you'll start to see signs warning you about danger. That would be the famous Crawler's Ledge. I know you've heard this before, but I'm gonna tell you again anyway. This trail is dangerous."

He looked at each of us in turn, his face heavy with warning. "On your left, mauka, you'll be penned in by rock. Unforgiving, straight up for many feet, rock. Only a few feet away, and sometimes less than that, is the makai. There will be nothing but empty space between you and a fall that will last only until your body smashes onto the rocks below. It might be carried out to sea in pieces, or it might lie there until it's picked apart by sea birds, depending on the tide and just where it falls. Don't be that dead body. I want you all going home and bragging to everyone you know about your prowess on one of the most perilous stretches you'll ever see."

He pulled a trekking pole out of his pack. "This ledge is when you will need this pole I made you bring. You will want to keep it on the makai, your right, to help you balance away from the edge. Do not," and he looked at Owen, "make the mistake of thinking you'll have any use for another pole. There might be a few places you would have room, but it won't help you. And the last thing you want is to push yourself away from the rock. You should be working with all your might to stay close to that rock. Got it?"

"Got it," Margot said, her voice bright with enthusiasm.

Poles in hands, we all hefted our packs back onto our shoulders again.

"Ready?"

We said we were. I wasn't so sure.

Somehow Margot got between Owen and me. I was still able to watch him, though. He'd stopped chattering, though whether that was due to his private conversation with Conroy or the dire description of what lay ahead I couldn't tell.

In less than half a mile, if I gauged correctly, we started to see the warning signs Conroy had predicted. They got more urgent as we went forward toward a cliff face that loomed ahead of us. And soon we were on it.

Conroy had not exaggerated. The trail, if it could be called that, was dizzying and spectacular. Some people say they feel the most alive when they're doing something that brings them close to death. I hadn't felt like that on my climb up Mount Chocorua, but I felt it in spades here on Crawler's Ledge.

Almost every step was a challenge. There were places where I felt safer than others, but for the most part every step was an opportunity to find out what it might mean that there's no bridge between life and death here on Kaua'i. And there was no help; there were no guardrails, no hand-holds. It was all up to me.

It was exhilarating. I loved it.

Although I was enthralled by what I was experiencing,

I managed to monitor Owen part of the time—not that there was much anyone could have done about it if he'd had trouble, though maybe we could have turned around. But he seemed to be doing as well as anyone else. I saw no signs that he was under the influence of anything that wasn't affecting me.

We were maybe halfway along the ledge part of the trail, by my reckoning anyway, and when a gust of wind came whipping out of nowhere. It lifted a small canvas cover completely off of the top of Owen's pack and sent it flying toward Margot.

Two things happened at once. Margot gave a little scream. And she disappeared over the edge.

The world seemed to stop. Reality had ended, and some other state had taken its place. For what felt like an eternity, I stared at the empty space where Margot had been. Then I saw Conroy drop to the ground and crawl toward the edge, so I did the same. Owen flattened himself against the rock, seemingly paralyzed. Behind me, Erik and Hugh also dropped to the ground. I inched forward until I could see over the edge, knowing I had to look and yet really not wanting to see what I was sure would be there; how could Margot be anything other than body parts?

But instead of bloody bones hundreds of feet below, there was a living Margot, on her right side, facing the cliff edge and gasping for breath. A ledge of rock, maybe eight feet below the trail, had stopped her fall. It extended about six feet away from the cliff and was maybe ten feet long. Margot was very close to the edge.

"Margot!" Conroy called. "Don't move! We'll get you up!"

He sat upright, shrugged out of his pack, and opened it. He pulled out a length of rope. Owen was still paralyzed, but I was watching Conroy, who had started tying knots in the rope at about every ten to twelve inches.

"Nathan! I'm going to crawl toward you and give you

one end of the rope. You move toward me, slowly. Don't cross in front of Owen. Erik, can you hold Nathan's feet? And Hugh, you stabilize Erik."

"What are we going to do?" I asked before starting my crawl forward.

"Each of us will hold one end of the rope. I'm hoping Margot isn't badly hurt, just had the wind knocked out of her. If I'm right, as soon as she's able, I'll drop the loop of rope down to her. Then you and I will help pull her up. Got that?"

I gazed at him in disbelief. But it did seem to be the only option, beyond leaving her there. "But you've got no one to hold you in place. What if you fall, too?" Neither of us looked at the frozen statue that was Owen, who was still on his feet and pressed against the rock face.

"A risk we'll have to take."

Another burst of wind whipped toward us just as Conroy flung one end of rope toward me, but I caught the end and started tying knots. I felt Erik grip my ankles. I looked down at Margot.

She was moving one of her arms, feeling in front of her for the edge, and when her fingers found it she jerked her arm back and gasped.

"Margot?" Conroy called. "Are you hurt?"

She flapped her hand a few times to indicate that she was trying to regain her breath. Maybe thirty seconds went by before I heard, "I don't think so."

"Can you flex your feet? One at a time."

She did.

"Is your vision normal?"

"Yes. Nothing double. One of these scenes is enough."

I felt an irrational sense of laughter trying to find its way out of my body, but I stifled it. I knew Margot was going for humor, but her voice was thin and very shaky.

"Very slowly, try to raise your left leg just a few inches straight up. See if anything hurts."

She did as Conroy told her and said, "Nope."

"Again, very slowly, see if you can bend your right knee and move that leg at all. Don't move it very far, just see if it hurts."

"It's fine," she said. "Can you get me out of here now?"

"Did you hear me tell Nathan what we're doing?"

"Yes."

"When I throw the loop, you grab it unless it goes over the edge. If it does, wait until we pull it back enough for you to reach it without moving."

"Okay."

It flew up, was caught by the wind, and did indeed go over the edge.

"Nathan, pull up some of the rope slowly. I'll do the same."

When it was within Margot's reach, she grabbed it and made a kind of gasping sob. She held it against her like the life-line it was.

"Hold it with both hands, and slowly pull on it so you can sit up and lean your back against the rock. Nathan and I will hold it taught."

Conroy and I pulled gently on the rope. It took her a few minutes, and even more tries, before she was able to do as he said.

"Does anything hurt now?"

"Just my pride."

Conroy chuckled and shook his head. "Do you want to rest for a minute?"

I saw her head nod. I could barely see the side of her face. Her eyes were tight shut, and tears streamed down her cheeks. I saw, rather than heard her take shuddering breaths.

My pack had shifted awkwardly on my shoulders. I was a little afraid it would slide up toward my head and overbalance me, but there didn't seem to be anything I could do about it at this point.

Finally Margot called up, "What next?"

"Put the rope in front of you below the waist strap of

your pack. Then use the rock behind you to help you get out of your pack. Lean against the rock. Let the pack fall to one side."

"That will be tricky."

"Yes, but you can do it. You know how to get a frame pack off your back, girl. You're intrepid."

Maybe that helped. In any case, Margot managed this feat.

"Okay," Conroy called, "Now keep the rope in front of you and, very carefully, move sideways away from your pack, and when you're far enough away from it, come to a standing position with your back still against the rock. Nathan and I will keep the rope taught."

It was painful to watch her do this, not because she was hurt, because she wasn't, but because she was so terrified. I was terrified for her. It was an eternity before she managed to stand fully. Her legs shook.

"Okay," she said, and her voice sounded a little more stable. "Now?"

"Now comes the hard part."

Margot let out a barking laugh.

"I want you to turn around so you face the cliff. Keep the rope around your waist, and turn until it's gone around you twice. Look up, not down. The ledge is plenty wide enough for you to do this safely; it just feels like it isn't. Once you've turned, facing the rock, you'll need to grasp the rope that leads up to me with your right hand, and grasp the other side that Nathan's holding in your left. We'll wait." To me he said, "If you can get any closer to me, do that."

As I crawled several inches toward Owen, I heard his strangled voice say, "What should I do?"

"Do you think you can get past me?" Conroy asked.

"I think so."

"Do it. Then drop, and hold my ankles."

Margot had closed her eyes again, and I saw her take three of four very deep, very shaky breaths. She kept her right hand pressed against the cliff. She started the turn slowly, and then in one quick movement she was facing the rock. Her left hand reached a little wildly for the rope on that side of her, found it, and gripped it tightly. Obediently looking up, she turned until there were two circles of rope around her waist. She worked her hands up, following the rope, and Conroy and I moved closer together, bringing the two rope lengths with us.

"Gather your strength now, Margot. When you're ready, I want you to grip the rope very tightly. Find a knot with each hand and hold onto that. You'll need to use your feet to brace yourself against the rock and push up as much as you can while Nathan and I pull the rope up. Do you understand?"

"I think so."

"It won't be easy, and it won't be quick. But from what you've told me about yourself, I know you can do this. Let me know when you're ready."

Conroy and I crawled closer together, Erik following behind me. I had no idea what Hugh was doing.

"Okay," Margot called. "Let's go."

It seemed to take forever. Margot grunted and struggled, and a few times one of her boots would slip and she'd give a little cry. She stopped a number of times to pant and re-stabilize herself. At one point Erik released one of my ankles and grasped the bottom of my frame pack with one hand and then the other. This seemed to give him more control on my position, because the shoulder straps were firmly on my shoulders.

Finally Margot's head appeared above the edge of the trail, dirty and tear-stained. With her teeth gritted, she managed to scramble up onto the trail. She crawled over to where she could sit with her back to the cliff and began to sob. Conroy immediately moved to sit beside her. He draped an arm around her shoulders and let her cry until she was ready to stop.

I watched him, feeling proud of my role in Margot's rescue, but also conflicted about Conroy. Since I'd met him, my feelings about him had bounced back and forth, around and around, and most recently had landed on disdain and disrespect. But now—well, shit. It amazed me to see how calm Conroy had remained, how well he had coached Margot, how he had known exactly what to do. And now, he just held her shoulders. He didn't speak, he just let her cry. It was the perfect thing to do.

We'd been sitting there for maybe five minutes, and Margot's weeping had subsided to the occasional catch of her breath, when a couple approached from behind. There was no way they could pass with us spread out on the narrow trail, so we all had to take off our packs and stand, plastered against the cliff face, to let them pass. It was hairy, but they managed. I watched them disappear out of sight. They'd said nothing but "Hi" and "Thanks." I don't think they had any sense of what had happened.

When they were gone, Margot said, "My pack."

Owen must have decided he was now part of the rescue. "Should have brought that up first."

I don't think Erik liked Owen any better than I did. He said, "I have more faith in a leader who puts his people above their gear."

Conroy gave Erik a wry grin and said, "I'll get the pack." I looked at him, aghast. He turned to me. "You guys need to hold onto the rope while I go down. I'll send the pack up on the rope, you send the rope back to me, and I'll climb back up. Got it?"

I don't know where this came from, but I said, "I should do it."

"You? Why?"

"I'm smaller and lighter. If I have trouble it will be easier to pull me up than you."

From behind me I heard Erik's voice. "Good-oh, mate."

Without waiting for Conroy to say anything, I crawled toward the edge.

I couldn't say why, but I wasn't nervous. This didn't seem like a big deal, though looking back I think it probably was. I watched Conroy throw one end of the rope over the edge and then move back toward Erik. I had an odd moment as I started to go over, rather like there was an abyss below me that went on forever, but I didn't let myself pause. The last thing I saw before going over was Margot's face, her eyes full of what looked to me like gratitude.

It wasn't difficult to lower myself to the ledge below. I sat with my back to the cliff, tied the pack securely, and called, "Haul it up!"

I listened to the scraping sounds of the pack as it rose, bumping into the cliff face as it went. A few bits of rock tumbled down onto me. I gazed out across the vast ocean from this tremendous height, with only a few feet of tenuous ledge between me and that paradise I wasn't ready to find myself entering. I had only a short time alone there, but it was long enough for me to feel overwhelmed by the glory of where I was and what I had just done. My heart seemed to swell, and I swear that I felt both Gram and Neil there with me.

I had found what I'd come here to find.

Conroy spoke to the group. "Before we go any farther, let's all make sure everything on our packs, everything we're wearing or carrying, is secured."

It was everything I could do not to look at Owen. Conroy, I thought, showed remarkable tact by not referring directly to what had happened.

Margot's trekking pole had gone all the way over the edge, never to be seen again by human eyes.

Conroy turned to Owen. "You brought two poles, right?

I'm sure you won't mind giving one of them to Margot."

For a split second I thought Owen would protest. But he pulled out his second pole and handed it to her.

She seemed reluctant, but she accepted it. "Um, Conroy," He looked at her and waited. "I don't think I can keep going."

I saw Conroy freeze for just a second. He took a deep breath before he spoke. "We're nearly half-way to the other side."

"And then tomorrow we'll have to come back again. I just can't do it."

Owen had a problem with this. "My trekking pole!"

Margot's "I'll reimburse you" was drowned out by Erik's drawling, "Aye, but what? It isn't a Gucci." Owen said nothing more.

I could almost see the wheels turning inside Conroy's head as he tried to decide how to respond to Margot. Then, for the second time that day, my voice spoke before I knew what it was going to say.

"I'll go back with her." Conroy started to shake his head, but I gave him an intense look. "I've found what I came here to find."

We locked eyes, and I saw his face change from concern to recognition as what I'd said registered, and as he realized there was no arguing with me. "Nathan, I don't know what to say."

I smiled at him. "Say 'Aloha.'"

He smiled back. "Aloha, Nathan." He held his hand out for me to shake. He turned to Margot. "Aloha, Margot."

"Aloha, Conroy. Thank you for everything."

I looked at Margot. "Ready?"

She let out a long breath, nodded, and smiled. "Ready."

CHAPTER EIGHTEEN

I let Margot lead. "I'll follow your pace," I told her. "I don't want you to go faster than you feel comfortable."

At first her pace was snail-slow; no surprise. Another gust of wind hit us, and Margot froze and then winced. She seemed to be trying to dig her fingers into the cliff face on her right side, but there was something wrong.

"Margot? Are you okay?"

"Yeah. My right shoulder's a little sore. I landed on it." She moved forward again.

It took us considerably longer to retrace our steps along the ledge than it had taken to get to where Margot had fallen.

As soon as we were clear of the dangerous part of the trail, Margot nearly collapsed onto a grassy spot and sat with folded arms on her bent knees, breathing hard. She bent her head forward. I sat beside her, silent, waiting patiently, taking in the scene, reveling in the feeling that Gram and Neil had come with me up from Margot's ledge and were still here, traveling back with us.

After several minutes, voice muffled because of her posture, Margot said, "You must think I'm a complete loser."

"I think you're incredibly brave," I told her. "I totally respect that you're in touch with yourself enough to know you needed to turn around, and you had the guts to say so. I mean it." I gave a short laugh, hoping she'd appreciate the humor in my next comment. "Just imagine if Owen had fallen. We'd still be back there trying to convince him just to sit up."

I heard her chuckle and then, without lifting her head, she said, "You had to go down for my pack. If that had been Owen, someone would have had to go down to get him *and* his pack."

I laughed aloud. Poor Owen.

"But we're being mean." Margot lifted her head, eyes forward toward the ocean. "There's always one."

"One what?"

"One person in a hiking group like Owen, someone who doesn't fit in, sometimes for reasons that aren't clear. Someone who feels left out and tries to compensate by acting like the life of the party."

I froze. What if that had been what was going on with Owen? What if his behavior had nothing to do with drugs, and the effort of being the life of the party just exhausted him more and more as the day wore on? Maybe when he was too tired to put on an act any longer, that was when he got anxious. Wishing I could text Conroy to say I might have been wrong about Owen, I barely heard Margot's next comment.

"I've been on a number of guided hikes like this one. It's predictable. Once or twice, I've been that one person. It can feel like hell."

I gave that the space it deserved. Then, "Would you sign up for another Finnegan's Walk?"

She turned her face toward me and grinned. "In a flash. That man knows what he's doing. He's prepared, competent, and very good in a crisis."

She waved a hand in the air and faced forward again. "Plus he's super easy on the eyes."

I laughed again. Should I say anything? A few seconds later I realized I didn't need to.

She turned toward me again. "How well do you know him? Forgive my forwardness here, but you've seen me in a pretty vulnerable state. So—are you lovers?" Her tone was completely matter-of fact, no emotion, no judgement, just honest curiosity.

I think my jaw dropped. "I—how—what?"

She laughed gleefully and let her arms fall. "Don't look so shocked, Nathan. I mean, don't get me wrong, you're a lot more discreet than Hugh. That poor guy...." She shook her head. "But I can see you and Conroy together. That makes sense to me."

"Okay. Why?"

She turned her body toward me and sat cross-legged. "You're both competent, experienced, strong, brave, and classy. And you're pretty easy on the eyes, yourself." She tilted her head. "Have I gone too far? You know, once you get me talking, I can say the stupidest things. It's like I don't know when to stop."

I shook my head and looked at the ground to pull up a few bits of plant material. "I wouldn't use the term 'lovers' to describe how I know Conroy. I mean, yeah, we know each other that way. But it's never been romantic."

I dropped the bits of plant, mutilated now. "I didn't come here because of Conroy. I came here because the way he described it to me gave me hope of coming to a kind of reconciliation for a couple of things I wasn't happy about in my life. I won't go into details, but I'll just say he wasn't wrong."

Another gleeful laugh. "See? Another point in his favor." She let a beat go by. Then, "How about you? Would you go on another walk with Conroy?"

I smiled, partly for her and partly for myself. "No."

Margot and I agreed to camp in the same spot as the night before, provided we could find it again and no one else had claimed it. We got there sooner than I expected, not having done a detour to the Hanakoa falls on the return trip, and got our tents set up. By the time we sat down to relax, Margot had told me more about herself than I think she would have expected to.

While it was true she'd signed up to give herself a break before job-hunting, she told me she'd started going on hiking and camping trips as a teenager to escape her home life. Her father was emotionally abusive, her mother was beaten down, depressed, and alcoholic. Her three brothers had tormented her, and though two of them left the house before she went to college, the attention from her father was becoming frightening.

"I figured, you know, either I got away, or I got raped. So I got away. Fortunately, I decided I liked going on these trips."

We were munching on whatever we had in our packs that didn't need to be cooked. I watched her face for long enough that she said, "What?"

"The first time I saw you," I told her, "I got an impression that was absolutely nothing like what you've just told me about your life."

She popped a slice of dried mango into her mouth. "Tell me."

"Health-food. Wholesome. Church-goer. Norman Rockwell."

At that last category, she laughed. "Oh my god! I hope none of the people he painted had a home life like mine."

"Do you think it influenced your choice of career?"

"Absolutely. I want to find people who are going through that and help it stop."

"I think we're headed in similar directions." So I explained the cryptic comment I'd made the day I picked her up; that is, I told her why addiction fascinated me. I told her about Alden, and about Ellie's friend who got hooked on fentanyl our freshman year. I told her about how addiction traps people into spirals of desperation, reward, guilt, and more desperation. I talked about some of the many reasons addiction can start.

"You've seen this first hand," I said, "if you saw much of your mother's problem."

"I guess so. But I didn't see it quite like you describe it. Probably because I felt like a victim of it."

"And probably also because she couldn't describe it to

you. I mean, I learned about it from Alden, but it was when he was in a clean period, before going back to it. But I can tell you that when he went back to it, I felt like a victim."

She offered me a slice of dried mango, and we both chewed thoughtfully for a minute. Then I asked, "Why this trip? Why the Kalalau?"

She waved an arm toward the ocean, which we could barely see from the campsite, there was so much tropical greenery in the way. "I'd never seen anything like this. I stumbled on Conroy's site while I was searching for information on tents, and I saw this trip advertised. I thought, 'Paradise. Yeah, I could take that.' So I signed up. It was all very spontaneous, very live-in-the-now. Very zen." She giggled. "And you?"

I thought for a minute; how much should I dump on her? How much do I want to say, and how much would she want to hear? It all seemed to center on music.

The year Neil died, there had been the song his fiancée played after his funeral, the message of which had been "Go grab your life and live it," along with my surprise that he'd liked bluegrass. Then there'd been another song, "Buy for Me the Rain," with a very similar message, a song Neil and loved and I'd never paid any attention to. Then there had been my discovery, during Gram's funeral arrangements, that she'd been very fond of particular hymns, which had been followed by my realization of her deep religious feelings.

To top things off, Conroy had lured me to paradise with beautiful images, yes; but the music of Keola Beamer and other slack-key guitarists had impressed me so much I'd bought their music to play on my own. And, of course, there was "Bali Ha'i," my special island, and "South Pacific," about the laugh of someone you can't resist. So, music had called to my spiritual need to connect with Neil and Gram in a way I should have done before they'd died, a connection that I'd thought maybe, just maybe I could feel under the influence of Kaua'i's magic.

I was about to tell Margot all of this, and I got out my phone, fully charged from my solar charger. I pulled up Keola Beamer's album, "Tales from the Dream Guitar," and I started the first song. I let it play, not sure at what point I'd start talking.

Margot spoke first. "That is so lovely! What is it?"

"That's the call. The call to me to find a connection I wasn't awake enough to make when I wish I had."

Before I could begin to tell her what that meant, I realized someone was approaching our campsite from uphill. Margot saw him first and gasped. I turned to look.

He was tall and skinny, dressed in jeans and a T-shirt. His clothes had no doubt once been whole but now had a few tears and holes. He looked clean enough, but he definitely had an unkempt look about him. His light brown hair was in braids that hung back over his shoulders, and his crinkly beard was full and long enough to tickle his collar bone. There was a dark green bandana tied over his skull. He carried something in a sack made of what might once have been a plaid flannel shirt.

He stopped walking about ten feet from us. He nodded first to Margot and then to me, and then he pointed to my phone. "I heard your music. I love that stuff."

In a flash, I realized who this guy was. Or, rather, *what* he was. I stood, moved toward him, and shook his hand. "I'm honored," I told him. His eyes and his smile told me we were on the same wavelength.

Margot had stood as well. "Nathan? What's going on?"

I turned toward her. "I think we are in the presence of one of the Kalalau outlaws." I looked back at the guy, whose mouth was lifted in a sly smile.

"Busted," he said.

"Outlaw?" Margot echoed.

I invited the guy to sit and introduced myself and Margot. He said his name was Wayland. I pulled out some dried apples and bread to offer him.

"Thanks," he said. "Appreciate it."

"I don't want to pretend I know very much about you," I told him. "Would you mind telling us a little about how you live here on the island?"

He must have talked for half an hour, barely stopping for breath. I figured it was likely he didn't see a lot of other people, so once he started talking, the words just kept following each other. He'd been living on the Na Pali Coast, he said, for three years now. He'd come to Oahu to surf for a year to get away from his hectic life in Chicago, where he'd been in finance in some way I didn't understand. But he'd been turned off by the commercialism on Oahu. Then someone had told him about Na Pali. Other than an occasional trip out to get supplies with money he still had from his former life, he'd been here ever since.

"Are there other outlaws?" Margot wanted to know.

"Sure. Some I like, some I don't. Mostly men. Sometimes a guy will have a woman with him, and sometimes she stays with him for a while or goes on to some other man, but mostly the women leave before they've been here more than a few weeks. It's a tough life for a woman, what with all the female-starved men around."

Margot looked a little concerned. I asked, "Is there any reason Margot should be worried?"

Wayland shook his head. "Not from me, and not from most of the guys here. We'd put a stop to things if it looked otherwise. Not to worry. But if you'll bring that music with you, I'd like to invite you both to dinner at my place."

"Dinner?"

"Caught a pig two days ago. Smoked most of it in another guy's smoker—which I helped him make—and gave him some of the pork, but I'd be real pleased if you'd join me tonight. I have some taro and some local greens as well." He grinned broadly, and I noticed a dark spot in his lower jaw where he was missing a tooth. "And I can offer you a fresh mango for dessert. Better than the dried stuff you're eating."

I could tell Margot was hesitant, but I believed what he'd said, and I kind of wanted to see where he lived. I asked Margot, "What do you think?"

"Look, Wayland," she said, "I appreciate your generosity, but I've already had enough excitement for one day. Going into the woods where I know there are guys sniffing around for someone like me? I don't think I want to do that."

She was right. I knew she was right, but I was still disappointed.

Wayland nodded and stood. "In that case, how about if I leave this with you, and I'll go back and fetch some mangoes?"

He bent over and set the cloth sack onto the ground near where Margot and I were still sitting, and he opened it. Smoked pork. He'd brought it with him, probably figuring we'd be reluctant to follow him into the wilderness.

"Wow," I said. But then the hairs on my neck tingled. Forcing myself to avoid glancing at all the stuff Margot and I had pulled out of our packs, a lot of which would have come in very handy for him and his friends, I looked up at him. "Um, you live alone?"

He gave me an assessing glance. "You afraid I'll bring an army of us down on you or something?"

I decided it was time I stood up again. I wasn't as tall as Wayland, and he stood slightly uphill from me, but it still made me feel more equal. "Like Margot said, we appreciate your generosity. But, hell, man, we don't know you. We don't know how you live, or who else lives nearby, or anything else about you. And from what I know about the outlaws, scavenging is a survival technique."

Wayland looked a little surprised, but he said nothing. Given his silence, I kept talking. "I've also heard that you seldom approach hikers, tourists, people like Margot and me. So, right now it seems like you want to trade smoked pork for music. That's fair, as long as that's all it is."

227

Wayland's head shook slowly side to side, and he looked almost sad. He glanced down at the pork and then back up at me. "See, now, this is exactly why I'm here. I couldn't take the suspicion all around me out there." He waved an arm in the general direction of civilization. "I couldn't bring myself to distrust everything and everyone. But, hey, I get it, you got a lady with you, and she feels vulnerable. That's fair, too. So I'll answer your question. I live alone. I'm going back to get mangoes. Fresh, juicy, delicious mangoes. And I offer you my pork. In return I'd love to hear some music and maybe have a little of the water I believe you've purified."

Our eyes met, and I saw nothing in his but openness. Again, I held my right hand out. "Deal."

He left the pork and disappeared back into the wilds of paradise.

"Are you okay with this, Margot? I should have asked before agreeing."

She grinned. "Why not? YOLO, right?"

"YOLO? Oh, got it." You only live once.

CHAPTER NINETEEN

While Wayland was gone, Margot and I purified more water and heated some of it to reconstitute another package of the lentil and rice she'd brought.

Maybe ten minutes later, Wayland came back. Alone. He had another cloth sack, this time holding three mangoes and some greens. We combined our bounty like friends who'd known each other for years. Working close together once or twice, I noticed Wayland's body odor was very slight. I would have expected otherwise. He must brave the goat pee and wash himself and his clothes in the streams, and that made me review in my mind whether I'd used enough purifier in our water. But I shook that thought away.

"Are there places around here where you can go into the ocean?" I asked once we sat down to eat. "Or do you stick to the streams for washing?"

He chuckled. "Good question. I have a kayak. Washed up one day with nothing and nobody in it. So I made a paddle. I can get it into the water some days, depending on the tides and the season and whether there's been a storm recently. The ocean, she stays upset for a while after a storm. But sometimes I can go in and fish, though I will say I've had a couple of close calls when I didn't think I'd make it back. So far, so good. And there are times it feels safe to splash around in the surf, maybe fish from the beach. But, yeah, I use the stream for most things."

Margot swallowed a bite of pork. "This is really good, Wayland. Thanks." The she asked, "The place where you live…. What's that like?"

He talked for quite a while, describing what he'd had when he got here, what he'd found to make things with, and sometimes how another resident—which is what he called himself—had helped him, or he had helped someone else.

"There's some competition for resources," he admitted, "but mostly that's not what living here is about. Most of the guys respect that." After swallowing a mouthful of lentils, he said, "I bet it would surprise you to know that I have a pizza oven." He grabbed a handful of greens and shoved them into his mouth.

Margot let out one of her musical laughs. "You're kidding!"

Wayland described a foundation of large stones he and another resident had set into place, with a large, flat stone set onto them. "The dirt around here is great for making things out of clay, so we formed it into a dome on top of the slab. I don't have a kiln, of course, but cooking things inside it kind of baked it enough."

"But... pizza?" Margot sounded like she didn't quite believe him.

"I won't go into all the steps, but I make flour from taro root. It's a bit of a pain to process, but once it's baked, I can use it to make pizza dough. No yeast, though, so the consistency isn't the same. But I have a garden where I grow greens and tomatoes and herbs and things. Onions. Garlic. And shaved pork is great on pizza." He waved a piece of pork at her. "You'd be surprised!"

As I listened to Wayland talk about his way of life here in the Kalalau, the creative ways he'd created a home for himself seemed much less important than the fact that he'd done them. I mean, the guy was literally in the middle of nowhere—no comforts, no conveniences, no ready-made supplies. But this place gave him such an overwhelming sense of belonging that nothing else mattered as much as being here.

I wanted that. As much as it had meant to have made that spiritual connection with Gram and Neil, as true as my statement to Conroy had been—finding what I'd come for—it wasn't the same as feeling like I belonged with them. Because

I didn't. They were dead. I was not. So one part of my quest was over. But not all of it.

We sat in silence for a few minutes, and then Wayland asked Margot, "So what was so exciting about your day?"

In the near darkness, I saw her close her eyes briefly and take a deep breath. She started to speak, but had to stop. Then she said, "Nathan, you tell him. I'm not ready to talk about it."

So I told Wayland about being on Crawler's Ledge, about the wind, about the flap of canvas that had flown into Margot's face, and about her body disappearing.

"Holy shit!" Wayland was obviously impressed. "But—she's here."

"She is. The local gods must have been protecting her, because she landed on a ledge not too far below the trail. It took a while, and a hell of a lot of Margot's courage, but we managed to haul her and then her pack back onto the trail."

"There were others?"

I gave him a brief description of our group, at which point Wayland asked for more details about how we'd rescued Margot. When I'd finished, he said, "I like this Conroy fellow. And as for you," he turned toward Margot, "I like you, too. You are one gutsy lady."

"Intrepid." Margot had found her voice again.

"What?" Wayland asked.

"When I was on the ledge, I was scared out of my mind. I'd never felt so alone, even though everyone up on the trail was doing everything they could to help me. At one point I had to do something I wasn't sure I could do. That's when Conroy called me intrepid. I liked that. It helped."

Wayland got up and stood in front of Margot. He reached his hands down, she took them, and he pulled her gently to her feet.

"Here in the Kalalau," he said, still holding her hands, "some of us have lived long enough and have worked hard enough and shared with others enough that we give each other special names. They reflect dominant characteristics. Mine is Pit Bull, because I never let anything get me, I just keep going. I keep my mind on my goal, and I don't get mad or frustrated. I just don't stop."

He dropped her hands and set his onto the top of her head. "I hereby declare you to be Intrepid. That is your Kalalau name. It will be with you always. You will live up to it in all you do." He dropped his hands to her shoulders and wrapped her in a brief embrace.

She did her best to say "Thank you, Pit Bull," her voice shaking with emotion.

They sat back down. In the minute or so of silence, I felt pleased for Margot—even proud of her—but also a little jealous. This was *my* special island. This was *my* spiritual quest. Margot had earned her name, but she could have earned it anywhere. For me, it was all about the Kalalau.

Wayland spoke next. He asked Margot, "Why did you choose the Kalalau for your trip?" She told him essentially what she'd told me. He turned to me and asked the same question.

What to say? How much to say? But I figured, hell, I'd probably never see Wayland or Margot again. Why not just tell them the truth? After all, I'd been about to spill all to Margot when Wayland had appeared.

So I talked. And talked. Margot and Wayland listened, made an occasional sympathetic sound or comment, but otherwise they just let me go on as long as I needed to. It was the first time I'd put it altogether for anyone, unless I counted that conversation with Conroy over Ethiopian yirgacheffes. Wayland seemed particularly interested when I talked about feeling Gram's and Neil's presence while I waited alone on the ledge.

After several seconds, Margot said, "So this trip really wasn't about Conroy. I didn't know whether to believe you or not, earlier." I saw her body jerk upright. "Oh. Um, Nathan, is it okay…."

I smiled and nodded. It was a risk, I knew, but I believed it was a small one. To Wayland, I said, "I'm gay. And Conroy is bi. We'd seen each other on and off for the past year. But like I'd told Margot, he isn't the reason I'm here. It's completely about my—I don't know, my spiritual quest, I guess."

I turned to Margot. "Tell me something. What was it that gave me away? I mean, how did you know there was anything personal between Conroy and me? Did you hear us laughing last night?"

"Oh, that was only the confirmation. I'd felt pretty sure before then."

"How? I mean, did I gaze at him a lot, or look like I was mooning over him, or something?"

She laughed. "No. I can't really imagine you doing that. At any rate, I didn't see you doing that. No, it wasn't the way you looked at Conroy. It was the way you looked at Hugh."

I made a face. "What are you talking about, girl?"

"Hugh was the one mooning over Conroy. I could tell Conroy wasn't thrilled, but I could also tell you—well, I'm not sure I understood quite what you were feeling. It wasn't exactly jealousy. And it wasn't like you hated Hugh. More like you pitied him."

That made sense, and I nodded again.

"There's one thing that I wondered about though," she said. "Conroy seems so—I think you said he was self-assured. That fits. And he's pretty savvy. So how on earth did he end up leading a hike with two different guys who'd been in a relationship with him? He seems smarter than that."

My turn to laugh. I told her and Wayland what Conroy had revealed to me in my tent, which made Margot laugh almost as hard as I'd laughed last night. But Wayland didn't laugh. He seemed to be thinking about something else entirely, as though the story about Conroy and Hugh were more a distraction than anything of substance.

While Margot and I were still chuckling, Wayland

stood and did the same thing to me he'd done to Margot. As I stood in front of him, having a pretty good idea what he was doing, I doubted him, I doubted his sincerity, I doubted his authenticity. How could he come up with a Kalalau name for me that had any real meaning in it? The word "intrepid" had come from Conroy. But I let Wayland do what he wanted to do.

"I hereby declare you to be Trailblazer." He dropped his hands to my shoulders, and I expected a hug, but he paused. "I was going to name you Seeker, because that fits your quest here. And I sense this is not your first time looking for yourself in the wilderness. But I think you will lead the way for others."

That couldn't be right. I'd been look for Neil, and for Gram. And I'd found them.

"Myself? I'm not looking for myself."

"Aren't you?" And he hugged me.

CHAPTER TWENTY

I didn't sleep very well that night. It rained on us, but that wasn't what kept me awake. Wayland's name for me, and the reason he said it fit, made me feel so many different things. Conflicting things. They flew around my head and landed nowhere. I just hoped I wasn't keeping Margot awake; she'd moved her tent so it was very close to mine after Wayland's visit, and I didn't blame her. I'd almost asked if she wanted to bring her sleeping bag into my tent; there was barely room, but there was room. But I also wanted her to feel intrepid.

God knows what I wanted myself to feel.

Just before I dozed off, it stopped raining. That was when I realized that coming back with Margot would mean I could make it to El Speed's wedding.

Despite the mud on the trail from the rain, we got back to the trailhead in the early afternoon, not stopping for lunch. We sat for a few minutes on Ke'e Beach, looking down the coast along that scene that had so filled me with euphoria a couple of days ago. I didn't expect that to happen again. But it did.

Margot sighed deeply. I did the same, and we smiled at each other.

"There's no place else in the world like this," she said.

"Agreed." I asked, "Do you know what you want to do now?"

"I guess I'll plow through that herd of chickens near the road and then see if that place I was staying can take me tonight. I'd reserved the same room for the end of the hike, but now...."

I brought an image of the place to the front of my mind. It had seemed a little run down, a number of pegs below my

235

resort, which was at least very comfortable. "Did you like it so well you particularly want to stay there again?"

She shrugged. "It's what I can afford."

I reached for my phone and was glad to see I had some reception. I called the office of my resort and asked if they had any openings for tonight.

"One only. Do you want to book?"

"How many adults will it accommodate?"

"There's two bedrooms, and the living room sofa folds out. It's a garden view, not ocean."

"But it has access to the same beach, right?"

"It does."

I booked it and rang off. To Margot, I said, "I've just booked the only room that was available at the resort. There are two bedrooms. I've got to pay for it anyway, so I'm offering you the other bedroom. For free."

Her jaw dropped. "You'd do that for me?"

"I'm blazing the trail. All you have to do is follow." I grinned at her.

She laughed musically into the sparkling air. "All right, but I'm buying dinner. No arguments."

We hefted our packs back on again. I said, "I'm not walking all the way back to the resort."

"So, what, you're flying?"

"Follow me."

I led the way slowly down the row of cars parked along the road, watching to see if it looked like anyone was leaving. Just ahead of us, I saw a young couple with a small child approaching a minivan, and I headed for them.

"Hi," I opened, speaking to the man and sounding as friendly as I could. "Sorry to approach you like this, but my friend and I got stranded by our group. Any chance you could give us a lift back to where we're staying? It's just a little over two miles from here."

The woman looked ready to agree, but the man was a little more suspicious. "Where's your group?"

Margot spoke up. "It's my fault, really. They're still out there," and she pointed south, "on the Kalalau Trail. We were on Crawler's Ledge, and I—well, I fell. I'm okay, but I didn't feel up to hiking any farther. Nathan gave up the rest of the hike to walk back with me."

What a concept, I thought; *just tell them the truth.*

The man looked at me with more respect than before, and to Margot, the woman said, "Oh, sweetie, are you sure you're all right?"

The man held his hand out. "Ron Hanson," he said. I gave him my name as we shook. He nodded toward the woman. "My wife Nancy, and that's little Rebecca. We're going all the way to Hanalei. Hop in."

Nancy was examining Margot, looking for signs of injury, finding only a few scrapes and a bruise or two. "You're so brave!"

I smiled at Nancy. "She's intrepid."

On the drive back, Margot gave them the full story of her fall, playing up my role in the rescue beyond what I think I deserved, but it made a good tale.

"So you met on this hike?" Nancy wanted to know. "You seem so natural together."

Margot and I exchanged a secret smile. I said, "Yeah, I think we'll stay in touch." I was sure it was what Nancy wanted to hear. And now, I was pretty sure it was true.

I texted Conroy that we'd made it back safely. I knew he wouldn't get it right away, but I was sure he'd want to know.

As promised, Margot treated me to dinner at the resort. Over grilled mahi-mahi and a bottle of wine, we talked about how the trip had affected us. Mostly what I said was that I wasn't sure what to make of Wayland's name for me.

"Oh, Nathan, it's perfect."

"Why?"

"I'm a watcher," she said. "I know I talk a lot, but I

observe people. Everyone on the hike was looking to you as much as to Conroy for leadership."

"Whoa. Not Erik."

She laughed, "Yes, Erik! I think he's not usually a follower, but there was something lost about him. Like he had some hole in his soul he was trying to fill. He wasn't looking to you for that, but he was looking to you as a source of stability."

"His wife just died of cancer."

"Oh, how sad. But see? Just proves my point. And as for Hugh, well… I don't know that he figured out on his own about you and Conroy, but he definitely had his eye on you. I think he couldn't figure you out, and he felt threatened without quite knowing why."

"What on earth are you basing this on?"

She took a sip of wine, examined my face for a minute, and took another sip. "There's a confidence about you. It's like—okay, maybe Wayland was right, that you're looking to find yourself. Everyone is, right? But some people seem lost in the process. You don't. It's like you know something other people wish they knew. It's seductive." This time she watched my eyes as she sipped from her glass.

"You mean like that look you're giving me right now?"

She grinned. "I was hoping you'd notice. I wanted you to get what I was talking about. It doesn't have to be about what you say to other people. Like, coming back with me the way you did? And the way you stood up to Wayland when he was unhappy that we didn't trust him? That all took confidence *and* leadership."

I shook my head. "Y'know, I've already told you that my initial impression of you is nothing like what you've turned out to be. And now I have to say that my picture of myself feels nothing like yours. Yours of me, I mean."

She smiled sweetly at me and popped the last bit of fish into her mouth. The next thing she said was, "So Conroy is bi?"

"He sure is."

"But not you?"

That got my attention. "Uh, no."

"Too bad. Sorry if that makes you uncomfortable. But really, it's too bad."

I'm sure I blushed. I was glad the lighting was fairly dim.

The next morning Margot and I walked down to the beach before breakfast. We spoke very little, just opened ourselves up to the stillness that wasn't really stillness, the calm that wasn't really calm. Conroy had been right about this place; it was everything, all at once.

I waded into the water up to my knees. The sun was up, sending multi-colored rays down through a few clouds to the sea. I looked down to admire the little polkadots of shadow that the sun created in the clear, moving water. And I noticed that my puka bead anklet was gone.

I froze, staring at my ankle, wracking my brain to remember when I'd seen the anklet last. I hadn't taken it off since I'd bought it, and I was positive I'd had it on last night. In fact, Margot had commented on it as we'd walked down to the beach just a little while ago. And now it was gone.

Well, I told myself, *you know where to get another one.*

But I wouldn't do that. The anklet had decided it wanted to stay here, and it had released itself to return to the sea it had come from. I was sorry not to have it, but at the same time I felt a sense of spiritual validation. The anklet belonged here. I did not.

Because I had a flexible plane reservation, I was able to get a seat on a flight that left in the afternoon without buying a whole new ticket. Margot hadn't done that, but she said she'd go with me and see if there was a stand-by seat she could get.

So we loaded everything into my rented Jeep and headed back toward Lihue.

We didn't talk much on the drive. There was some kind of intimate understanding between us, something not physical or sexual. It was very easy to be in her company. It had been that way since her fall. At first I wondered if I had changed or she had, and then I decided that after being forced to be so helpless and vulnerable, and so beholden to others, it was no longer necessary for her to try and create or maintain any particular impression. In fact, it would have been ridiculous. So the Margot I'd been with since we'd turned around on the hike was the real Margot. And I had a feeling she'd seen something like the real me.

We hugged long and hard as I got ready to board my flight. We'd already exchanged contact information.

"I hope what you told Nancy was true," Margot said. "Let's stay in touch."

"Wouldn't have it any other way." Thinking of what awaited her at home, I wanted to tell her to stay safe, but I didn't want to take her mind back to what she was trying so hard to leave behind. I wanted Kaua'i's spirit to stay with her at least a little longer. I was sure it would stay with me forever.

My flight reservation might have been flexible, but it did not guarantee me a particular seat. I had to choose from what was available, and I ended up near the back of the plane; at least it was an aisle seat with no one next to me, though there was a young girl, maybe eight, in the window seat. I pacified myself over this annoyance by contemplating how surprised El Speed would be to see me. I just hoped it wouldn't be an unpleasant surprise.

I killed the screen on the back of the seat in front of me, settled in with my earbuds firmly in place, and did my best to ignore the thuds on the back of my seat as the six-year-old behind me banged his feet over and over. The banging stopped and started a few times as the hours went by. Once or twice, the girl pushed her way past me, once to go to the restroom and once to talk to someone in the row behind me, evidently her mother from the bits of conversation I overheard.

At some point after the flight attendants had served the meal and retrieved the dishes, the kid behind me must have dozed off. So did I.

A sudden lurch brought me suddenly and completely awake.

A woman's voice came over the sound system. "The captain has turned on the fasten seat belt sign. Please stay in your seats with your seat belts firmly fastened until further notice."

Another lurch caused the flight attendant in the aisle ahead to move in a drunken manner as she headed toward her own seat.

The woman behind me stood and leaned over the middle seat. "Theresa, are you buckled in?"

I glanced over; she was not. She had pulled her legs up under her and was clutching her knees, her eyes huge and her forehead so puckered it looked painful. She was obviously terrified.

A male voice came over the sound system and announced itself as the captain. "We're encountering some turbulence. The ride might get a little bumpy. We're about ninety minutes from landing, so just remain seated."

I unfastened my own seatbelt and stood. "I'll help her," I told the woman. Theresa's wild eyes landed on my face and her arms shot out and grabbed me. I decided the best place for her would be the middle seat. Somehow I wrestled her into it and fastened the belt.

The woman said, "Thank you!"

Before I could take my seat again, the plane seemed to rise a few feet into the air. I felt my weight lift up almost to the point where my feet left the floor. Then the plane seemed to fall about five feet, and I nearly landed on Theresa. A few passengers let out little screams.

As I struggled to maneuver myself back into my seat, a task which should have been simple, I wondered if the weightlessness of space felt anything like this.

As soon as I was fastened back in my seat, the plane lurched again, up and then a hard fall.

It happened again and again. Each time the fall stopped, it was as though the metal belly had hit the ground, and I could feel and hear everything in the luggage compartment land hard. My hands gripped the arms of my seat.

No one spoke. I'm sure that everyone, like me, was waiting for the next gut-wrenching lurch.

It came. The worst one of all. More screams. I heard myself gasp, my grip on the seat arms tightened, and I wondered whether it was possible that a wing would snap off. It occurred to me that we could all die today. I closed my eyes. My breathing was shaky and fast, and my stomach hurt from clenching.

When the screams lessened I heard the unmistakable sound of air hissing violently as it rushed from one place to another. On a plane, that could mean only one thing: the air, the air we would all die without, was leaving the cabin. Fast.

Suddenly that thing the flight attendants tell you about—that thing that no one listens to because we've heard it so many times before and because, really, it isn't going to happen to us—happened. The air masks fell.

Rather automatically I grabbed mine. I had no idea why or how fast the air was leaking. Before I could get my mask on I heard the woman behind me yell, "Theresa!"

Help others first. That's how the spiel went.

I took a deep breath, which did not feel very satisfying, and reached for Theresa's mask. She was screaming and crying, her arms flailing helplessly.

The spiel doesn't tell you about this part, I thought as I wrestled with the girl to capture her arms. I couldn't say now how it was that I got that mask on her, but I know the plane lurched at least twice more before I succeeded, tossing me around. The screams of people up and down the aisle barely registered in my ears, which were popping ferociously. My body was trying to breathe without much success. My eyes felt like they were bugging out of my head.

Finally, my own mask back on, I buckled myself in. And that's when panic hit me. My mask wasn't working! I smelled something burning! This can't be right! Just before I ripped it off again I realized I was breathing; it was working after all. *They don't tell you about* that, *either.*

Adrenalin coursing through me, I looked over at Theresa to be sure she hadn't done what I wanted to do with that mask. But no; she was breathing, mask in place, still terrified, her eyes glued to my face.

The next lurch felt different from the others in a way I couldn't have described. With both hands, Theresa reached for me. I gave her my hand and we clung to each other.

I heard the pilot's voice again, very muffled; he must have had a mask on as well. His voice was so calm it was almost unnatural.

"We have a leak in the cabin. Please be sure your masks are fully over your nose and your mouth. I'm descending to a lower altitude where the air will be breathable. Don't be alarmed at the downward direction the plane will take. Leave your masks on until further notice."

I wanted to close my eyes again, but I didn't dare. Being able to see wasn't going to help me, but whatever happened, I wanted to know about it. Mostly what I could see was a plastic jungle of tubing, the umbilical connections between masks and the source of life that was breathable air hanging in curled lines that resembled so many Amazonian vines.

Unbelievably, there were a few people without masks standing, or trying to stand as the plane's motions made that nearly impossible. At first some of them were struggling to speak. One of the flight attendants was trying to help them, but they were irrational and combative, and the attendant had to give up and go back to her own mask.

Then the people without masks got quieter. They hung onto the edges of seat backs or staggered about aimlessly. Then, two rows in front of me, a man collapsed onto the floor.

Hypoxia. Where had I heard about that? No doubt in one of my psych classes, but I couldn't think which one it would have been. Was the guy dead? No, wait; not immediately. But his organs were going to start shutting down.

Then a woman farther up the aisle dropped. The flight attendant who'd tried to help earlier rushed toward her, and a male passenger helped get the unconscious woman into a seat so they put get a mask on her.

No time for thought. Or fear. Or courage, for that matter. I wrenched my hand away from Theresa, tore off my mask, and ran to the man in the aisle. He'd been in an aisle seat, but he was so heavy that I couldn't manage to get him into it.

It was clear the plane was descending rapidly—no doubt as rapidly as the pilot could safely do that—and getting my arms and legs to function as expected just wasn't happening. Then another man was with me, and together we got the unconscious guy seated and masked.

As I stood back and nodded at my helper, I realized I was breathing. There was just enough oxygen now that I could manage without the mask—barely. The guy who had helped me looked toward the flight attendant, who was leading anyone without a mask to a seat, and he and I both went to help.

Finally everyone was seated and masked. The guy who had fainted, the one I'd gone to help initially, was breathing. He still looked out of it, but his chest was rising and falling. I was taking deep breaths that were only partially satisfying, but it was enough. Back in my seat, I put my mask on again and gave Theresa my hand once more.

As the plane landed, it was obvious the pilot had notified someone of our plight, because there was a large fleet of ambulances waiting, and beyond them were a couple of buses. We taxied to a stop out on the tarmac rather than going to a gate.

Those of us who had used our masks were asked to stay seated while the attendants and paramedics or EMTs removed anyone who'd fainted or had not used a mask. There were also a couple of doctors doing assessments. It took a while for one of them to get to the back of the plane. She deemed me fine, but she took Theresa and her family away, I think more because of hysteria than anything else. Theresa's mother gave me a hard hug before she followed the doctor.

I made it down the stairs, one of the last to leave, but when my feet touched the tarmac my knees buckled and I fell sideways. An EMT rushed forward and helped me up. It took a couple of minutes to convince him that I'd worn a mask and was just feeling a little overwhelmed. Adrenaline, I decided, can play mean tricks on a person.

Inside the airport, I learned that my flight back to Boston had been canceled due to weather in the Midwest, and I was assigned to a plane leaving the next afternoon. I had two reactions to this. One was that I wasn't altogether sure I ever wanted to get on another plane again in my life. The other was anxiety about getting to Maine in time for the wedding.

I checked into a room at an airport hotel and sat on the side of the bed where I could see out the window. The room was billed as "bay view" rather than "waterfront," but I was barely seeing anything, anyway. I was still feeling rattled after my collapse on the tarmac. What the fuck was that about? I got all the way through the ordeal, past the fear of maybe dying in a plane that crashed into the ocean. I'd helped calm the terrified Theresa, giving her mother the space to tend to the six-year-old who'd attacked my seat. I'd been instrumental in possibly saving a couple of lives. And *then* I fall apart?

I stood and shook myself off, thinking that maybe if I unpacked just the clothes and stuff I'd need overnight, that would give me something productive to do; maybe it would take my mind off the shakiness I was still feeling.

Unpacking done, I stood at the window, hands on hips. What now? I could be, like, totally adult and take a cab into the city. But then what? I knew no one there, I had no particular destination for the short amount of time I'd have, and I'd need to find someplace to have dinner. Alone.

Still undecided, I took a hot shower. And I decided to stay put. I'd have dinner at the hotel, maybe even room service. And until then, I'd wander around outside. While checking in, I'd seen a sidewalk down by the waterfront. I put on khaki slacks and a white shirt, sleeves rolled up above my elbows, and headed downstairs.

Outside, between the hotel and the water, was a small expanse of grass, then a sidewalk, then a smaller strip of grass, and then a kind of breakwater made of tumbled rocks. The sidewalk went for quite a way, along the length of the hotel. I walked back and forth a couple of times, stopping now and then to gaze out over the water. A little to the north was the airport, with the predictable planes taking off and landing. At a distance across the water, according to the map on my phone, were towns I'd never heard of: San Leandro; Hayward; Union City.

Finally I grew tired of walking back and forth. I headed for the far end of the sidewalk, away from where cars dropped visitors off, and I carefully picked my way out onto those tumbled rocks. It took a little effort to find one I could sit on comfortably, but I found one very close to the water and settled down. Knees bent, arms around my legs, I listened to the quiet lapping sounds coming from the water's edge, punctuated by the whine of plane engines. I was finally starting to calm down, almost to the point of exhaustion.

And then I started to chuckle. The gentle laughter just kept coming as seemingly unconnected thoughts chased each other in and out of my head.

How ironic it would have been if I'd survived Crawler's Ledge only to die in a plane crash. And I'm here to tell you, there's nothing quite like nearly dying to put things into perspective.

So many aspects to Ocean. I'd seen one aspect near my resort, benign as long as I kept my place; then there had been the ocean along the Na Pali Coast, treacherous and beautiful; then the ocean beneath my struggling plane, massive with unbridled power and with complete disregard for the lives of humans; and finally this water here, curling like a kitten just past my feet.

As my laughter faded into deep breathing, thoughts similar to some I'd had on Kaua'i came to me. That is, the ocean was the ocean. The differences, the characteristics were creatures of interaction—the interaction between the ocean and what it encountered. Or, in the case of the enormity of the middle of the Pacific, what it didn't encounter. With nothing to make the ocean stop and figure out how to interact with a shoreline, what was it?

Maybe life was an ocean. And again, as on Kaua'i, it came to me that my life experiences were like a series of beaches, with the characteristics of them—and of me— changing according to which beach I encountered.

I had no idea what to do with these thoughts. Had I spent too much time alone on Kaua'i? And here I was again, alone, thinking weird thoughts.

Perspective. It pared away the unimportant, and what

was left was your own set of priorities.

To Ocean I whispered my thoughts as they came to me, almost like prayers.

"Neil, I wish I had told you how much you meant to me. I wish I'd thanked you for always looking out for me, and for Nina, for always being there for us. I wish I'd paid more attention to who you were.

"Gram, I wish I'd paid more attention to you. I wish I'd asked you more questions about your life. I wish I'd been more aware of how much you had suffered, and I wish I'd found a way to let you know how profoundly grateful I am for how you raised three grandchildren all by yourself. I wish I'd told you how much I love you.

"Nina, I can't make the same mistake with you. I want to know who you are as a person, not just as the sister who challenges and aggravates me. I was all wrong about Margot. Maybe I'm all wrong about you, too, and you're not the hard-shelled, fearless person you want the world to see."

When I stopped whispering, I realized that tiny droplets of salt water, like ocean water, were making their slow, trailing way down my face. I left them there.

"Alden, you're another person I thought I knew. I loved you, or I loved what I knew of you. I don't blame you for leaving the way you did, because you had no choice. But I do blame you for not ever contacting me again. It hurt so much—it still hurts—because I have to believe that what you felt for me was insignificant next to the feeling you wanted from fentanyl. I needed you to talk to me about that. I needed closure. I don't forgive you for not giving me that.

"Daniel, I hope if ever again I meet someone like you—someone who seems much more responsible, much more capable, much more adult than he is—I will recognize that disconnect. You were not good for me. You led me on, and I let you do that. We were both wrong."

I closed my eyes and took a few more deep breaths.

"Conroy." I stopped whispering long enough to smile

as that scene from *Into the Woods* came back to me. Prince Charming was not as simple as adultery. He was not as simple as any one thing, or any two things he did. Like the prince, Conroy was not a bad fellow. But he was not good for me. "You told me about the duality of Kaua'i, the good and the bad, the paradise and the hell. Maybe you connect with that place so well because you are so steeped in duality. To you I say only, 'Aloha.'"

By the time the light from the sun behind me disappeared beyond the hills to the southwest, my feet were tingling from lack of circulation, and the rock under my ass had drained a significant amount of warmth from me. It was a minute or so before I could stand upright and get enough feeling back in my legs to work my way across the tumbled rocks toward the hotel.

Back in my room, I perused the room-service menu. The choices were decidedly more limited than I would expect to see in the dining room. I wasn't sure that mattered; there were things here I could enjoy. I could even order a half-bottle of wine. I picked up the phone handset.

I put it down again and went to stand at the window. Would I rather have dinner alone in my room or in a room full of strangers? Where would I feel more alone?

I decided that what mattered was that I at least had other people to look at. So I headed down.

To get to the dining room, I had to pass through what the hotel called its "great room," a large bar area, really, with upholstered chairs around small tables. It overlooked the waterfront sidewalk I'd been pacing earlier. I stopped to look out and saw a couple of people at an outdoor table, the darkening sky beyond them, and low flames coming from some kind of fire pit. I couldn't resist; I went out.

There were three separate fire pits, round and free-standing, made of some kind of stone or concrete. In the center of each one was a jumble of something that looked like glass chards, and the flames came up through them. I'd never seen anything like them before. I walked over to a table for two where no one was sitting and examined the base until I saw a propane tank. I sat down to enjoy the new experience.

My eyes were fixed on the flames, my head for once blissfully empty of thoughts, when a woman approached. She set down a basket of bread and a bowl of nuts and asked me what I'd like to drink.

I don't know why this came to me. Maybe it was just one more thing I'd never done. I asked, "What kinds of scotch do you have?"

"Blend or single malt?"

Blend sounded boring. I couldn't have said why. "Single malt." Whatever that meant.

"We have several in the ten year group, three in the eighteen, and we have The Macallan twenty-five."

I figured the prices were going up with the years. "The Macallan twenty-five, please." I could afford it. Plus I didn't want to make her go through the names in the other categories, which would mean nothing to me anyway. And I thought, you know, why not start with something good?

"Sir, I need to ask for identification. Hotel policy."

I chuckled. Conroy had warned me. I proved my age to her satisfaction and she headed off. I went back to staring at the flaming glass.

When my drink appeared, I wasn't sure what to do next. Should I just toss it back like so many people did in films and on TV? Wait. That was usually from a shot glass, and it was vodka or maybe tequila. This glass was large, with a thick, heavy base. No; I should sip it.

I picked the glass up and gently swirled the liquor around. Then I lifted it to my nose and inhaled.

Wow.

What had I done? Could I actually consume this elixir?

Hell, why not? I tilted the glass gently and allowed just

the tiniest bit of the scotch into my mouth. I closed my eyes and let the intensity fill my head before I swallowed. I had to fight the urge to cough. Thank the gods I hadn't taken a larger mouthful.

I set the glass down and reached for a piece of bread. It was in little cubes, rich with olive oil or butter or both, with slightly singed onion bits on the crust. It was delicious.

I'd barely finished the second cube of bread when the woman was back. "Is everything to your liking, sir?"

"Yes. Thanks. Um, do I need a reservation for the dining room?"

"I'd be glad to take care of that for you, Mr. Bartlett. What time would like to dine?"

I told her eight thirty and went back to my flaming glass and my scotch. What kind of beach had I landed on this time? I'd never in my life been called Mr. Bartlett, except by one professor at school who'd insisted on addressing all his students in that formal way.

Whether I felt like an adult or not, whether I really was one or not, I was being taken seriously here as one. Who knew all you had to do was throw a little money around and order a high-end single malt scotch?

"Is it all right if I join you?"

I looked up at the man who had spoken. It was a little difficult to see him in the dimming light, but what I could see was very pleasant: tall, slender, pale blue polo shirt over jeans, dark hair just long enough to reveal a slight curl. He might have been twenty-five or thirty-two; I couldn't tell. Could I decline? Did I want to? I didn't give myself time to think; I gestured toward the empty chair.

"Dennis Bond," he said, extending his right hand.

"Nathan Bartlett."

"I hope I'm not intruding."

I shook my head. "I've spent enough time alone today."

"What are you drinking?"

It was as good a place to start as any, I decided. He had

what he referred to as a Glenfiddich eighteen. Then he went on to describe a trip he'd taken to Scotland to tour various single malt producers, so I gathered that his drink was not a blend. It was a good fifteen minutes, by my reckoning, before he asked anything about me other than my brand of scotch. Finally he asked, "Where's home for you, Nathan?"

"New Hampshire." That reply was met with silence and seemed likely to die a lonely death, so I added, "I've just been hiking on Kaua'i. The Kalalau Trail. Do you know it?"

I felt like someone else. I sounded like someone else. Someone other than who I was.

He did not know anything about Hawai'i, he said. So I told him about the trail, about Crawler's Ledge, and about my role in rescuing a damsel in distress from the jaws of a ravenous ocean. Not, I admit, in so many words. Still, it was fun to spin the tale. I was just describing the chickens on Ke'e Beach when my wait person reappeared.

"Mr. Bartlett, your table is ready for you. Are you dining alone or will there be two in your party?"

I glanced at Dennis, took in his attractive face, his expectant expression, and told her, "Alone, I think." I stood and shook Dennis' hand. "A pleasure," I told him, which was at least partly true.

It felt like the most adult thing I'd done in my life.

CHAPTER TWENTY-ONE

After a blissfully smooth flight, I got into Logan around nine, the nearly-dark night sky aglow with city lights. It felt as though I'd come through some kind of time tunnel, or maybe a wormhole from another dimension, or at least another universe.

The bittersweet energy of Kaua'i had been nearly obliterated by my experience in the damaged airplane, but my contemplation outside the hotel had helped me recover some equilibrium. It had helped me maintain something of the exotic pull of paradise. The life-beach represented by the hotel had also made me feel as though I'd passed through some portal to a new and different life.

Landing in Boston threatened this fresh new feeling. Being back in New England seemed likely to throw me back into my old life, my old way of being, my old way of feeling.

It was obvious Nina had been to the house at some point in the last week, because I hadn't left things as organized as I found them. Gram's room was now completely empty of anything personal, and other than my room, there was nothing directly relating to our family anywhere in sight. Nina must have taken a lot of stuff to the storage unit.

As I was walking around the house, taking inventory, I got a text from Conroy thanking me for keeping him informed about my return trip with Margot. *You're a class act, Nathan. If you get to Austin in the next ten months, let me know!*

Yeah. Right. Austin? That ain't happenin'. Then my eyes went back to "class act." In Conroy's book, what would that mean? Did I earn that praise for keeping my distance while he was leading a group? Was it for never clinging to him at any point in our acquaintance, letting him retain control?

Yeah. That was it. He had to be the leader. He had to be on top, for sex or whatever else was going on. He had to be in charge.

With a painful shock, I remembered something Nina had said when I'd told her about my trip. I'd barely heard her words, and I'd put them out of my mind immediately. Because they were true.

Conroy was a hammer. I was a nail. Without the nail, the hammer is nothing. But with or without the hammer, the nail is still the nail.

I was fucking sick and tired of being the nail. I didn't want to be the hammer, either, but I vowed there'd be no more "nail" in my character, no more of being the one to take it, whatever "it" was.

God damn it, I wanted a *partner*.

I took a quick shower, scrubbing to see if I could find a new version of myself, to see if there was anything beneath the level of "fool" I felt like. Then I sent a quick text off to Nina.

Home safe. Off to Maine, El Speed's wedding.

She replied: *Call me when you're back.*

I climbed into the bed in my old room but I couldn't close my eyes. Something was different. Very different. And then it hit me.

Gram and Neil weren't here anymore. They weren't haunting the rooms, the halls, the air all around me. Kaua'i had freed them. I hoped it had freed me, too.

In the morning it was raining. Supposedly that's good luck for a wedding, but I didn't think El Speed and Ellie would need much in the way of luck; I bet they'd have preferred sunshine.

I figured the drive to Lewiston would take just over two hours. I still had the invitation El Speed had sent me, which said the ceremony would begin at one and a reception would follow immediately. There were directions to the park where the wedding would take place.

As though I had willed it, the sun came out when I was half-way to Lewiston. Other than a couple of sections of highway under construction, the drive was uneventful—a good thing, because my mind was bouncing all over the place. Would El Speed be glad to see me, or was he too pissed off? Did Ellie hate me because I'd been unwilling to cancel my trip for them? At one point I yelled "SHIT!" out loud; it had never once occurred to me that I should get a gift. After that I tried playing slack-key guitar music to mellow things out, but it felt all wrong. All I could do was keep driving.

Balloons, all colors, reflecting bright sunlight and bouncing in a light breeze, grabbed my attention at the park entrance. They were tied to a sign that pointed toward a huge white tent past the parking area, lots of people milling around it. There was no doubt where to go. In fact, there was a line of long pieces of plywood leading from the parking lot right into the tent and over to one side. The only reason I could think of for that was if Ellie's dress was very long, and she didn't want to get grass stains on it.

I'd met El Speed's parents a couple of times when they'd come to campus. I wasn't entirely sure I'd recognize them, but they recognized me.

"Nathan!" Mrs. Speed called when she saw me. "Oh, Larry will be so thrilled you could come!" She wrapped me in a hug, her large frame smelling of something a little too sweet. She wore a pink straw hat with a very wide brim, but she was so tall that it didn't interfere with the hug.

Mr. Speed shook my hand enthusiastically. "Larry said

you'd be in Hawai'i."

"I was. But I decided to come back early." That was sort of true.

"Larry will be so glad to see you."

Most of the tent was filled with white folding chairs. They weren't terribly stable on the uneven ground, but they were serviceable. Mrs. Speed insisted that I sit with her, so I did. I asked about the plywood as we sat down.

"Ellie's best friend Laura uses a wheelchair," Mrs. Speed told me. "The plywood is her path over the ground. We didn't want to take any chances." She pointed to the bride's side of the tent.

And sure enough, a young woman in a wheelchair had her own place at the far end of the front row. A man in a folding chair beside her was chatting with her. They both looked completely comfortable, but I felt something in me stir, something unsettling.

I couldn't tell from here what it was that made Laura need the chair. It looked like her legs were fine, and if her chair hadn't had wheels I wouldn't have had any idea she needed it. She waved her hands enthusiastically as she talked to the man beside her.

"That's her boyfriend, Tim, talking to her," Mrs. Speed explained. Her voice barely above a conspiratorial whisper, she added, "I think they'll be engaged before the summer is out. Maybe today! Weddings are great for that."

My mind went blank as I watched Laura and Tim. I told myself I was just tired after a near-death experience, two airplane flights, and a long drive to Maine. But now, looking back, I suspect that I just didn't have a place in my imagination for what their life would be like.

Two different thoughts about Ellie came to me. One was that I liked her even better now, and any resentment I was holding onto over the incident of the mosquito shaming went up in flames. The other was that she was a better human being than I was. I didn't know what it would take for me to see a disabled person rather than their disability, let alone to call that person my best friend. It hit me that I had become all about physical vigor, strength, and stamina. Sure, I had respected that Margot was brave enough to admit her reluctance to continue on Crawler's Ledge, but I admired her for carrying a pack that was heavier for her than it would have been for me, and for carrying it without complaint while she kept up with a group of men.

The "mountain man" identity had become so much a part of me—and evidently so important in terms of how I thought of people—that I didn't know what to make of someone in a wheelchair. I didn't know how to assess them. I didn't know how to figure out who they were.

Everyone got quiet all of a sudden as El Speed and his best man took their positions in the front. Both of them looked happy in a nervous kind of way. And then El Speed saw me. His face froze for just a second, and then a huge grin spread across it. I lifted my chin and grinned back.

At that point, from somewhere I couldn't see, music began. It was hard to tell what the instrument was, but it was definitely not a recording. I was about to look around to see what it was when I noticed El Speed's posture change, and his gaze lifted to a spot behind the audience. With everyone else, I glanced back to see that Ellie, on her father's arm, was walking toward the front. I took in her simple white dress. The skirt was not quite floor-length, and it looked like it was made from many layers of wispy cotton that flowed gently as she moved. Then I looked back at El Speed.

I will never forget the look on his face. If he had been a five-year-old child watching Santa Claus scattering presents under the tree on Christmas morning, he couldn't have looked more ecstatic.

As I'd expected, I didn't get a lot of time with El Speed at the reception. In fact, even before I had a chance to speak with him, Ellie came to find me and pulled me a little away from the crowd.

"Nathan, Larry and I are both so glad you're here. But I have to tell you how angry I was when you said you weren't coming."

I felt defensive immediately. "I tried to explain that to him."

"Yeah, he told me what you said. It made no sense."

"It would have if he'd let me talk. And I told him I'd come see both of you after you get back from Nova Scotia."

The look she gave me made me think she was weighing what I'd said against how angry she still was.

"You called it a spiritual quest."

"It was. I needed a kind of absolution. It had to do with Neil, and with Gram."

"You needed to go on a hike for that?"

"I needed to go on a hike to a very particular place for that."

She gazed at me for maybe five seconds. "I'm sure you've heard that expression that life is about the journey. But, Nathan, it's not about the trail."

Suddenly it hit me what it was about Ellie that was in the way of my feeling comfortable around her. What she'd said was just like something Nina would have said; I could almost hear Nina's voice. It was probably a good thing that I saw El Speed approaching before I could make some wise-crack retort. Instead, I smiled at the man I hoped, I prayed, was still my best friend.

He smiled, too, and we embraced as we had after our graduation ceremony. Words weren't necessary.

El Speed kept one arm around my shoulder and beckoned to Ellie with the other, and we had a short group hug.

"So you're coming for a visit, yeah? When Ellie and I get back?"

"I would love that."

"We've rented a house just outside Orono. There's a spare bedroom. Consider it yours. You can tell me all about this demon-casting trip."

I'd known they were both going to the University of Maine, Ellie's alma mater, for graduate work, so the rented house was not a surprise. "Starting right in on the next phase of your academic careers, eh?" It was an obvious statement, uttered more to cover my awkward feeling than to establish anything important.

"What about you?" Ellie asked me. "Aren't you going for an advanced degree is psych?"

"Maybe next year. I need a little space to think."

She asked, "Are you staying in the house in Concord?"

"Nina and I are going to sell that. It's almost through probate, I think."

"So—?"

I shrugged. She turned to El Speed as if for help.

He said, "Apply to Orono! Why not?"

I laughed. "I'll consider it, I promise."

I left in time to get back to Concord before dark, stopping on the way to get groceries. I didn't look forward to preparing meals alone, eating them alone, washing dishes alone, but it was better than going to a restaurant. Eating out alone had seemed fine in Hanalei and at the airport hotel, but here it felt wrong. Here it felt not alone, but lonely.

I called Nina around nine.

"So you're back. Have a good time?"

"How much time do you have?"

She laughed. It surprised me.

"So, Nathan, how much do you like being in that house all alone?"

"I think you know the answer to that."

"If you're ready to sell, probate's over. I'll find a few days in the next couple of weeks to come up and help get the house ready. You'll be around, right?"

"Oh, yeah, I'll be here." No more trips to paradise for me. At least, not this summer. And I needed to figure out where the hell I was going to go.

There was a pause, and then she said, "I have a proposal for you."

"Oh, I can't wait to hear this."

"Be nice, Nathan. I'm trying to help you. This loft, Luc's loft, has three bedrooms in it. He's traveling now, and he'll be away part of August and the second half of September. Why don't you come stay here and I can help you figure out what you want to do next? That way the house can be ready at any time for a buyer, and you won't have to worry about keeping the place looking nice for walk-throughs and open houses and all that crap. You've never been to New York City, have you?"

"Uh, no. Never have."

"It kind of sucks in the summer—hot, smelly—but it's still New York. And it's lovely in the fall. So—?"

"Um, can I think about this a little?"

"Sure. I figured you'd want to. We can talk when I come up, yeah?"

Eyes closed, I nodded, though of course she wouldn't know that. "Sounds good."

I spent all day Sunday at the house, most of it sitting in Gram's lawn chair in the garden. It was a gorgeous day, sunny and just slightly crisp, with that sense in the air that change is about to happen. In fact, it was very much like the day, almost exactly a year ago, that I'd met Conroy.

I missed Conroy. I missed the intensity, the energy, the voice, the laugh, and the attention. And I missed the sex, even though he always wanted it his way. I considered calling him, but I was pretty sure he'd already put me so far in his rear view mirror that he could barely remember what I looked like. He'd disappeared into a fog of ocean mist and waterfall spray. And now, he was busy getting used to his latest temporary life in Austin, and I had no part in that.

I considered calling Margot, but when I picked up my phone I realized I didn't really want to talk. Not to anyone. Not at all.

I needed some time to say goodbye to this house. Maybe the ghosts were gone, but I was still here. The memories were still here. And the idea of leaving all this behind, jumping into some unknown future, was making me feel small and frightened.

I needed to think.

While my eyes followed the flight of bees and hornets fighting their way through the weeds that had taken over Gram's vegetable garden, images of my time on Kaua'i moved across my mind like the slideshow I'd seen on Conroy's computer screen. There was the chicken when I landed in Lihue. There was that great little red Jeep. There was the drive up the coast and the sweetness of Hanalei, where I'd found my puka bead anklet that had returned itself to the sea. There was the feeling of—geez, I don't know, zen, maybe? A zen-like feeling that came over me during those two days I was alone in paradise. And then Conroy, who'd told me about paradise, who'd convinced me to visit it, had destroyed that feeling. Or, he'd at least put a hole in it.

I stood and walked around the garden's perimeter, eyes down to see if any of Gram's plants from last year had re-planted themselves and were growing vegetables. As I walked, I asked myself if that zen-like feeling was still somewhere inside me. And I realized something better had come to stay instead. I'd felt it out on Crawler's Ledge, and walking back to the trailhead, and during that final morning on the beach, and yet again at the hotel.

As I searched visually for vegetables, my mind went to Wayland. He'd said I was a seeker. I *was* a seeker. That felt right. I'd never thought of myself that way in the past, but when I tried it on, it was not just comfortable. It was like a second skin. Until recently, I don't think it would have fit me so well. Until recently, I'd been more of a searcher.

Searching brings with it the implication that there's something in particular that needs to be found, like a vegetable. Or it might be something that's missing, something essential that's lacking. You'd search for something that already existed as an image or a concept in your mind, something specific. Seeking, on the other hand, requires you to keep your mind open, to be ready to receive new ideas and new directions, new paths.

I had arrived in Kaua'i searching. Searching had been my life up until that trip. Kaua'i had helped me find some of what I sought. But it had also shown me that finding what I'd wanted was not the end of my journey.

It seemed to me now that the act of climbing a mountain involved searching. You search for trail markers. You search for the best places to put your feet. You search for where to ford a stream or a river. But when you reach the summit, you open yourself up to what's possible beyond searching. You are a seeker. There's a problem in that approach, though, because you can climb all the mountains you want. But you can't live on the summit.

I would go and stay for a while with Nina. I would re-orient myself on my path to help understand and treat addiction. Addiction was searching. It seemed to me that if it were replaced with seeking, there might be something helpful in that transformation.

I couldn't pretend I wasn't still searching for that feeling of belonging that was so elusive. And I'd reached even this incomplete state of seeking only after searching. If this was true for others, then would it help if they understood what it was they were searching for? And would a realization about that help them transform into seekers? Was the transformation to Seeker the thing we were all really searching for?

ON THE KALALAUA TRAIL

Was Wayland right? Could I blaze a trail that others could follow? Or was I just going in circles?

I had to figure this out. Maybe, even as a seeker, I had more searching to do. And seeking meant leaving myself open, which would take courage. I wasn't entirely sure where to search for that.

The End

ACKNOWLEDGMENTS

Years ago, I realized that the maxim "Write what you know" is woefully inadequate for the kind of writing I want to do. So sometimes my characters find themselves in situations requiring expertise or knowledge I don't have. When this happens, I rely on someone who knows more about the situation than I do.

On The Kalalau Trail features a very important character— Conroy Finnegan—who leads hikes and guided walks professionally. Although I have been a participant in this kind of activity a number of times, leading a hike is a specialty.

Enter Nelson Earl. Nelson is a professional who has led hikers and trekkers to various locations, many of them quite challenging. He knows how to organize a group hike, how to gauge someone's competence for the location's demands, and how to prepare individuals for what they'll encounter. His guidance for me—helping to ensure that Conroy's role is described accurately and credibly—was invaluable to my story.

Many thanks, Nelson. Hike on!

A Reading Group Guide

ON THE KALALAU TRAIL
(Trailblazer Series, Book 2)

Robin Reardon

ABOUT THIS GUIDE

The suggested questions are included to enhance your group's reading of Robin Reardon's novel, *ON THE KALALAU TRAIL* , Book 2 of the *TRAILBLAZER* series.

DISCUSSION QUESTIONS

Note: The questions in this guide contain spoiler information. It is recommended that you finish the book before reading through the questions.

1. Nathan believes that his grandmother, who'd raised him and his siblings, has accepted his homosexuality as well as she could have. How do you see that aspect of their relationship? If someone close to you, someone you thought was straight, reveals to you that they are gay, would that change how you feel about them? If so, how?

2. Conroy's reaction to the "ladder" dog is fairly harsh. Do you see it as warranted? How would you have reacted? What does Conroy's reaction tell you about him as a person?

3. What's your take on the initial interaction between Nathan and Conroy? When Conroy disappears at the summit of Cannon Mountain, do you think it's deliberate? Were you surprised when he appeared beside Nathan on the viewing platform?

4. Nathan describes how his first (and, so far, only) romantic relationship ended in his freshman year at college: his boyfriend, Alden Armstrong, relapsed back into his addiction to fentanyl and disappeared from Nathan's life. Nathan was left feeling as though he could never have meant as much to Alden as Alden had meant to him, because to Alden, fentanyl would always mean more than anything else. Can you put yourself in Nathan's position? Would you have felt as he did? Can you put yourself in Alden's position? Do you think your addiction would become the most important thing in your life?

5. Conroy hates dogs. He tells Nathan, "They look at you like they expect you to save them from something. Like you're God. I don't want that responsibility. And I don't respect them for trying to lay it on me." How do you see this aspect of Conroy's personality playing out with people?

6. When Nathan and Nina are driving to Concord, just having learned that their grandmother had died, Nathan is distraught that she died alone. Nina tells him, "Everyone dies alone." Do you agree? What does this tell you about Nina?

7. Nathan is appalled when he realizes that El Speed is not aware, or has not remembered, that many tragedies and problems are blamed on "the gays" by homophobic bigots, many of whom are in positions of influence and power. If you are gay, do you think your straight friends would be similarly unaware? If you are not gay, do you think Nathan would have been more mollified with your awareness than he was with El Speed's?

8. After Nathan's grandmother dies, he comes to the same painful conclusion he'd reached after Neil had died: that is, he hadn't known her nearly as well as he'd thought. Having this realization about two of the most important people in his life, Nathan feels profound shame, and he becomes convinced that going to Kaua'i will help him gain perspective and possibly even provide some degree of reconciliation. He's convinced this is the reason he needs to go on the trip. He's also convinced that he's not following Conroy as he had followed Daniel Cooke. Are you convinced?

9. When El Speed's wedding date is rescheduled so that it conflicts with Nathan's trip to Hawai'i, Nathan decides

he needs to take the trip badly enough to miss the wedding. What did you think about Nathan's decision and his reasons for it? What did you think of El Speed's reaction? Does the fact that the two friends had been growing apart affect what you think about Nathan's choice?

10. At El Speed's wedding, Nathan sees Ellie's friend Laura in a wheelchair. He learns that Laura might soon be engaged to an able-bodied man, and he has trouble imagining their life together. Do you? He also realizes he's begun to set great store in the ability of himself and others to be strong, to be willing to take risks and to persevere in harsh physical environments—that is, he now sees himself as a "mountain man," and he's unsure how to relate to someone like Laura. If you are able-bodied, do you think you would have trouble relating to someone who relied completely on a wheelchair or who had some other limiting physical disability? If you have physical disabilities, how does Nathan's reaction to Laura strike you?

11. At the end of the story, Nina invites Nathan to come and stay with her while he figures out what he wants to do next in his life. What do you think will happen? Will she be able to help him? Or now that they are coming into their own in terms of who they are as people, will the differences between them be even more pronounced than when they were growing up? What do you think of Nina?

12. Nathan is called a seeker by Wayland, the Kalalau outlaw. Nathan sees this as different from searching. Do you agree? In what aspects of your life have you been a searcher? Are there ways in which you are, instead, a seeker?

Bonus Question

In *On Chocorua*, Nathan is sitting on a bench one lovely autumn day. He collects a few colorful leaves to admire. A young woman, passing by, admires them as well. She asks if Nathan is going to keep them. He shakes his head and tells her, "I don't have a better place for them than right here." In *On The Kalalau Trail,* there is something colorful that Nathan must leave more or less where he found it. What is it?

PLAYLIST FOR
ON THE KALALAU TRAIL

Every time I write a story, I'm influenced—and sometimes haunted—by some number of musical pieces. *On The Kalalau Trail* was no exception.

I've included a playlist for anyone interested in exploring any of the music that influenced my writing of *Kalalau*.

- "Live It" (Cherryholmes)
- "Hurricane" (David Wilcox)
- "Buy for Me the Rain" (Nitty Gritty Dirt Band)
- "Bali Ha'i" (Richard Rodgers / Oscar Hammerstein)
- "Some Enchanted Evening" (Richard Rodgers / Oscar Hammerstein)
- "Before This World / Jolly Springtime" (James Taylor)
- "Tales of the Dream Guitar" (album; Keola Beamer)

Additional slack-key guitar musicians whose recordings I listened to while writing:

- Keoki Kahumoku
- Sonny Lim
- Brian Kessler
- John Keawe

If you enjoyed this book, please consider posting a review on the online sites of your choice. This is the best way to ensure that more titles by this author will become available.

If you would like to be notified with news about this author's work, including when new titles are released, you can sign up for Robin's mailing list at robinreardon.com/contact.

ABOUT THE AUTHOR

Robin Reardon is an inveterate observer of human nature, and her primary writing goal is to create stories about all kinds of people, some of whom happen to be gay, transgender, or intersex—people whose destinies should not be determined solely by their sexual orientation. Her secondary writing goal is to introduce readers to concepts or information they might not know very much about.

Robin's motto is this: The only thing wrong with being gay is how some people treat you when they find out.

Interests outside of writing include singing, nature photography, and the study of comparative religions. Robin writes in a butter yellow study with a view of the Boston, Massachusetts skyline.

Robin blogs (And now, this) about various subjects that influence her writing, as well as about the writing process itself, on her website.

OTHER WORKS BY ROBIN REARDON

Novels
ON CHOCORUA (Book 1 of the Trailblazer series)
AND IF I FALL
WAITING FOR WALKER
THROWING STONES
(Published by **IAM Books**)
EDUCATING SIMON
THE EVOLUTION OF ETHAN POE
A QUESTION OF MANHOOD
THINKING STRAIGHT
A SECRET EDGE
(Published by Kensington Publishing Corp.)

* * *

Essay
THE CASE FOR ACCEPTANCE: AN OPEN LETTER TO
HUMANITY
(Published by **IAM Books**)

* * *

Short Stories
GIUSEPPE AND ME
A LINE IN THE SAND
(Published by **IAM Books**)

Made in the USA
San Bernardino, CA
15 December 2019